COLD CHILLS

Novels

THE SCARF
SPIDERWEB
THE KIDNAPER
THE WILL TO KILL
SHOOTING STAR
PSYCHO
THE DEAD BEAT
FIREBUG
TERROR
THE COUCH
THE STAR STALKER
SNEAK PREVIEW
IT'S ALL IN YOUR MIND
NIGHT WORLD
AMERICAN GOTHIC

Short Story Collections

THE OPENER OF THE WAY
TERROR IN THE NIGHT
PLEASANT DREAMS

BLOOD RUNS COLD
NIGHTMARES
YOURS TRULY JACK THE RIPPER
MORE NIGHTMARES
ATOMS AND EVIL
HORROR 7
THE HOUSE OF THE HATCHET
BOGEY MEN
TALES IN A JUGULAR VEIN
THE SKULL OF THE MARQUIS DE
   SADE
CHAMBER OF HORRORS
15 GRUSEL STORIES
THE LIVING DEMONS
DRAGONS AND NIGHTMARES
LADIES DAY/THIS CROWDED EARTH
BLOCH AND BRADBURY
FEAR TODAY, GONE TOMORROW
CONTES DE TERREUR
THE KING OF TERRORS
THE EIGHTH STAGE OF FANDOM

COLD CHILLS

ROBERT BLOCH

DOUBLEDAY & COMPANY, INC.
GARDEN CITY, NEW YORK
1977

"The Gods Are Not Mocked" Copyright © 1968 by Davis Publications, for *Ellery Queen's Mystery Magazine,* August 1968.
"How Like a God" Copyright © 1969 by Galaxy Publishing Corp., for *Galaxy,* April 1969.
"The Movie People" Copyright © 1969 by Mercury Press, Inc., for *Fantasy and Science Fiction,* October 1969.
"The Double Whammy" Copyright © 1969 by Ultimate Publishing Co., Inc., for *Fantastic Stories,* February 1970.
"In the Cards" Copyright © 1970 by UPD Publishing Co., for *Worlds of Fantasy,* Winter 1970–71.
"The Animal Fair" Copyright © 1971 by Playboy, for *Playboy,* May 1971.
"The Oracle" Copyright © 1971 by Penthouse International, Ltd., for *Penthouse,* May 1971.
"The Play's the Thing" Copyright © 1971 by HSD Publications, Inc., for *Alfred Hitchcock's Mystery Magazine,* May 1971.
"Ego Trip" Copyright © 1972 by Penthouse International, Ltd., for *Penthouse,* March 1972.
"Forever and Amen" Copyright © 1972 by Robert Bloch, for *And Walk Now Gently Through the Fire,* edited by Roger Elwood, Chilton Book Co., 1972.
"See How They Run" Copyright © 1973 by Davis Publications, for *Ellery Queen's Mystery Magazine,* April 1973.
"Space-Born" Copyright © 1973 by Franklin Watts, Inc., for *Children of Infinity,* edited by Roger Elwood.
"The Learning Maze" Copyright © 1974 by Robert Bloch, for *The Learning Maze,* edited by Roger Elwood, Julian Messner, 1974.
"The Model" Copyright © 1975 by Montcalm Publishing Corp., for *Gallery,* November 1975.

Library of Congress Cataloging in Publication Data

Bloch, Robert, 1917–
   Cold chills.

   CONTENTS: The gods are not mocked.—How like a god.—The movie people. [etc.]
   1. Science fiction, American. I. Title.
PZ3.B62043Cm [PS3503.L718]   813'.5'4
ISBN: 0-385-12421-X
Library of Congress Catalog Card Number 76–24039

CONTENTS

This book is for the ladies in my life—Nestunia Zelisko, Miss Hillman, Mrs. Alexander—and, of course, Elly.

INTRODUCTION

"Where do you get the ideas for your stories?"

I quoted this question when I introduced my very first collection, way back in 1945.

Then I tried to answer it. But apparently my explanation wasn't very convincing, since people are still asking me the same question today.

So let's start all over again.

Where do I get the ideas for my stories?

God only knows.

But that's sufficient, because God keeps on providing me with plots, year after year.

Or is it the Devil?

Some readers seem to think so. They find a diabolical element in my work; a bit of brimstone in my buildups, a smidge of sulphur in my solutions.

Whatever the source, I've reason to be grateful. But the questions—and the readers—keep nagging.

Perhaps you and I can find the answer together.

When this book was being assembled, the editor suggested I offer a personal comment about each story included here. Now I'm not exactly keen on the *and-then-I-wrote* approach. It may be fine for composers, but—considering the type of subject matter in my tales—I'm more of a decomposer.

My late friend, motion picture director Fritz Lang, always told audiences who asked about his work, "My films speak for me." And that's how I feel about my stories.

But where did they come from? Just how and why did these particular ideas pop into my head and out of my typewriter?

The contents of this collection were written during the past seven years. Meanwhile I was also writing films, teleplays, suspense novels, and letters to my creditors. Such projects take a great deal of time and energy. Even so, ideas for short stories—inspired by God or the Devil—kept germinating. And ever so often I had to write them down. Or out.

Down and out. That would be a pretty accurate description of my status if I attempted to make a living from short stories alone. There just aren't enough outlets for such material, so it's not the economic incentive that makes me continue. And yet I keep on publishing a science fiction story here, a fantasy yarn there, a psychological horror tale somewhere else.

In checking out the contents of this volume I note that it contains fourteen stories—coming from no less than twelve different sources.

Unlike some of my contemporaries, I'm not identified with a single genre, and my readers—like the stories—are scattered all over the place. People who are aware of my science fiction may not be familiar with the psychological suspense efforts; mystery buffs don't necessarily find the fantasies. No reader can keep track of the entire output of a writer who jumps around as much as I do.

Of course jumping around has a certain value—it's harder, they say, to hit a moving target—but in order to reach a broader spectrum of readership I've got to somehow put it all together. Hence this collection.

All well and good. But it still doesn't answer the question about where the ideas come from.

Now it occurs to me, as it may have occurred to you, that blaming either God or the Devil for my efforts sounds a bit pretentious. The world being what it is, both of them must have more important things to do.

On the other hand, God may occasionally tire of noting each sparrow's fall, and the Devil may grow weary of pushing them out of their trees. In such a case, it's possible they'd turn to reading for relaxation, even as you and I.

If so, it would be only natural for them to take an interest in science fiction, fantasy, and psychological suspense. For in this age of realism, of anti-heroes and telling it like it is, much of the mainstream writing has become muddied.

In speculative and imaginative fiction, however, the moral issues can remain clear. The approach may be scientific or supernatural, but the subject matter is age-old and ageless; the problem of good and evil. And surely both God and the Devil would find this intriguing.

So perhaps it *is* important enough for them to try and influence the writers of such modern morality plays, which may in turn influence readers in their search for salvation or damnation.

As I've told you, I'm not sure about who or what influenced me. But following the conclusion of each story included here I'll set down something of the circumstances under which it was written.

In that way, maybe we can both come to a better understanding of why I write—and why you read—stories designed to give you *Cold Chills*.

—*Robert Bloch*

The Gods Are Not Mocked

Harry Hinch was a funny man and he sold funny things. He had a groovy little hole-in-the-wall shop near the Strip with a big burlap sack hanging in the window and a sign reading *What's Your Bag?* and inside he stocked goodies for everyone.

There were lurid paperbacks and off-brand LPs, of course, and campy photographic blowups of Theda Bara, but Harry's store wasn't just one of those places catering to UCLA drop-outs. Naturally he sold psychedelic prints and Nazi helmets and Iron Crosses and Mellow Yellow and sunflower seeds, but he had some swinging specialties, too. Like dirty Mother's Day cards, for instance. And leather goods—a whole counter of gloves, high-heeled boots, riding crops, and dog whips. For the birds he stocked kinky lingerie; bras in the shape of two clutching, hairy hands; and a G-string designed to look like an open mouth with two rows of sharp-pointed teeth.

But Harry was proudest of the items he dreamed up on his own. Along with the usual bumper stickers and buttons—*Virginity Causes Cancer, Dracula Sucks,* and *Mary Poppins Is a Junky*—he pushed a line of originals like *It Takes Two to Make a Love-in, Flower-Children Are Pansies,* and *Keep Incest in the Family.*

To look at him, sitting up front behind the cash register, you'd never think he was a mover and shaker. There are a dozen duplicates of Harry in the sidewalk scofferies on the Strip—they're all a little on the short side, dress very tight and Mod, and when their hairlines start to recede they sprout the usual compensation on their chins. They plant grass, they sell tickets for trips you can't book with a travel agency, they'll match you with an ideal partner without using a computer. But most of them aren't really *creative*, like Harry was.

He was the one who did the *I'm a Flaming Heterosexual* button and the bumper sticker that says, *Caution—This Car Is Driven by Helen Keller*. Bumper stickers were a "thing" with old Harry. Every night he sat up turning out jollies like *Be Charitable—Contribute to the Delinquency of Minors,* and *Dr. Fu Manchu Is Alive and Performing Abortions in Pasadena.*

Of course not everybody dug Harry. Some cubes said he was hung-up on put-downs. But you've got to expect such flap from the senior citizens; their idea of black comedy ended with Amos 'n Andy. The fuzz did everything they could to nail him for running an illegal letter drop, pushing pot, and a few other sideline scuffles, but Harry just kept on laughing and scratching.

It was always a freak-out scene at Harry's shop, with the hogs and choppers parked outside and the hippies and the teeny-boppers balling it up inside. He kept it cool and quiet, and the only noise was the ringing of the cash register.

When the crunch came, Harry was clean. It wasn't his problem when a juvie named Kim Carmichael wiggled her miniskirt at old Grabber. Sure, they met at his shop, but Harry didn't set up the action. Harry didn't claim he was a chemistry major, and if he sold Grabber a few sugar cubes that didn't prove he knew they were loaded.

Old Grabber had come on strong for Kim Carmichael, but Harry never told him to cut out with her riding tail-gunner on his chopper; Harry never told him to suck the cubes he bought, and Harry definitely didn't tell him to sail off that sharp curve on top of Mulholland and total the chopper, himself, and Kim Carmichael.

When Harry got the word he knew it was either split out or cop out and he wasn't about to take any chances of getting busted. So he hung his *God Is Dead and I'm Going to the Funeral* sign on the front door and faded fast.

'Way past Baldy, up in the National Forest, Harry had a little pad—just a shack, a real nothing scene, but a place where he could get away from the heat.

That's where Harry headed for, right into the old boondocks, 'way out in the toolies with big trees and the mountains and the high lonesomes all around. He holed up in his cabin and waited; in a week or so the fuzz would cool it and meanwhile he was safe as the pill because nobody knew where he was hanging in.

The only thing was that he was all alone and it gets dark pretty early in the woods and very quiet. Harry never realized how much he was used to hearing the cut-outs blasting and the transistor sets blaring and the rumble of the freeways blending all the sounds together for background music. And he missed the lights and the wiggy crowds that kept him company in the shop, even the sickies that talked to themselves. Harry just wasn't with the country-and-western bit, and by the time the sun went down that first night he was ready to climb the walls.

When he knew he was uptight, Harry decided to take his mind off things by doing a little occupational therapy with a bottle of juice he'd packed along. A couple of blasts and he felt better, but he still wasn't comfy-cozy about the dark shadows and the way the wind started to shiver in the tall trees around the cabin.

So he belted another slug and settled down to work. No point just sitting there and thinking about the news report—how the old chopper went sailing off down a sixty-foot drop and landed right on Grabber's spine, then smashed Kim Carmichael's arms, legs, and face—

No, it was better to do a little serious constructive work, and Harry had pen and paper and he was creative and with it, and in no time at all he was lining out some new copy for stickers. *Kick Your Hobbit*, for the Tolkien crowd, and a Zen thing, *Big Buddha Is Watching You*, and then, *Reality Is a Put-on*.

But there were shadows moving outside and the wind kept moaning and he didn't like the trees in the first place, to hell with the conservationists, and that gave Harry another inspiration; so he wrote down *Smokey the Bear Is a Pyromaniac*.

That really broke him up; he'd always hated that damned smart-aleck picture and the slogan about forest fires and for two cents and another belt from the bottle he'd start a fire himself and burn down the whole lousy setup and the Boy Scouts and the mothers and the veterans and the fuzz and the rest of the squares that bugged him, that were always bugging Harry to believe in their stinking superstitions about God and Freud and Law and Order and Love and Happiness. It was all a big yak and Harry had to laugh; he was still laughing when Dr. Carmichael walked in.

Dr. Carmichael or Professor Carmichael—Harry didn't know which it was, and it didn't matter. All he knew when the guy introduced himself was that this Carmichael was Kim Carmichael's father.

He must have tailed Harry up to the cabin all the way from town when he took off, and he'd hung around waiting until it got dark to make his move.

There he was, standing in the doorway, saying nothing except, "I'm Carmichael—Kim's father," and doing nothing but stare at Harry. He was a tall, skinny gray-haired cat—taught sociology or ethics or some such crud out at the U—and Harry could have taken him in one fast chop. Except that the old guy was holding an Astra .25 with the safety off. A very small gun, but the kind that makes a very big hole at close range.

"Sit down," said Carmichael, and Harry sat down. He wasn't exactly loving every minute of it, but one thing he knew for sure. Carmichael wasn't about to kill him, not after telling him to sit. He wouldn't be shooting off anything but his mouth, and this Harry could take.

He took it for about ten minutes, took it with a very straight face—all the usual jazz about, "You murderer, you killed my daughter just as surely as if you drove that motorcycle off the cliff yourself," and a lot more. Harry couldn't have cared less until Carmichael started getting to him. *Him*, personally.

"I've seen your store," Carmichael said. "I've seen the sickness you sell—the sickness of our times. Oh, I know all the rationalizations. The fix is in, the dice are loaded, you can't win for losing, all the world's a Theatre of the Absurd, life's just another Happening, and why play anything straight?

"So you and your kind put down heroes in the name of humor, you put down society in the name of satire, you put down culture and call it comedy.

"But you're not a funny man, Harry. Behind the laughter there's hatred, and behind the hatred is fear. That's the real reason for the put-downs, isn't it? Because you're afraid of everything and everyone. There's a name for your disease—paranoid fixation. You're a carrier, you infect everything you touch.

"You infect the mumbling misfits who come to your shop—the idle, would-be idol-smashers who foist their fears and vent their aggressions on the world of reality. And you infect the healthy ones, too—girls like Kim who mistake your hostility for profundity—"

"Get off my back," said Harry.

"I'm not on your back," Carmichael told him. "You're carrying your own monkey. The simian syndrome—huddling behind the bars of your cage and making faces at the world because it frightens you. Monkey sees, monkey does, and because there are thousands of others just like you, you think you've got a grasp on the truth.

"But for every thousand pedestal-topplers and icon-breakers, there are millions who still believe otherwise. And perhaps their belief is stronger than yours.

"Have you ever really thought about this faith you spend your life trying to destroy—the sustaining faith that most of the world maintains in its illusions? Belief sanctifies, you know. Belief *makes* heroes, creates beauty and honor and decency and all the other phenomena which you laugh at. You paranoid types can't stand heroes, can you, Harry? Not even the make-believe ones in art and literature and the mass media of TV and films. But in terms of belief they do exist, you know. Hamlet is far more *real* to us than Shakespeare, and though Conan Doyle is dead, Sherlock Holmes still has a life of his own.

"I suspect you *do* realize this, and that's why you put down the villains, too—with all the snickering about Dracula and King Kong and the little wind-up toy Frankenstein's Monster that loses its trousers when it starts to reach out for you. These things scared you when you were a kid and you're still scared; so you've got to laugh at them and pretend they're not real."

Carmichael looked down at the table and saw what Harry had been writing and he shook his head.

"*Smoky the Bear Is a Pyromaniac*," he said. "Why, Harry? Why? Is it because you were afraid of the Three Bears when Mommy told you the story? Is it because you secretly believe there is such a creature? Well, if there's any power in faith, then the belief of millions of youngsters constitutes a force you'll never laugh away with a cheap put-down. Maybe you have good reason for your fear, Harry. Belief creates our gods, and the gods are not mocked."

That is what Carmichael told Harry before he went away.

At least he *says* he told Harry and went away, but we have only his word for it.

We do know, from a guy named Rogers who happened to be bedding down in his camper about a half mile away on the lake, that the lights went out in Harry's cabin around midnight; probably right after Harry finished the last of his whiskey.

A little while later, the growling started. The growling, and the screams.

You could hear them echoing all over the lake, but by the time Rogers stumbled through the pitch-black woods and reached the cabin there was no sound except the whispering of the wind.

Harry was dead by then; nobody could have survived the ripping and the chewing. Perhaps Carmichael was lying, maybe *he* was the crazy one and came back to descend on Harry in the darkness, to bite and slash and tear. He could even have planted that strange object on the cabin's earthen floor alongside Harry's body—the crushed and crumpled Boy Scout hat, with its rank animal odor.

Maybe so.

But nobody ever explained the pawprints.

*   *

I may not be the most logical person in the world, but at least I can be chronological.

"The Gods Are Not Mocked" is the earliest-written story in this collection: it appeared in the August 1968 issue of *Ellery Queen's Mystery Magazine*.

Frankly, I was puzzled to see a fantasy printed there. Apparently the editors had doubts too, because they prefaced the tale with a warning in bold, black letters—BE SURE TO READ THIS FIRST. And then went on to tell the readers that this story was in bad taste, and they were violating their rules by publishing it.

To me, if any bad taste is involved, it's not in the story itself but in the reality which inspired me to write the yarn.

You see, I happen to dislike the type of put-down described here. This may surprise people who've heard me speak at various science fiction gatherings and conventions, for I quite frequently do a bit of roasting. But there's a definite distinction involved. To begin with, I take pains to let the audience know I'm not serious. And more importantly, my targets are quite capable of turning the tables on me: I make it a rule never to single out someone whom I know is unable to respond in kind.

But in many instances the bumper sticker is just a cheap shot and its alleged humor merely an excuse for an expression of vicious hostility. This hostility is directed at utter strangers, not to amuse, but to wound a victim who is not present and has no opportunity to answer back.

And to add insult to injury, the driver of the car bearing the sticker can't even take credit for the sentiment, since he didn't originate it. All he did was buy it and paste it on. I guess this irks the writer in me: I hate to see somebody take bows for another author's work.

Petty as this may be, I find it immoral.

Incidentally, my original title for this story was "The Funny Man." The editors changed it to "The Gods Are Not Mocked," and perhaps they divined my inspiration for writing this piece.

If so, chalk one up for God.

How Like a God

I

To *be* was sweet.

There was meditation—a turning-in upon one's self. There was contemplation—a turning-out to regard others, and otherness.

In meditation one remained contained. In contemplation there was a merging, a coalescence with the rest.

Mok preferred meditation. Here Mok enjoyed identity and was conscious of being *he, she* or *it,* endlessly repeated through the memory of millenniums of incarnations. Mok, like the others, had evolved through many life-forms on many worlds. Now Mok was free of the pain and free of the pleasures, too, free of the illusions of the senses which had served the bodies housing the beings which finally became Mok.

And yet, Mok was not wholly free. Because Mok still turned to the memories for satisfaction.

The others preferred contemplation. They enjoyed coalescing, mingling their memories, pooling their awareness and sharing their sense of being.

Mok could never share completely. Mok was too conscious of the differences. For even without body, without sex, without physical limitation imposed by substance in time and space, Mok was aware of inequality.

Mok was aware of Ser.

Ser was the mightiest of them all. In coalescence, Ser's being dominated every pattern of contemplation. Ser's will imposed harmony on the others, but only if the others surrendered to it.

To *be* was sweet. But it was not sweet enough.

Upon this, Mok meditated. And when coalescence came again, Mok did not surrender. Mok fixed firmly upon the concept of freedom—freedom of choice, the final freedom which Ser denied.

There was agitation amongst the others; Mok sensed it. Some attempted to merge with Mok, for they too shared the concept, and Mok opened to receive them, feeling the strength grow. Mok was as strong as Ser now, stronger, calling upon the will and purpose born of memories of millions of finite existences in which will and purpose were the roots of survival. But that survival had been temporary, and this would be permanent, forever.

Mok held the concept, gathered the strength, firmed the purpose—and then, quite suddenly, the purpose faded. The strength oozed away. The others were gone; nothing was left but Mok and the concept itself. The concept to—

Mok couldn't grasp the concept now. It had vanished.

All that remained was Mok and Ser. Ser's will, obliterating concept and purpose and strength, imposing itself upon Mok, invading and inundating Mok's awareness. Mok's very *being*. But without concept there was no purpose, without purpose there was no strength, without strength Mok could not preserve awareness, and without awareness there was no being.

Without being there was no Mok.

When Mok's identity returned he was in the ship.

Ship?

Only memories of distant incarnations told Mok this was a ship, but it was unmistakably so: a ship, a vessel, a transporter, a physical object, capable of physical movement through space and time.

Space and time existed again, and the ship moved through

them. The ship was confined in space and time, and Mok was confined in the ship, which was just large enough to house him as he journeyed.

Yes, *he*.

Mok was *he*. Confined now, not only in the prison of space and time, nor in the smaller prison of the ship, but in the prison of a body. A male body.

Male. Mammalian. A spine to support the frame, arms and legs to support and grasp, eyes and ears and nose and other crude sensory receivers. Flesh, blood, skin—yellowish fur covering the latter, even along the lashing tail. Lungs for oxygen intake, which at the moment was supplied by an ingenious transparent helmet and attached pack mechanism.

Ingenious? But this was clumsy, crude, primitive, a relic of remote barbaric eras Mok could only vaguely recall. He tried to meditate, tried to contemplate, but now he could only *see*—see through the transparency of the helmet as the ship settled to rest and its belly opened to catapult him forth upon the frigid surface of a barren planet where a cold moon wheeled against the icy glitter of distant stars.

The ship, too, had a form—a body that was in itself vaguely modeled on mammalian concept, almost like one of those giant robots developed by life-forms in intermediate stages of evolution.

Mok stared at the ship as it rested before him on the sterile, starlit slope. Yes, the ship had a domed cranial protuberance and two metal arms terminating in claws. Claws to open the belly of the ship, claws that had lifted Mok's body forth to disgorge him from the belly in a parody of birth.

Now, as Mok watched, the ship's belly was closing again, sealing tightly while the metallic claws returned to rest at its sides. And flames of force were blasting from the pediment.

The ship was rising, taking off.

Mok had been embodied in the confines of the ship, imprisoned in this, his present form. The ship had carried him to this world and now it was leaving him here. Which meant that the ship must be—

"*Ser!*" he screamed, as the realization came, and the sound of his voice echoing in the hollow helmet almost split his skull. But Ser did not answer. The ship continued to rise, the rising accelerated, there was a roar and a glimmer and then an incandescence which faded to nothingness against the black backdrop of emptiness punctured by glittering pinpoints of light flickering down upon the world into which Mok had been born.

The world where Ser had left him to die . . .

II

Mok turned away. His body burned? *Burned?* Mok searched archaic memories and came up with another concept. He wasn't burning. He was freezing. This was cold.

The surface of the planet was cold, and his skin—*fur?*—did not sufficiently protect him. Mok took a deep breath, and that in turn brought consciousness of the inner mechanism: circulation, nervous system, lungs. Lungs for breath, supplying the fuel of life.

The feeder-pack on his back was small. Its content, scarcely enough to fill his needs on the flight here, would soon be exhausted.

Was there oxygen on the surface of this planet? Mok glanced around. The rocky terrain was devoid of vegetation, and that was not a promising sign. But perhaps the entire surface wasn't like this; in other areas at lower levels, plant-life might flourish. If so, functioning existence could be sustained.

There was only one way to learn. Mok's prehensile appendages—not exactly claws, not quite fingers—fumbled clumsily with the fastenings of the helmet and raised it gingerly. He took a shallow breath, then another. Yes, there was oxygen present.

Satisfied, Mok removed helmet and pack, along with the control mechanism strapped to his side. There'd be no further need of this apparatus here.

What he needed now was warmth, a heated atmosphere.

He glanced toward the bleak, black bulk of crags looming across the barren plain. He moved toward them slowly, under the silent, staring stars, toiling up a slope as a sudden wind tore at his shivering body. It was awkward, this body of his, a clumsy mechanism subject to crude muscular control. Only atavism came to his aid as half-perceived memories of ancient physical existence enabled him to move his legs with proper coordination. Walking—climbing—then crawling and clinging to the rocks— all was demanding, difficult, a challenge to be met and mastered.

But Mok ascended the face of the nearest cliff and found the opening, a crevasse with an inner fissure that became the mouth of a cave. A dark shelter from the wind, but it was warmer here. And the rocky floor sloped into deeper darkness. The pupils of his eyes accommodated, and he could guide himself in the dim tunnelway, for his vision was that of a feral nyctalops.

Mok crept through caverns like a giant cat, gusts of warm air billowing against his body to beckon him forward. Forward and down, forward and down. And now the heat rose about him in palpable waves, the air singed with an acrid scent, and there was a glowing from a light source ahead. Forward and down toward the light source, until he heard the hissing and the rumbling, felt the scalding steam, breathed the lung-searing gases, saw the spurting flames in which steam and gas were born.

The inner core of the planet was molten!

Mok went no further. He turned and retreated to a comfortable distance, moving into a side passageway which led to still other offshoots. Here tortuous tunnels branched in all directions, but he was safe in warmth and darkness; safe to rest. His body—this corporeal prison in which he was doomed to dwell—needed rest.

Rest was not sleep. Rest was not hibernation, or estivation, or any of a thousand forms of suspended animation which Mok's memory summoned from myriad incarnations in the past. Rest was merely passivity. Passivity and reflection.

Reflection. . . .

Images mingled with long-discarded verbal concepts. With their aid, while passive, Mok formulated his situation. He was in the body of a beast, but there were subtle differentiations from the true mammal. Oxygen was needed, but not the respite of true sleep. And he felt no visceral stirrings, no pangs of physical hunger. He would not be dependent, he knew, upon the ingestion of alien substance for continued survival. As long as he protected his fleshly envelope from extremes of heat and cold, as long as he avoided excessive demands upon muscles and organs, he would exist. But despite the difference which distinguished him from a true mammal, he was still confined to his feral form. And his existence was bestial.

Sensation surged within him, a flood of feeling Mok had not

experienced in aeons, a quickening, sickening, burning, churning evocation of emotion. He knew it now. It was fear.

Fear.

The true bondage of the beast.

Mok was afraid, because now he understood that this was planned, this part of Ser's purpose. Ser had committed him to this degradation and modified his mammalian aspect so that he could exist eternally.

That was what Mok feared. Eternity in *this* form!

Passive no longer, Mok flexed and rose. Summoning cognition to utmost capacity, Mok searched within himself for other, inherent powers. The power to merge, to coalesce—that was gone. The power to transmute, to transfer, to transport, to transform— gone. He could not change his physical being, could not alter his physical environment, save by physical means of his own devising within the limitations of his beast's body.

So there was no escape from this existence.

No escape.

The realization brought fresh fear, and Mok turned and ran. Ran blindly through the twisting corridors, fear riding him as he raced, raced mindlessly, endlessly.

Somewhere along the way a tunnel burrowed upward. Mok toiled through it, panting and gasping for breath; he willed himself to stop breathing but the body, the beast-body, sucked air in greedy gulps, autonomically functioning beyond his conscious control.

Scrambling along slanted spirals, Mok emerged once more upon the outer surface of his planetary prison. This was a low-lying area, distant and different from his point of entry, with vegetation vividly verdant against a dazzling dawn—a valley, capable of supporting life.

And there was life here! Feathery forms chattering in the trees, furry figures scurrying through undergrowth, scaly slith-erers, chitinoidal burrowers buzzing. These were simple shapes, crudely conceived creatures of primitive pursuits, but alive and aware.

Mok sensed them, and they sensed Mok. There was no way of communicating with them except vocally, but even the soft sounds issuing from his throat sent them fleeing frantically. For Mok was a beast now, who feared and was feared.

He crouched amongst the rocks at the mouth of the cavern from which he had come forth and gazed in helpless, hopeless confusion at the panic his presence had provoked, and the soft sounds he uttered gave place to a growling groan of despair.

And it was then that they found him—the hairy bipeds, moved cautiously to encircle him until he was ringed by a shambling band. These were troglodytes, grunting and snuffling and giving off an acrid stench of mingled fear and rage as they cautiously approached.

Mok stared at them, noting how the hunched, swaying figures moved in concert to approach him. They clutched rude clubs, mere branches torn from trees; some carried rocks scooped up from the surface of the slope. But these were weapons, capable of inflicting injury, and the hairy creatures were hunters seeking their prey.

Mok turned to retreat into the cavern, but the way was barred now by shaggy bodies, and there was no escape.

The troglodytes pressed forward now, awe and apprehension giving place to anger. Yellow fangs bared, hairy arms raised. One of the creatures—the leader of the pack—grunted what seemed a signal.

And they hurled their rocks.

Mok raised his arms to protect his head. His vision was blocked, so that he heard the sound of the stones clattering against the slope before he saw them fall. Then, as the growls and shrieks rose to a frenzy, Mok glanced up to see the rocks rebounding upon his attackers.

Raging, they closed in to smash at Mok's skull and body with their clubs. Mok heard the sounds of impact, but he felt nothing, for the blows never reached their intended target. Instead, the clubs splintered and broke in empty air.

Then Mok whirled, confused, to face his enemies. As he did so they recoiled, screaming in fright. Breaking the circle, they retreated down the slopes and into the forest, fleeing from this strange thing that could not be harmed or killed, this invincible entity—

This invincible entity.

It was Mok's concept, and he understood, now. Ser had granted him that final irony—invincibility. A field of force, surrounding his body, rendering him immune to injury and death. No doubt it also immunized him from bacterial invasion. He was in a physical form, but one independent of physical needs to sustain survival; one which would exist, indestructibly, forever. He was, in truth, imprisoned, and eternal.

For a moment Mok stood stunned at the comprehension, blankly blinded by the almost tangible intensity of black despair. Here was the ultimate horror—doom without death, exile without end, isolation throughout infinity. *Alone forever.*

Numbed senses reasserted their sway, and Mok glanced around the empty stillness of the slope.

It wasn't entirely empty. Two of the troglodytic creatures sprawled motionless on the rocks directly below him. One was bleeding from a gash in the side of his head, inflicted by a rebounding club, the other had been felled by a glancing blow from a stone.

These creatures weren't immortal.

Mok moved toward them, noting chest movement, the soft sussurration of breath.

They weren't immortal, but they were still alive. Alive and helpless. Vulnerable, at his mercy.

Mercy. The quality Ser had refused to show Mok. There had been no mercy in condemning him to spend eternity here alone.

Mok halted, peering down at the two unconscious forms. He made a sound in his throat, a sound that was curiously like a chuckle.

Perhaps that was a way out, after all, a way to at least mitigate his sentence here. If *he* showed mercy now, to these creatures—he might not always be alone.

Mok reached down, lifting the body of the first creature in his arms. It was heavy in its limpness, but Mok's strength was great. He picked up the second creature carefully, so as not to injure it further.

Then, still chuckling, Mok turned and carried the two unconscious forms back into the cavern.

III

In the warm, firelit shelter of the deeper caverns, Mok tended to the creatures. While they slumbered fitfully, he ascended again to the surface and foraged for their nourishment in the green glades. He brought food and, calling upon distant memories, fashioned small clay pots in which to carry water to them from a mountainside spring.

After a time they regained consciousness and they were afraid —afraid of the great beast with the bulging eyes and lashing tail, the beast they knew to be deathless.

It was simple enough for Mok to fathom the crude construct of growls and gruntings which served these life-forms as a principal means of communication, simple enough to grasp the limited concepts and references symbolized in their speech. Within these limitations he attempted to tell them who and what he was and how he had come to be here, but while they listened they did not comprehend.

And still they feared him, the female specimen more than the male. The male, at least, evinced curiosity concerning the clay pots, and Mok demonstrated the fashioning method until the male was able to imitate it successfully.

But both were wary, and both reacted in terror when confronted with the molten reaches of the planet's inner core. Nor could they become accustomed to the acrid gases, the darkness enveloping the maze of far-flung fissures honeycombing the substrata. As they gathered strength over the passage of time, they huddled together and murmured, eyeing Mok apprehensively.

Mok was not too surprised when, upon returning from one of his food-gathering expeditions to the surface, he discovered that they were gone.

But Mok *was* surprised by the strength of his own reaction— the sudden responsive surge of *loneliness*.

Loneliness—for those creatures? They couldn't conceivably serve as companions, even on the lowest level of such a relationship; and yet he missed their presence. Their mere presence had in itself been some assuagement to his own inner agony of isolation.

Now he realized a growing sympathy for them in the helplessness of their abysmal ignorance. Even their destructive impulses excited pity, for such impulses indicated their constant fear. Beings such as these lived out their tiny span in utter dread; they trusted neither their environment nor one another, and each new experience or phenomenon was perceived as a potential peril. They had no hope, no abstract image of the future to sustain them.

Mok wondered if his two captives had succeeded in their escape. He prowled the passages searching for them, visioning their weary wanderings, their pathetic plight if they had become lost in the underground fastnesses. But he found nothing.

Once again he was alone in the warm beast-body that knew neither fatigue nor pain—except for this new pang, this lonely longing for contact with life on any level. Ancient concepts came to him, identifying the nuances of his reactions, all likened and linked to finite time-spans. *Monotony. Boredom. Restlessness.*

These were the emotive elements which forced him up again from the confined comfort of the caves. He prowled the planet, avoiding the bleak, cold wastes and searching out the areas of lush vegetation. For a long period he encountered only the lowest life-forms.

Then one of his diurnal forays to the surface brought him to a stream, and as he crouched behind a clump of vegetation he peered at a group of troglodytes gathered on its far bank.

Vocalizing in their pattern of growls and grunts, he ventured forth, uttering phonic placations. But they screamed at the sight of him, screamed and fled into the forest, and he was left alone.

Left alone, to stoop and pick up what they had abandoned in their flight—*two crude clay containers, half-filled with water.*

Now he knew the fate of his captives.

They had survived and returned to their own kind, bringing with them their newly acquired skill. What tales they had told of their experience he could not surmise, but they remembered what he had taught them. They were capable of learning.

Mok had no need of further proof, and the incentive was there; the compound of pity, of concern for these creatures, of his own need for contact on any level. And here was a logical level indeed—there would never be companionship, that he understood and accepted, but this other relationship was possible. The relationship between teacher and pupil, between mentor and supplicant, between the governing power and the governed.

The governing power. . . .

Mok turned the clay containers this way and that, noting the clumsiness with which they had been fashioned, noting the irregularities of their surface. He could so easily correct that clumsiness, he could so surely smooth and reshape that clay. Govern the earth, govern the creatures, impart and instruct that which would shape them anew.

And then the ultimate realization came.

This would be duty and destiny, function and fulfillment. Within the prison of space and time, he would mold the little lives.

Now he knew his own fate.

He would be their god.

IV

It was a strange role, but Mok played it well.

There were obstacles, of course. The first to be faced was the fear in which they held him. He was an alien, and to the primitive minds of these creatures, anything alien was abhorrent. His very appearance provoked reactions which prevented him from approaching them, and for a time Mok despaired of overcoming this communication barrier. Then, slowly he came to realize that their fear was in itself a tool he could employ to positive ends. With it he could invoke awe, authority, awareness of his powers.

Yes, that was the way. To accept his condition and stay apart from them always, confident that in time their own curiosity would drive them to seek him out.

So Mok kept to the caves, and gradually the contacts were made. Not all of the hominids came to him, of course, only the boldest and most enterprising, but these were the ones he awaited. These were the ones most fitted to learn.

As he expected, the experience of his captives became a legend, and the legend led to worship. It was useless for Mok to discourage this, impossible even to make the attempt in the light of their primitive reasoning, a barter-system must prevail. Offerings and sacrifices were the price they must pay in return for wisdom. Mok scanned his own primordial memories, assigning an order to the learning he imparted: the gift of fire, the secret of cultivation, the firing of clay, the shaping of weapons, the subjugation and domestication of lesser life-forms, the control and eradication of others. Slowly a more sophisticated system of com-

munication evolved, first on the verbal and then on the visual
level.

The creatures disseminated his wisdom, absorbing it into their
crude culture. They learned the uses of wheel and lever, then
reached the gradual abstraction of the numeral concept. Now
they were capable of making their own independent discoveries;
language and mathematics stimulated self-development.

But in times of crisis there was still a need for further enlight-
enment. Natural forces beyond their limited powers of control
brought periodic disaster to life-patterns on the surface of the
planet, and with every upheaval came a resurgence of the worship and sacrifices Mok secretly abhorred. Yet these creatures
seemed to feel the necessity of making recompense for the skills
he could grant them and the bonus these skills conferred, and
Mok reluctantly accepted this.

It was harder for him to accept the continuation of their fear.

For a time he hoped that as their enlightment increased they
would revise their attitudes. Instead, their dreads actually increased. Mok attempted to observe their progress at firsthand,
but there was no opportunity for open contact and communication, and his mere appearance provoked panic. Even
those who sought him in secret, or led the rituals of worship,
seemed to be afraid of acknowledging the fact, lest it lessen their
own superior status within the group. Acknowledging and ac-
claiming the existence of their god, they nevertheless avoided
his physical presence.

Perhaps it was because sects and schisms had sprung up, each
with its own hierarchy, its own dogma regarding the true nature
of what they worshipped. Mok remembered, wryly, that in organized religion the actual presence of a god is an embar-
rassment.

So Mok refrained from further visitations, and as time passed
he retreated deeper and deeper into the caverns. Now it was almost unnecessary for him to maintain even token contact, for
these creatures had evolved to a stage where they were capable
of self-development.

But even gods grow lonely, and take nurture in pride. Thus it
was that at rare intervals, and in utmost secrecy, Mok ventured
forth for a hasty glimpse of his domain.

One evening he came forth upon a mountaintop. Here the
stars still glittered coldly, but there was an even greater glitter
emanating from the expanse below—the huge city-complex towering as a testament to the wisdom of these creatures, and his
own.

Mok stared down, and the sweet surges of pride coursed
through him as he contemplated what he had wrought. These
toys, these trifles with which he played, now toyed and trifled
with the prime forces of the universe to create their own destiny.

Perhaps he, as their god, was misunderstood, even forgotten
now. But did it matter? They had achieved independence, they
did not need him any more.

Or did they?

The concept came, and it was more chilling to Mok than the
wind of mountain night.

These creatures created, but they also destroyed. And their
motivations—their greeds, their hungers, their lusts, their fears—
were still those of the beasts they had been. The beasts they
could become again, if spiritual awareness did not keep pace
with material attainment.

There was still a need here, a need greater than before. And
now Mok felt no pride, only perplexity which pierced more
poignantly than pain.

How could he help them?

"You cannot."

The communication came, and Mok whirled.

Absorbed, he had not sensed the silent streaking of the ship
from sky to surface, but it was here now, remembered and recognized. The ship which had captured and conveyed him, the
strangely shaped ship which *was* Ser—

It hovered incandescently against the horizon of infinity, and
as if communication had been a signal, Mok found himself
caught up in a long-discarded reaction. He was *contemplating*
Ser.

And in that colloquy, Ser's concepts flowed to him.

"Valid. You cannot fulfill their needs. Already you have done
too much."

Despite conscious volition, Mok felt the stubborn resurgence
of his pride. But there was no need to formulate the reasons, for
Ser's contemplation was complete.

"You are in error. I sensed your rebellion, overcame you, brought you here—but it was not a punishment. You were placed for a purpose. Because this pride, this urge to invest identity through achievement, could be of use at this time, in this place. Like the others."

"*Others?*" Confusion colored Mok's contemplation.

"Did you conceive of yourself as the only rebel? Not so. There have been more, many more. And they have served their purposes on other worlds throughout the cosmos. Worlds where the seeds of life needed cultivation and careful nurturing. I chose them for their tasks, just as I chose you. And you have not failed."

Mok considered, then communicated with an energy which surprised him.

"Then let me continue! Endow me with what is necessary to help them now!"

Ser's concept came. "It is not possible."

Mok contemplated in final effort. "But it is my right to do so. I am their god."

"No," Ser answered. "You have never been their god. You were chosen for what you were—to be their devil."

Devil. . . .

There was no contemplation now, only maddening meditation as Mok scanned through concepts long discarded from incarnations long lost save in immutable memory. Concepts of *good, evil, right, wrong*—concepts embodied in the primitive religions of a million primitive pasts. God arose from those concepts, and so did the embodiment of an opposing force. And in all the legends in each of the myriad myths, the pattern was the same. A rebel cast down from the skies to tempt with teaching, to furnish forbidden knowledge at a price. A being in the form of a beast, skulking in darkness, in the pit where inner fires flamed forever. And he had been this being; it was true, he was a devil.

Only pride had blinded him to the truth—the pride which had prompted him to play god.

"A pride of which you have been purged," Ser's communication continued. "One can sense in you now only mercy and compassion for these creatures and their potential peril. One can sense love."

"It is true," Mok acknowledged. "I feel love for them."

Ser's assent came. "With your aid, these creatures evolved. But you have evolved too—losing pride, gaining love. In so doing, you cannot function for them as their devil any longer. Your usefulness here is ended."

"But what will happen?"

The answer came not as a concept but as an accomplishment.

Suddenly Mok was no longer in the tawny body of the beast. He was in the ship, hovering and gazing down at that body; gazing down at the creature which lashed its tail and stared up at him with bulging eyes. The creature which now contained the essence of Ser.

And Ser communicated. "For a span you shall take my place, as you once desired. You will seed the stars, instill order in chaos, lead the others in contemplation. You will do so in understanding, and in love."

"And you?" Mok asked.

The being in the bestial body formed a final concept. "I take your role and your responsibility. There is that within me which must also be purged, and it may be I will destroy much of what you have created here. But in the end, even as their devil, I may bring them to an ultimate salvation. The cycle changes."

Mok willed the celestial machine in which his essence dwelt, willed it to rise, and like a fiery chariot it ascended to the realms of glory awaiting him in the skies beyond.

As he did so, he caught a fleeting glimpse of Ser.

The beast had turned to descend the mountain. Padding purposefully, the devil was entering his kingdom.

Mok's comprehension faltered. *Cycle?* Ser had been a god and now he was a devil. Mok had been a devil and now he was a god. But he could never have become a god if Ser hadn't willed the exchange of roles.

Was this Ser's intent all along—to allow Mok to evolve as devil and then usurp his identity?

In that case, Ser was actually a devil from the beginning, and Mok had been right in opposing him, for Mok was truly godlike.

Or were they all—Mok, Ser, the others, even the primitive mammalian creatures on this planet—both gods *and* devils?

It was a matter, Mok decided, which might require an eternity of contemplation. . . .

* *

Blame Judy-Lynn del Rey for that one.

Judy-Lynn Benjamin was her name when I first met her at the 1968 World Science Fiction Convention. She was associate editor of *Galaxy*, and in her official capacity she asked me to write a story for the magazine. In her unofficial capacity she became such an instantaneous good friend that neither I nor my wife Elly could refuse her anything. Besides, she sneakily sent me the cover illustration for an upcoming issue of the magazine and commanded me to write a story around it.

Staring at the offbeat Reese artwork depicting a reptilian figure in a space suit and a rocket blasting off the surface of a barren planet, I felt trapped and desperate. During the previous four years I'd become heavily involved in film and television work, and done very little short fiction. Now I was committed to write not just a story, but one dealing specifically with the subject matter of this illustration. In effect, I was being told, "Here's the cart—now go build yourself a horse to put in front of it." And I had a deadline to meet.

In such a situation I did the sensible thing: I panicked.

Then I sat down and wrote "How Like a God" in a single sitting for the April 1969 issue.

As you've noted, it deals with both God and the Devil. Perhaps in this emergency the two of them were forced into an unwilling collaboration so that I'd complete the assignment on time.

Rendering unto God and giving the Devil his due, I'd say this story scores half a point for each.

The Movie People

Two thousand stars.

Two thousand stars, maybe more, set in the sidewalks along Hollywood Boulevard, each metal slab inscribed with the name of someone in the movie industry. They go way back, those names; from Broncho Billy Anderson to Adolph Zukor, everybody's there.

Everybody but Jimmy Rogers.

You won't find Jimmy's name because he wasn't a star, not even a bit player—just an extra.

"But I deserve it," he told me. "I'm entitled, if anybody is. Started out here in 1920 when I was just a punk kid. You look close, you'll spot me in the crowd shots in *The Mark of Zorro*. Been in over 450 pictures since, and still going strong. Ain't many left who can beat that record. You'd think it would entitle a fella to something."

Maybe it did, but there was no star for Jimmy Rogers, and that bit about still going strong was just a crock. Nowadays Jimmy was lucky if he got a casting call once or twice a year; there just isn't any spot for an old-timer with a white muff except in a western barroom scene.

Most of the time Jimmy just strolled the boulevard; a tall, soldierly-erect incongruity in the crowd of tourists, fags and freakouts. His home address was on Las Palmas, somewhere south of Sunset. I'd never been there but I could guess what it was—one of those old frame bungalow-court sweatboxes put up about the time he crashed the movies and still standing somehow by the grace of God and the disgrace of the housing authorities. That's the sort of place Jimmy stayed at, but he didn't really *live* there.

Jimmy Rogers lived at the Silent Movie.

The Silent Movie is over on Fairfax, and it's the only place in town where you can still go and see *The Mark of Zorro*. There's always a Chaplin comedy, and usually Laurel and Hardy, along with a serial starring Pearl White, Elmo Lincoln, or Houdini. And the features are great—early Griffith and DeMille, Barrymore in *Dr. Jekyll and Mr. Hyde,* Lon Chaney in *The Hunchback of Notre Dame,* Valentino in *Blood and Sand,* and a hundred more.

The bill changes every Wednesday, and every Wednesday night Jimmy Rogers was there, plunking down his ninety cents at the box office to watch *The Black Pirate* or *Son of the Sheik* or *Orphans of the Storm.*

To live again.

Because Jimmy didn't go there to see Doug and Mary or Rudy or Clara or Gloria or the Gish sisters. He went there to see himself, in the crowd shots.

At least that's the way I figured it, the first time I met him. They were playing *The Phantom of the Opera* that night, and afterward I spent the intermission with a cigarette outside the theatre, studying the display of stills.

If you asked me under oath, I couldn't tell you how our conversation started, but that's where I first heard Jimmy's routine about the 450 pictures and still going strong.

"Did you see me in there tonight?" he asked.

I stared at him and shook my head; even with the shabby hand-me-down suit and the white beard, Jimmy Rogers wasn't the kind you'd spot in an audience.

"Guess it was too dark for me to notice," I said.

"But there were torches," Jimmy told me. "I carried one."

Then I got the message. He was in the picture.

Jimmy smiled and shrugged. "Hell, I keep forgetting. You wouldn't recognize me. We did *The Phantom* way back in 'twenty-five. I looked so young they slapped a mustache on me in Make-up and a black wig. Hard to spot me in the catacombs scenes—all long shots. But there at the end, where Chaney is holding back the mob, I show up pretty good in the background, just left of Charley Zimmer. He's the one shaking his fist. I'm waving my torch. Had a lot of trouble with that picture, but we did this shot in one take."

In weeks to come I saw more of Jimmy Rogers. Sometimes he was up there on the screen, though truth to tell, I never did recognize him; he was a young man in those films of the twenties, and his appearances were limited to a flickering flash, a blurred face glimpsed in a crowd.

But always Jimmy was in the audience, even though he hadn't played in the picture. And one night I found out why.

Again it was intermission time and we were standing outside. By now Jimmy had gotten into the habit of talking to me and tonight we'd been seated together during the showing of *The Covered Wagon.*

We stood outside and Jimmy blinked at me. "Wasn't she beautiful?" he asked. "They don't look like that any more."

I nodded. "Lois Wilson? Very attractive."

"I'm talking about June."

I stared at Jimmy and then I realized he wasn't blinking. He was crying.

"June Logan. My girl. This was her first bit, the Indian attack scene. Must have been seventeen—I didn't know her then, it was two years later we met over at First National. But you must have noticed her. She was the one with the long blond curls."

"Oh, *that* one." I nodded again. "You're right. She was lovely."

And I was a liar, because I didn't remember seeing her at all, but I wanted to make the old man feel good.

"Junie's in a lot of the pictures they show here. And from 'twenty-five on, we played in a flock of 'em together. For a while we talked about getting hitched, but she started working her way up, doing bits—maids and such—and I never broke out of extra work. Both of us had been in the business long enough to know it was no go, not when one of you stays small and the other is headed for a big career."

Jimmy managed a grin as he wiped his eyes with something which might once have been a handkerchief. "You think I'm kidding, don't you? About the career, I mean. But she was going great, she would have been playing second leads pretty soon."

"What happened?" I asked.

The grin dissolved and the blinking returned. "Sound killed her."

"She didn't have a voice for talkies?"

Jimmy shook his head. "She had a great voice. I told you she was all set for second leads—by nineteen thirty she'd been in a dozen talkies. Then sound killed her."

I'd heard the expression a thousand times, but never like this.

Because the way Jimmy told the story, that's exactly what had happened. June Logan, his girl Junie, was on the set during the shooting of one of those early ALL TALKING—ALL SINGING—ALL DANCING epics. The director and camera crew, seeking to break away from the tyranny of the stationary microphone, rigged up one of the first traveling mikes on a boom. Such items weren't standard equipment yet, and this was an experiment. Somehow, during a take, it broke loose and the boom crashed, crushing June Logan's skull.

It never made the papers, not even the trades; the studio hushed it up and June Logan had a quiet funeral.

"Damn near forty years ago," Jimmy said. "And here I am, crying like it was yesterday. But she was my girl—"

And that was the other reason why Jimmy Rogers went to the Silent Movie. To visit his girl.

"Don't you see?" he told me. "She's still alive up there on the screen, in all those pictures. Just the way she was when we were together. Five years we had, the best years for me."

I could see that. The two of them in love, with each other and with the movies. Because in those days, people *did* love the movies. And to actually be *in* them, even in tiny roles, was the average person's idea of seventh heaven.

Seventh Heaven, that's another film we saw with June Logan playing a crowd scene. In the following weeks, with Jimmy's help, I got so I could spot his girl. And he'd told the truth—she was a beauty. Once you noticed her, really saw her, you wouldn't forget. Those blond ringlets, that smile, identified her immediately.

One Wednesday night Jimmy and I were sitting together watching *The Birth of a Nation*. During a street shot Jimmy nudged my shoulder. "Look, there's June."

I peered up at the screen, then shook my head. "I don't see her."

"Wait a second—there she is again. See, off to the left, behind Walthall's shoulder?"

There was a blurred image and then the camera followed Henry B. Walthall as he moved away.

I glanced at Jimmy. He was rising from his seat.

"Where you going?"

He didn't answer me, just marched outside.

When I followed I found him leaning against the wall under the marquee and breathing hard; his skin was the color of his whiskers.

"Junie," he murmured. "I saw her—"

I took a deep breath. "Listen to me. You told me her first picture was *The Covered Wagon*. That was made in 1923. And Griffith shot *The Birth of a Nation* in 1914."

Jimmy didn't say anything. There was nothing to say. We both knew what we were going to do—march back into the theatre and see the second show.

When the scene screened again we were watching and waiting. I looked at the screen, then glanced at Jimmy.

"She's gone," he whispered. "She's not in the picture."

"She never was," I told him. "You know that."

"Yeah." Jimmy got up and drifted out into the night, and I didn't see him again until the following week.

That's when they showed the short feature with Charles Ray— I've forgotten the title, but he played his usual country-boy role, and there was a baseball game in the climax with Ray coming through to win.

The camera panned across the crowd sitting in the bleachers and I caught a momentary glimpse of a smiling girl with long blond curls.

"Did you see her?" Jimmy grabbed my arm.

"That girl—"

"It was Junie. She winked at me!"

This time I was the one who got up and walked out. He followed, and I was waiting in front of the theatre, right next to the display poster.

"See for yourself." I nodded at the poster. "This picture was made in 1917." I forced a smile. "You forget, there were thousands of pretty blond extras in pictures and most of them wore curls."

He stood there shaking, not listening to me at all, and I put my hand on his shoulder. "Now look here—"

"I *been* looking here," Jimmy said. "Week after week, year after year. And you might as well know the truth. This ain't the first time it's happened. Junie keeps turning up in picture after picture I know she never made. Not just the early ones, before her time, but later, during the twenties when I knew her, when I knew exactly what she was playing in. Sometimes it's only a quick flash, but I see her—then she's gone again. And the next running, she doesn't come back.

"It got so that for a while I was almost afraid to go see a show —figured I was cracking up. But now you've seen her too—"

I shook my head slowly. "Sorry, Jimmy. I never said that." I glanced at him, then gestured toward my car at the curb. "You look tired. Come on, I'll drive you home."

He looked worse than tired; he looked lost and lonely and infinitely old. But there was a stubborn glint in his eyes, and he stood his ground.

"No, thanks. I'm gonna stick around for the second show."

As I slid behind the wheel I saw him turn and move into the theatre, into the place where the present becomes the past and the past becomes the present. Up above in the booth they call it a projection machine, but it's really a time machine; it can take you back, play tricks with your imagination and your memory. A girl dead forty years comes alive again, and an old man relives his vanished youth—

But I belonged in the real world, and that's where I stayed. I didn't go to the Silent Movie the next week or the week following.

And the next time I saw Jimmy was almost a month later, on the set.

They were shooting a western, one of my scripts, and the director wanted some additional dialogue to stretch a sequence. So they called me in, and I drove all the way out to location, at the ranch.

Most of the studios have a ranch spread for western action sequences, and this was one of the oldest; it had been in use since the silent days. What fascinated me was the wooden fort where they were doing the crowd scene—I could swear I remembered it from one of the first Tim McCoy pictures. So after I huddled with the director and scribbled a few extra lines for the principals, I began nosing around behind the fort, just out of curiosity, while they set up for the new shots.

Out front was the usual organized confusion; cast and crew milling around the trailers, extras sprawled on the grass drinking coffee. But here in the back I was all alone, prowling around in musty, log-lined rooms built for use in forgotten features. Hoot

Gibson had stood at this bar, and Jack Hoxie had swung from this dance-hall chandelier. Here was a dust-covered table where Fred Thomson sat, and around the corner, in the cut-away bunkhouse—

Around the corner, in the cut-away bunkhouse, Jimmy Rogers sat on the edge of a mildewed mattress and stared up at me, startled, as I moved forward.

"You—?"

Quickly I explained my presence. There was no need for him to explain his; casting had called and given him a day's work here in the crowd shots.

"They been stalling all day, and it's hot out there. I figured maybe I could sneak back here and catch me a little nap in the shade."

"How'd you know where to go?" I asked. "Ever been here before?"

"Sure. Forty years ago in this very bunkhouse. Junie and I, we used to come here during lunch break and—"

He stopped.

"What's wrong?"

Something *was* wrong. On the pan make-up face of it, Jimmy Rogers was the perfect picture of the grizzled western old-timer; buckskin britches, fringed shirt, white whiskers and all. But under the make-up was pallor, and the hands holding the envelope were trembling.

The envelope—

He held it out to me. "Here. Mebbe you better read this."

The envelope was unsealed, unstamped, unaddressed. It contained four folded pages covered with fine handwriting. I removed them slowly. Jimmy stared at me.

"Found it lying here on the mattress when I came in," he murmured. "Just waiting for me."

"But what is it? Where'd it come from?"

"Read it and see."

As I started to unfold the pages the whistle blew. We both knew the signal; the scene was set up, they were ready to roll, principals and extras were wanted out there before the cameras.

Jimmy Rogers stood up and moved off, a tired old man shuffling out into the hot sun. I waved at him, then sat down on the moldering mattress and opened the letter. The handwriting was faded, and there was a thin film of dust on the pages. But I could still read it, every word. . . .

Darling:
I've been trying to reach you so long and in so many ways. Of course I've seen you, but it's so dark out there I can't always be sure, and then too you've changed a lot through the years.

But I *do* see you, quite often, even though it's only for a moment. And I hope you've seen me, because I always try to wink or make some kind of motion to attract your attention.

The only thing is, I can't do too much or show myself too long or it would make trouble. That's the big secret—keeping in the background, so the others won't notice me. It wouldn't do to frighten anybody, or even to get anyone wondering why there are more people in the background of a shot than there should be.

That's something for you to remember, darling, just in case. You're always safe, as long as you stay clear of close-ups. Costume pictures are the best—about all you have to do is wave your arms once in a while and shout, "On to the Bastille," or something like that. It really doesn't matter except to lip-readers, because it's silent, of course.

Oh, there's a lot to watch out for. Being a dress extra has its points, but not in ballroom sequences—too much dancing. That goes for parties, too, particularly in a DeMille production where they're "making whoopee" or one of von Stroheim's orgies. Besides, von Stroheim's scenes are always cut.

It doesn't hurt to be cut, don't misunderstand about that. It's no different than an ordinary fadeout at the end of a scene, and then you're free to go into another picture. Anything that was ever made, as long as there's still a print available for running somewhere. It's like falling asleep and then having one dream after another. The dreams are the scenes, of course, but while the scenes are playing, they're real.

I'm not the only one, either. There's no telling how many others do the same thing; maybe hundreds for all I know, but I've recognized a few I'm sure of and I think some of them have recognized me. We never let on to each other that we know, because it wouldn't do to make anybody suspicious.

Sometimes I think that if we could talk it over, we might

come up with a better understanding of just how it happens, and why. But the point is, you *can't* talk, everything is silent; all you do is move your lips and if you tried to communicate such a difficult thing in pantomime you'd surely attract attention.

I guess the closest I can come to explaining it is to say it's like reincarnation—you can play a thousand roles, take or reject any part you want, as long as you don't make yourself conspicuous or do something that would change the plot.

Naturally you get used to certain things. The silence, of course. And if you're in a bad print there's flickering; sometimes even the air seems grainy, and for a few frames you may be faded or out of focus.

Which reminds me—another thing to stay away from, the slapstick comedies. Sennett's early stuff is the worst, but Larry Semon and some of the others are just as bad; all that speeded-up camera action makes you dizzy.

Once you can learn to adjust, it's all right, even when you're looking off the screen into the audience. At first the darkness is a little frightening—you have to remind yourself it's only a theatre and there are just people out there, ordinary people watching a show. They don't know you can see them. They don't know that as long as your scene runs, you're just as real as they are, only in a different way. You walk, run, smile, frown, drink, eat—

That's another thing to remember, about the eating. Stay out of those Poverty Row quickies where everything is cheap and faked. Go where there's real set-dressing, big productions with banquet scenes and real food. If you work fast you can grab enough in a few minutes, while you're off-camera, to last you.

The big rule is, always be careful. Don't get caught. There's so little time, and you seldom get an opportunity to do anything on your own, even in a long sequence. It's taken me forever to get this chance to write you—I've planned it for so long, my darling, but it just wasn't possible until now.

This scene is playing outside the fort, but there's quite a large crowd of settlers and wagon-train people, and I had a chance to slip away inside here to the rooms in back—they're on camera in the background all during the action. I found this stationery and a pen, and I'm scribbling just as fast as I can. Hope you can read it. That is, if you ever get the chance!

Naturally, I can't mail it—but I have a funny hunch. You see, I noticed that standing set back here, the bunkhouse, where you and I used to come in the old days. I'm going to leave this letter under the mattress, and pray.

Yes, darling, I pray. Someone or something *knows* about us, and about how we feel. How we felt about being in the movies. That's why I'm here, I'm sure of that; because I've always loved pictures so. Someone who knows *that* must also know how I loved you. And still do.

I think there must be many heavens and many hells, each of us making his own, and—

The letter broke off there.

No signature, but of course I didn't need one. And it wouldn't have proved anything. A lonely old man, nursing his love for forty years, keeping her alive inside himself somewhere until she broke out in the form of a visual hallucination up there on the screen—such a man could conceivably go all the way into a schizoid split, even to the point where he could imitate a woman's handwriting as he set down the rationalization of his obsession.

I started to fold the letter, then dropped it on the mattress as the shrill scream of an ambulance siren startled me into sudden movement.

Even as I ran out the doorway I seemed to know what I'd find; the crowd huddling around the figure sprawled in the dust under the hot sun. Old men tire easily in such heat, and once the heart goes—

Jimmy Rogers looked very much as though he were smiling in his sleep as they lifted him into the ambulance. And I was glad of that; at least he'd died with his illusions intact.

"Just keeled over during the scene—one minute he was standing there, and the next—"

They were still chattering and gabbling when I walked away, walked back behind the fort and into the bunkhouse.

The letter was gone.

I'd dropped it on the mattress, and it was gone. That's all I can say about it. Maybe somebody else happened by while I was out front, watching them take Jimmy away. Maybe a gust of wind carried it through the doorway, blew it across the desert in a hot Santa Ana gust. Maybe there *was* no letter. You can take your choice—all I can do is state the facts.

And there aren't very many more facts to state.

I didn't go to Jimmy Rogers' funeral, if indeed he had one. I don't even know where he was buried; probably the Motion Picture Fund took care of him. Whatever *those* facts may be, they aren't important.

For a few days I wasn't too interested in facts. I was trying to answer a few abstract questions about metaphysics—reincarnation, heaven and hell, the difference between real life and reel life. I kept thinking about those images you see up there on the screen in those old movies; images of actual people indulging in make-believe. But even after they die, the make-believe goes on, and that's a form of reality too. I mean, where's the borderline? And if there *is* a borderline—is it possible to cross over? *Life's but a walking shadow—*

Shakespeare said that, but I wasn't sure what he meant.

I'm still not sure, but there's just one more fact I must state.

The other night, for the first time in all the months since Jimmy Rogers died, I went back to the Silent Movie.

They were playing *Intolerance,* one of Griffith's greatest. Way back in 1916 he built the biggest set ever shown on the screen— the huge temple in the Babylonian sequence.

One shot never fails to impress me, and it did so now; a wide angle on the towering temple, with thousands of people moving antlike amid the gigantic carvings and colossal statues. In the distance, beyond the steps guarded by rows of stone elephants, looms a mighty wall, its top covered with tiny figures. You really have to look closely to make them out. But I did look closely, and this time I can swear to what I saw.

One of the extras, way up there on the wall in the background, was a smiling girl with long blond curls. And standing right beside her, one arm around her shoulder, was a tall old man with white whiskers. I wouldn't have noticed either of them, except for one thing.

They were waving at me . . .

*   *

Long ago and far away—on the other side of the generation gap—the silent movies were important. To people like myself, who grew up in an era before radio, television, and air transportation brought us into contact with the far corners of the earth, movies were our window on the world. We attended regularly, and the stars and players we saw on the screen frequently became more familiar to us than our own cousins, uncles, and aunts. We learned to love the films and the actors featured in them. And for some of us, first loves last forever.

Luckily for me, I got to Hollywood just in time to meet some of the people who'd represented romance to me in my childhood. Names like Monte Blue, Francis McDonald, Chester Conklin, and Julia Faye may not mean anything to youngsters today, but I remembered them fondly. And I'll always be grateful for the opportunity to reminisce with Boris Karloff and play baseball with Buster Keaton. In 1964, when Elly and I were married, our wedding cake was the gift of Joan Crawford. No sense denying it; I'm hung up on silent films and those who made them. And I think some of that feeling comes through in "The Movie People."

The idea itself occurred to me because I'd seen some of my favorite films repeatedly in revivals—and each time I discovered something new, something I'd overlooked before. One day I got to wondering. What if that "something new" turned out to be *people?*

After that, the story wrote itself. To those who find it difficult to reconcile it with the sort of thing I'm usually associated with, I can only say that it must have been written on an off day.

But those who believe that "God is love" will have no doubt as to just where this particular story came from.

The Double Whammy

Rod pulled the chicken out of the burlap bag and threw it down into the pit.

The chicken squawked and fluttered, and Rod glanced away quickly. The gaping crowd gathered around the canvas walls of the pit ignored him; now all the eyes were focused on what was happening down below. There was a cackling, a scrabbling sound, and then a sudden sharp simultaneous intake of breath from the spectators.

Rod didn't have to look. He knew that the geek had caught the chicken.

Then the crowd began to roar. It was a strange noise, compounded of women's screams, high harsh laughter teetering on the edge of hysteria, and deep hoarse masculine murmurs of shocked dismay.

Rod knew what *that* sound meant, too.

The geek was biting off the chicken's head.

Rod stumbled out of the little tent, not looking back, grateful for the cool night air that fanned his sweating face. His shirt was soaked through under the cheap blazer. He'd have to change again before he went up on the outside platform to make his next pitch.

The pitch itself didn't bother him. Being a talker was his job and he was good at it; he liked conning the marks and turning the tip. Standing up there in front of the bloody banners and spieling about the Strange People always gave him his kicks, even if he was only working for a lousy mudshow that never played anywhere north of Tennessee. For three seasons straight he'd been with it, he was a pro, a real carny.

But now, all of a sudden, something was spooking him. No use kidding himself, he had to face it.

Rod was afraid of the geek.

He crossed behind the ten-in-one tent and moved in the direction of his little trailer, pulling out a handkerchief and wiping his forehead. That helped a little, but he couldn't wipe away what was inside his head. The cold, clammy fear was always there now, night and day.

Hell of it was, it didn't make sense. The Monarch of Mirth Shows had always worked "strong"—out here in the old boondocks you could still get away with murder, particularly if you were only killing chickens. And who gives a damn about chickens, anyway? The butchers chop off a million heads a day. A chicken is just a lousy bird, and a geek is just a lousy wino. A rumdum who hooks up with a carny, puts on a phony wild-man outfit and hops around in the bottom of a canvas enclosure while the talker gives the crowd a line about this ferocious monster, half man and half beast. Then the talker throws in the chicken and the geek does his thing.

Rod shook his head, but what was inside it didn't move. It stayed there, cold and clammy and coiled up in a ball. It had been there almost ever since the beginning of this season, and now Rod was conscious that it was growing. The fear was getting bigger.

But why? He'd worked with half-a-dozen lushes over the past three years. Maybe biting the head off a live chicken wasn't exactly the greatest way to make a living, but if the geeks didn't mind, why should he care? And Rod knew that a geek wasn't really a monster, just a poor old futz who was down on his luck and hooked on the sauce—willing to do anything, as long as he got his daily ration of popskull.

This season the geek they took on was named Mike. A quiet guy who kept out of everybody's way when he wasn't working; under the burnt-cork make-up he had the sad, wrinkled face of a man of fifty. Fifty hard years, perhaps thirty of them years of hard drinking. He never talked, just took his pint and curled up in the canvas on one of the trucks. Looking at him then, Rod was never spooked; if anything, he felt kind of sorry for the poor bastard.

It was only when the geek was in the pit that Rod felt that ball of fear uncoil. When he saw the woolly wig and the black face, the painted hands that clutched and clawed—yes, and when he saw the grinning mouth open to reveal the rotting yellow teeth, ready to bite—

Oh, it was getting to him all right, he was really uptight now. But nobody else knew. And nobody *would* know. Rod wasn't about to spill his guts to anyone here on the lot, and how would it look if he ran off to some head-shrinker and said, "Hey, Doc, help me—I'm afraid I'm gonna turn into a geek." He knew better than that. No shrinker could help him, and come what may he'd never end up geeking for a living. He'd lick this thing himself; he had to, and he would, just as long as no one else caught on and bugged him about it.

Rod climbed the steps, removing his jacket and unbuttoning his wet shirt as he moved up into the darkness of the trailer.

And then he felt the hands sliding across his bare chest, moving up over his shoulders to embrace him, and he smelt the fragrance, felt the warmth and the pressure even as he heard the whispered words. "Rod—darling—are you surprised?"

Truth to tell, Rod wasn't surprised. But he was pleased that she'd been waiting for him. He took her in his arms and glued his mouth to hers as they sank down on the cot.

"Cora," he murmured. "Cora—"

"Shhhh! No time to talk."

She was right. There wasn't time, because he had to be back on the bally platform in fifteen minutes. And it wasn't a smart idea to talk anyway, not with Madame Sylvia sneaking around and popping up out of nowhere just when you least expected her. Why in hell did a swinging bird like Cora have to have an old buzzard like Madame Sylvia for a grandmother?

But Rod wasn't thinking about grandmothers now, and he wasn't thinking about geeks, either. That was what Cora did to him, that was what Cora did *for* him, dissolving the cold fear in warm, writhing, wanting flesh. At times like these Rod knew why he couldn't cut out, why he stayed with it. Staying with it meant staying with her, and this was enough; this was everything, with ribbons on it.

It was only later, struggling into his shirt, hearing her whisper, "Please, honey, hurry and let's get out of here before she comes looking for me," that he wondered if it was really worth it. All this horsing around for a fast grope in the dark with a teen-age spik who practically creamed her jeans every time the old lady looked cross-eyed at her.

Sure Cora was a beautiful job, custom-made for him. But when you got right down to it she was still a kid and nobody would ever mistake her brain for a computer. Besides, she was a spik—well, maybe not exactly, but she was a gypsy and that added up to the same thing.

Walking back to the bally platform for the last pitch of the evening, Rod decided it was time to cool it. From now on the chill was in.

That night the show folded and trucked to Mazoo County Fair Grounds for a ten-day stand. They were all day setting up and then the crowds surged in, rednecks from the toolies up in the hills; must have been a couple thousand coming in night after night, and all craving action.

For almost a week Rod managed to keep out of Cora's way without making it too obvious. Her grandmother was running the mitt camp concession on the other end of the midway, and Cora was supposed to shill for her; usually she was too busy to sneak off. A couple of times Rod caught sight of her signaling to him from down in the crowd around the bally platform, but he always looked the other way, pretending he didn't see her. And once he heard her scratching on the trailer door in the middle of the night, only he made out that he was asleep, even when she called out to him, and after about ten minutes she went away.

The trouble was, Rod didn't sleep anywhere near that good; seemed like every time he closed his eyes now he could see the pit, see the black geek and the white chicken.

So the next time Cora came scratching on the door he let her in, and for a little while he was out of the pit, safe in her arms. And instead of the geek growling and the chicken cackling he heard her voice in the darkness, her warm, soft voice, murmuring, "You do love me, don't you, Rod?"

The answer came easy, the way it always did. "Course I do. You know that."

Her fingers tightened on his arms. "Then it's all right. We can get married and I'll have the baby—"

"Baby?"

He sat up fast.

"I wasn't going to tell you, honey, not until I was sure, but I am now." Her voice was vibrant. "Just think, darling—"

He *was* thinking. And when he spoke, his voice was hoarse. "Your grandmother—Madame Sylvia—does she know?"

"Not yet. I wanted you to come with me when I tell her—"

"Tell her nothing."

"Rod?"

"Tell her nothing. Get rid of it."

"Honey—"

"You heard me."

She tried to hold him then but he wrenched himself free, stood up, reached for his shirt. She was crying now, but the louder she sobbed, the more he hurried dressing, just as if she wasn't there. Just as if she wasn't stuttering and stammering all that jazz about what did he mean, he couldn't do this, he had to listen, and if the old lady found out she'd kill her.

Rod wanted to yell at her to shut up, he wanted to crack her one across the mouth and *make* her shut up, but he managed to control himself. And when he did speak his voice was soft.

"Take it easy, sweetheart," he said. "Let's not get ourselves all excited here. There's no problem."

"But I told you—"

He patted her arm in the darkness. "Relax, will you? You got nothing to worry about. You told me yourself the old lady doesn't know. Get rid of it and she never will."

Christ, it was so simple you'd think even a lame-brain like Cora would understand. But instead she was crying again, louder than ever, and beating on him with her fists.

"No, no, you can't make me! We've got to get married, the first time I let you, you promised we would, just as soon as the season was over—"

"As far as I'm concerned, the season's over right now." Rod tried to keep his voice down, but when she came at him again, clinging, somehow it was worse than feeling her fists. He couldn't stand this any more; not the clinging, not the wet whimpering.

"Listen to me, Cora. I'm sorry about what happened, you know that. But you can scrub the marriage bit."

The way she blew up then you'd have thought the world was coming to an end, and he had to slap her to keep the whole damn lot from hearing her screech. He felt kind of lousy, belting her one like that, but it quieted her down enough so's he could hustle her out. She went away still crying, but very quietly. And at least she got the message.

Rod didn't see her around the next day, or the one after. But in order to keep her from bugging him again, he spent both nights over at Boots Donahue's wagon, playing a little stud with the boys. He figured that if there was any trouble and he had to peel off fast, maybe he could turn a few extra bucks for the old grouch-bag.

Only it didn't exactly work out that way. Usually he was pretty lucky with the pasteboards, but he had a bad run both evenings and ended up in hock for his next three paychecks. That was bad enough, but the next day was worse.

Basket Case gave him the word.

Rod was just heading for the cook tent for breakfast when Basket Case called him over. He was lying on an old army cot outside his trailer with a cigarette in his mouth.

"How's for a light?" he asked.

Rod cupped a match for him, then stuck around, knowing he'd have to flick the ashes while Basket Case had his smoke. And a guy born without arms or legs has a little trouble getting rid of a butt, too.

Funny thing, the Strange People never got to Rod, no matter how peculiar they looked. Even Basket Case, who was just a living head attached to a shapeless bundle of torso, didn't give him the creeps. Maybe it was because old Basket Case himself didn't seem to mind; he just took it for granted that he was a freak. And he always acted and sounded normal, not like that rumdum geek who put on a fright wig and blacked up and made noises like a crazy animal when he went after a chicken—

Rod tried to push away the thought and pulled out a cigarette for himself. He was just getting a match when Basket Case looked up at him.

"Heard the news?" he asked.

"What news?"

"Cora's dead."

Rod burned his fingers and the match dropped away.

"Dead?"

Basket Case nodded. "Last night. Madame Sylvia found her in the trailer after the last show—"

"What happened?"

Basket Case just looked at him. "Thought maybe you could tell me that."

Rod had to choke out the words. "What's that crack supposed to mean?"

"Nothing." Basket Case shrugged. "Madame Sylvia told Donahue the kid died of a ruptured appendix."

Rod took a deep breath. He forced himself to look sorry, but all at once he felt good, very good. Until he heard Basket Case saying, "Only thing is, I never heard of anyone rupturing their appendix with a knitting needle."

Rod reached out and took the cigarette from Basket Case to dump his ashes. The way his hand was trembling, he didn't have to do anything but let them fall.

"The appendix story is just a cover—Madame Sylvia doesn't want the fuzz nosing around." Basket Case nodded as Rod stuck the cigarette back between his lips. "But if you ask me, she knows."

"Now look, if you're saying what I think you're saying, you'd better forget it—"

"Sure, I'll forget it. But *she* won't." Basket Case lowered his voice. "Funeral's this afternoon, over at the county cemetery. You better show your face along with the rest of us, just so it doesn't look funny. After that, my advice to you is cut and run."

"Now wait a minute—" Rod was all set to go on, but what was the use? Basket Case *knew*, and there was no sense putting on an act with him. "I can't run," he said. "I'm into Boots Donahue for three weeks' advance. If I cop out, he'll spread the word around and I won't work carny again, not in these parts."

Basket Case spat the cigarette out. It landed on the ground beside the cot and Rod stamped it out. Basket Case shook his head. "Never mind the money," he said. "If you don't run, you won't be working anywhere." He glanced around cautiously and when he spoke again his voice was just a whisper. "Don't you understand? This is the crunch—I tell you, Madame Sylvia knows what happened."

Rod wasn't about to whisper. "That old bat? You said yourself she doesn't want any truck with the fuzz, and even if she did, she couldn't prove anything. So what's to be afraid of?"

"The double whammy," said Basket Case.

Rod blinked at him.

"Want me to spell it out for you? Three seasons ago, just before you came with the show, fella name of Richey was boss canvasman. Mighty nice guy, but he had a problem—he was scared of snakes. Babe Flynn was working them, had a bunch of constrictors, all standards for her act and harmless as they come. But Richey had such a thing about snakes he wouldn't even go near her wagon.

"Where he went wrong was, he went near Madame Sylvia's wagon. Cora was pretty young then, just budding out you might say, but that didn't stop Richey from making his move. Nothing serious, only conversation. How the old lady found out about it I don't know and how she found out he was spooked on snakes I don't know either, because he always tried to hide it, of course.

"But one afternoon, last day of our stand in Red Clay it was, Madame Sylvia took a little walk over to Richey's trailer. He was standing outside, shaving, with a mirror hung up on the door.

"She didn't say anything to him, didn't even look at him—just stared at his reflection in the mirror. Then she made a couple of passes and mumbled something under her breath and walked away. That's all there was to it.

"Next morning, Richey didn't show up. They found him lying on the floor inside his trailer, deader'n a mackerel. Half his bones were broken and the way the body was crushed you'd swear a dozen constrictors had been squeezing his guts. I saw his face and believe me it wasn't pretty."

Rod's voice was husky. "You mean the old lady set those snakes on him?"

Basket Case shook his head. "Babe Flynn kept her snakes locked up tight as a drum in her own trailer. She swore up and down nobody'd even come near them the night before, let alone turned 'em loose. But Richey was dead. And that's what I mean about the double whammy."

"Look." Rod was talking to Basket Case, but he wanted to hear it himself, too. "Madame Sylvia's just another mitt reader, peddling phony fortunes to the suckers. All this malarkey about gypsy curses—"

"Okay, okay." Basket Case shrugged. "But if I were you I'd cut out of here, fast. And until I did, I wouldn't let that old lady catch me standing in front of a mirror."

"Thanks for the tip," Rod said.

As he walked away, Basket Case called after him. "See you at the funeral."

But Rod didn't go to the funeral.

It wasn't as if he was afraid or anything; he just didn't like the idea of standing at Cora's grave with everybody looking at him as if they knew. And they damned well did by now, all of them. Maybe it would be smart to ease out of here like Basket Case said, but not now. Not until he could pay off what he owed to Donahue. For the next three weeks he'd just sweat it out.

Meanwhile, he'd watch his step. Not that he believed that crazy story about the double whammy—Basket Case was just putting him on, it had to be a gag. But it never hurt to be careful.

Which is why Rod shaved for the evening performance that afternoon. He knew the old lady was at the funeral like everybody else; she wouldn't be creeping up behind him to capture his soul from his reflection in the mirror—

Damned right she wouldn't!

Rod made a face at himself in the glass. What the hell was the matter with him, anyway? He didn't buy that bit about the curse.

But there *was* something wrong. Because for a moment when Rod looked into the mirror he didn't see himself. Instead he was staring into a black, grinning face, with bloodshot, red-rimmed eyes and a twisted mouth opening to show the yellow fangs—

Rod blinked and the face went away; it was his own reflection peering back at him. But his hand was shaking so that he had to put the razor down.

His hand was still shaking when he reached for the bottle on the top shelf, and he must have spilled more of the whiskey than he managed to get into the glass. So he took a slug straight from the bottle instead. And then another, until his hands were steady again. Good for the nerves, a little snort now and then. Only you had to watch that stuff, not let it run away with you. Because if you didn't, pretty soon you got hooked and some day before you knew what was happening, you wound up in the woolly wig and the blackface, down there in the pit waiting for the white chicken—

The hell with that noise. It wasn't going to happen. Just a couple of weeks and he'd be out of here, no more carny, nothing to bug him ever again. All he had to do now was keep his cool and watch his step.

Rod watched his step very carefully that evening when he walked up to the bally platform and adjusted his mike for the pitch. Standing before the bloody banners he felt good, very good indeed, and the couple of extra belts he'd taken from the bottle just for luck seemed to have unwound that ball of fear inside his head. It was easy to make his pitch about the Strange People—"All there on the inside, folks, on the *in*side"—and watch the marks flocking around down below. The marks—*they* were the real freaks, only they didn't know it. Shelling out their dough to gawk at poor devils like Basket Case, then paying extra for the SPECIAL ADDED ATTRACTION, ADULTS ONLY, in the canvas pit behind the ten-in-one tent. What kind of a pervert would pay money to see a geek? What was the matter with people like that?

And what was the matter with him? Standing there beside the pit, holding the burlap bag and feeling the chicken fluttering helplessly inside, Rod felt the fear returning to flutter within himself. He didn't want to look down into the pit and see the geek crouching there, growling and grimacing like a real wild man. So he looked at the crowd instead, and that was better. The crowd didn't know he was afraid. Nobody knew he was spooked, let alone what scared him.

Rod talked to the crowd, building his pitch, and his hands started to fumble with the cord around the neck of the burlap bag, getting ready to open it and dump the chicken into the pit.

And that's when he saw *her*.

She was standing over to one side, right up against the edge of the canvas; just a little old woman dressed in black, with a black shawl draped over her head. Her face was pinched, her skin was brown and leathery, wrinkled into a permanent scowl. An old lady, nobody gave her a second glance, but Rod saw her.

And she saw *him*.

Funny, he'd never noticed Madame Sylvia's eyes before. They were big and brown and staring—they stared right at him now, stared right *through* him.

Rod wrenched his gaze away, forced his fingers to open the sack. All the while, mechanically, he was talking, finishing the buildup as he reached for the chicken, pulled it out, flung the clucking creature down to that other creature in the pit—the creature that growled and grabbed and oh my God it was biting now—

He couldn't watch and he had to turn his head away, seeing the crowd again as they shrieked and shuddered, getting their kicks. And *she* was still standing there, still staring at him.

But now her clawlike hand moved, moved over the rim of the canvas to extend a pointing forefinger. Rod knew what she was pointing at; she was pointing at the geek pit. And that wrinkled face *could* change its expression, because she was smiling now.

Rod turned and groped his way out into the night.

She knew.

Not just about him and Cora, but about everything. Those eyes that stared at him and through him had also stared *inside* him—stared inside and found his fear. That's why she'd pointed and smiled; she knew what he was afraid of.

The midway lights were bright, but it was darker behind the canvas sidewalls except where a patch of moonlight shone on the big water barrel setting next to the cook tent.

Rod's face was damp with sweat; he headed for the barrel and soaked his handkerchief in the water to wipe his forehead. Time for another pitch pretty soon, and the next show. He had to pull himself together.

The cool water helped to clear his head, and he dipped his handkerchief again. That was better. No sense flipping just because a nutty old dame gave him a dirty look. This business about gypsies and the evil eye and the double whammy was all a crock. And even if there *was* something to it, he wouldn't let her get to him. He wasn't about to stand in front of any mirrors—

Then he glanced down at the water in the barrel, saw his features reflected in the moonlight shining there. And he saw her face, standing right behind him. Her eyes were staring and her mouth was mumbling, and now her hands were coming up, making passes in the air. Making passes like an old witch, she was going to turn him into a geek with the double whammy—

Rod turned, and that's the last thing he remembered. He must have passed out, fallen, because when he came to he was still on the ground.

But the ground was somehow different than the earth outside the tent; it was covered with sawdust. And the light was stronger, it was shining straight down between the canvas walls of the pit.

He was in the pit.

The realization came, and Rod looked up, knowing it was too late, she'd caught him, he was in the geek's body now.

But something else was wrong, too; the pit was deeper, the canvas walls much higher. Everything seemed bigger, even the blur of faces crowded around the sides of the pit way up above. *Way up above*—why was he so small?

Then his eyes shifted as he heard the growling. Rod turned and looked up again, just in time to see the black grinning face looming over him, the giant mouth opening to reveal the rotting yellow teeth. It was only then that Rod knew what she had really done to him, as the huge hands grabbed out, pulling him close. For a moment he squawked and fluttered his wings.

Then the geek bit off his head.

*   *

Way back in 1946, literary pundit Christopher Morley outraged his fellow critics by flatly declaring that William Lindsay Gresham's *Nightmare Alley* was the best novel of the year.

I agreed. People who know the title only through viewing the Tyrone Power film on television don't realize what they've missed by not reading the book. For my money, Bill Gresham was one hell of a writer.

Although we never met, we carried on an intermittent correspondence over the years. I was surprised to learn that Gresham and his wife were *Weird Tales* fans: they even had a copy of my first book, *The Opener of the Way*, which flattered me enormously.

As for Gresham's work, it was undoubtedly responsible in part for influencing the style of my own first novel, *The Scarf*, which The Dial Press published in '47. And like the late Henry Kuttner, I was fascinated by his account of carnival geeks. Several times I skirted around the subject in stories of my own, but it wasn't until February 1970 that my own particular concept appeared in *Fantastic*.

Now there may be some controversy as to which came first, the chicken or the geek, but I'm sure there's little room for doubt as to the source of this particular tale.

Gresham may have inspired it, but the Devil made me do it.

And Colonel Sanders would never approve.

In the Cards

"Saturday night?" Danny said. "What do you mean, I'll die on Saturday night?"

Danny tried to focus his eyes on the old woman but he couldn't make it—too smashed. She was just a big fat blur, like the cards spread on the table between them.

"I am truly sorry," the old woman murmured. "I can only read what I see. It is in the cards."

Danny grabbed for the edge of the table and stood up. The

smell of incense in the darkened room was making him sick. It wasn't easy to stand and it wasn't easy to laugh, either, but he managed.

"Hell with you, sister. You and the cards too."

The old woman stared at him but there was no anger in her eyes, only compassion, and somehow that was even worse.

"I'm not gonna die on Saturday night," Danny told her. "Not me. You're talking to Danny Jackson, remember? I'm a star. A big star. And you, you're just a—"

Standing there, lurching there in the darkness, he told her what she was, using a vocabulary ripened and enriched by thirty years in show biz.

Her eyes never flickered, her glance never wavered, and there was still nothing in her gaze but pity when he finally ran out of breath.

And ran out of the reeking room, her pity pursuing him.

"You will die on Saturday night."

Damned echo in his ears, even when he gunned the Ferrari and roared away from the curb. The car swayed, playing tag with the yellow line; good thing it was so late and the street was clear of traffic.

It was late and he was bombed, bombed clean out of his silly skull. Had to be, or he'd never have driven all the hell down to South Alvarado just to roust a phony, faking old fortuneteller out of bed and lay a fifty-dollar bill on her for a phony, faking fortune, the old witch, the old bitch—

But they were all bitches, all of them, and Lola was the worst.

Danny made it out to Bel Air, avoiding Sunset and coming up Pico until he could cut over on a side street through Westwood. When you're on the sauce you learn the right routes to take, the routes that get you safely through the streets, safely through the minutes and the hours and the days and the nights, even when your nerves are screaming and Lola is screaming too.

And of course Lola *was* screaming, she'd been waiting up for him and she cut loose the minute he opened the front door.

"Goddam it, where were you, don't you realize you've got a six o'clock call tomorrow morning—?"

There was a lot more, too, but Danny slammed the door on it, the door of the guest room. He hadn't slept in the same bed with Lola for three months, and it wasn't just because of what Dr. Carlsen had told him about his ticker, either.

It was better here in the bedroom, dropping his clothes and flopping down on the old king-size, away from the bitch, away from the witch.

Only the witch didn't go away. Here in the dark, Danny could see her eyes again, staring at him as if she understood, as if she *knew*. But nobody knew what the Doc had told him, not Lola, not the studio, not even his own agent. So how could some old bag take one look at him and figure it out?

In the cards. It's in the cards.

Her eyes, he remembered her eyes when she'd said it. They were so deep and black. Black as the Ace of Spades lying there on the table. The Queen of Spades had turned up, too, and that's when she made that crack about him dying on Saturday night.

Tomorrow was Wednesday. Wednesday, Thursday, Friday, Saturday—

To hell with it. That's what he'd told the old klooch and that's what he told himself. Tomorrow was Wednesday and he'd better think about that; Lola was right, he did have a six o'clock call, the test was shooting, and this is what counted. Not counting the days until Saturday, just the few short hours until that test.

Wednesday. Named after Woden, the god of war and battles. Danny's name had been Kuhlsberg once, not Jackson, and he knew, he remembered. Wednesday was war, all right, and it was a battle just getting out of bed with that head of his pounding away. Thank God he could sneak out before Lola woke up, and get through the foggy streets before the traffic began to build up on the San Diego Freeway.

But the fight was just beginning, the fight to smile there under the lights while Benny plastered on the old pancake make-up and fitted the little wings to the perspiring temples where the hairline had eroded. The perspiration was just the alcohol oozing out of him, it wasn't flop-sweat, because Danny knew he had nothing to worry about. The test was just a formality, all they wanted was six minutes of film to show the network brass and the agency people in New York. The series was all set, Fischer had told him that last week, and Fischer never conned him. Best damned agent in the business. So no panic, he knew his lines, all he had to do was step out onto the set and walk through the scene. If there were any fluffs, Joe Collins would cover for him. Joe was a good man, he'd never carry a lead himself but he was a real pro. And Rudy Moss was a hell of a director and an old buddy of his. They were all friends here, and they all knew how much was riding for them on this series.

"Ready for you, Mr. Jackson."

Danny smiled, stood up, strolled out to where Joe Collins was waiting on the set. He found his chalk marks, somebody from the camera unit dragged out his tape, the mike-boom came down and he tested his voice for gain. Then they hit the lights and Rudy Moss gave him his cue for action and they rolled.

They rolled, and he blew it.

The first take he forgot the business with the cigarette. They cut and started from the top, and he got fouled up in his cross-over to Joe, stepped right out of camera before he realized it. So they rolled again, and by this time he was uptight and Moss didn't like what he was getting, so it was back and take it from the top once more. Then Danny started losing lines—but those things happen. The only trouble was, he had to stand there under those lights and there were interruptions when a plane went over and ruined the sound and somebody came barging in right on the middle of his long speech and then Joe jumped one of his cues and the idiot script girl threw him the wrong prompt and he was sweating, wringing wet, and his hands started to twitch and Moss was very patient and it was Take Sixteen and no break for lunch and he could see the looks the crew was giving him and finally they wrapped it up at three-thirty, eight and a half solid hours for a lousy dialogue bit, nothing but two-shots and close-ups, and it was a bomb.

Everybody was very polite and they said, "Nice work, Mr. Jackson," and "Great," and "You did it, boy," but Danny knew what he'd done.

The fight was over and he'd lost.

No sense going home because Lola would ask him how did it go and Fischer would be calling and to hell with it. There was a little joint out on the ocean, below Malibu, where the lights were nice and dim and you could get a good steak to anchor the martinis.

That was the right answer, and though he scraped a fender getting out of the parking lot after they closed up the place, he made it without pain. Lola wasn't waiting up for him tonight—tonight, hell, it was morning already, Thursday morning—but the bed in the guest room felt better than ever.

Until he closed his eyes and saw what was in the cards. Thursday morning. *Thursday. And two days from now—*

If the old bitch was so good at telling fortunes, if she could see everything in the cards, why hadn't she tipped him off about the test? There was a *real* life-and-death matter for you, and she never even mentioned it. Of course she didn't; what could she or anybody else see in a lousy pack of playing cards? That's all they were, ordinary playing cards, and she was just a cheap grifter and Saturday was just another day of the week.

And this was Thursday. Thursday noon, now, with Danny getting up and groping his way into the john and shivering in the shower and shaving and stumbling downstairs and finding the note and reading it twice, three times, before it finally sank in.

Lola gone. Left him. *"Sorry . . . tried to get through to you . . . can't stand watching you destroy yourself . . . please . . . need help . . . try to understand."* God, the phrases in that note, like daytime soaper dialogue. But it all added up. Lola was gone.

Danny called her mother's place in Laguna. No answer. Then he tried her sister up at Arrowhead. Nothing. By this time he'd cased the joint, seen that she'd cleared out the works, everything; must have taken her all day to pack the station wagon. She meant it; probably been planning the caper for weeks. Next thing he'd be getting a call from some hotshot lawyer, one of those Lear-jet boys. Christ, the least she could have done was waited to find out if he was going to get the series.

The series! Danny remembered now, he was due in Projection Room Nine at two o'clock; they were screening the test.

But it was after one now, and besides, he didn't need to see the running. He knew what they had in the can—six minutes of worms.

So he climbed in the car and went to Scandia for lunch instead; at least he intended to have lunch, but by late afternoon he hadn't gotten any further than the bar.

That's where his agent caught up with him, somewhere between the fifth and the sixth bloody mary.

"Thought I'd find you here," Fischer told him. "Get moving."

"Where we going?"

"Up to the office. I'd hate to have all these nice people here see me hit you right in the mouth."

"Get off my back, Fischer."

"Get off your butt." He hauled Danny from the stool. "Come on, let's go."

Fischer's office was on the Strip, only a few blocks away. But by the time they got there, Danny was up the wall; he knew what Fischer was going to say.

"No calls," Fischer told the girl on the board. Then he took Danny into the private office *behind* his private office and closed the door.

"All right," Fischer said. "Tell me."

"You saw the test?"

Fischer nodded, waiting. His mouth was grim, but the hard face and the hard talk never fooled Danny; he knew it was just an act. Fischer was a sweet guy inside, always bleeding for his clients. You could see the compassion in his eyes, it was there now, the same look of pity that the fortuneteller had—

Danny wanted to explain about the fortuneteller but he knew how it would sound and besides it wouldn't do any good. All he could do was say, "I wasn't loaded. I swear to God I wasn't loaded."

"I know that. And nobody said you were. I wish you *had* been —I've seen you play a scene with a couple of drinks under your belt and come off great." Fischer shook his head. "Everybody on the set knew what was wrong with you yesterday, but even that wouldn't matter. The trouble is, everybody in the projection room could see it today, up there on the screen. You were hung over."

"It was that bad, huh?"

"That bad?" Fischer sighed, swiveled his chair around to face Danny. "Do I have to spell it out for you, Danny? A guy makes three pictures in a row, all bombs, and he's had it. Sure, I know that Metro thing wasn't your fault, but the word is out and I haven't had an offer for six months. When it comes to films, you're scrubbed. Moynihan tells me—"

"Never mind about Moynihan," Danny said. "He's my business manager. He shouldn't even be talking to you."

"Who else can he talk to when you won't listen?" Fischer opened a folder on his desk, glanced at a type-sheet. "You owe eighty-three on the house and nine on the cars. You're in hock on the furniture, that's another twenty including the redecorating. Your checking account is minus zero. And if they yank your credit cards, you won't have enough left to buy a bagel at Linny's."

Cards? Why did he have to mention cards? Danny felt a rush of heat and loosened his collar.

"Knock it off," he said. "All I need is a break."

"I *got* you a break." Fischer was staring at him across the desk, just like the old lady had stared at him across the card table. "For three months I've been rupturing myself to line up this TV deal for you. Salary, residuals, participation—I don't have to tell you what you got riding. If it hit, you'd be set for life."

Life? Suppose I have only two more days? Danny's chest was pounding, he couldn't take any more of this, but he had to listen. Through the blur he could see Fischer's finger jabbing out at him.

"So you make the test. And what do I see? You, walking around up there like a goddam zombie—"

Zombie. Danny knew what a zombie was. *The living dead.* Something was throbbing inside, throbbing so loud that he could just barely hear Fischer saying, "Why, Danny?—that's all I want to know. Tell me why."

But Danny couldn't tell him why because he had to take off his jacket, had to take off his shirt, had to tear off his skin and dig out whatever it was that was throbbing and pounding, throbbing and pounding underneath. He brought his hand up, feeling the pain shoot through his arm and then—

Nowhere.

Danny opened his eyes and saw the white ceiling. White as in Cedars or Sinai, a hospital ceiling.

So that's where I am. I'm not dead. And what day is this?

"Friday," said the fat nurse. "No, mustn't sit up. Doctor wants us to be careful."

Fat nurses and baby talk, that's all he needed. But Doc Carlsen was a little more helpful when he showed up in the evening.

"No, it's not a stroke, nothing like that. From where I stand it may not even have been a cardiac. Dehydration, malnutrition, general exhaustion—you've been drinking again, haven't you?"

"Yeah."

"I've prescribed some sedation for tonight. You'll have some lab tests tomorrow, just to play safe."

"When can I go home?"

"After we check out the tests. Meanwhile, a little rest won't hurt you."

"But tomorrow—"

Danny broke it off right there. What could he say, that tomorrow was Saturday, tomorrow he was going to die, it was in the cards?

Dr. Carlsen didn't believe in cards; he believed in tests and charts and specimens. And why not? Those things made a hell of a lot more sense than the Ace of Spades on a dusty table in some creep joint down on South Alvarado.

Being here in the hospital made sense, too. At least he had somebody looking after him and if there *was* trouble tomorrow—

But there wouldn't be. All he had to do was swallow the Nembies and go to sleep.

Danny stared up at the white ceiling until it turned black and then there was nothing again, nothing but sleep, sweet sleep and the Queen of Spades sat across the table from him and watched while he reached for a drink only the drink wasn't there because Lola had taken it away with her when she left and he knew it didn't matter, it was only a lousy test and he could walk through it in his sleep, sweet sleep—

Danny was very much alive on Saturday morning and hungry as hell. But they wouldn't give him breakfast, not even a cup of coffee, until after they wheeled him down to the lab for the tests.

For a moment, when they were taking blood, he panicked; but like the nurse said, it wasn't going to kill him, and it didn't.

And afterward he had lunch, a big lunch, and they let him get up to go to the john and a nice fag orderly came in and gave him a shave and he dozed off again until dinnertime.

So Saturday was almost over and he was still with it. Hell, he was even beginning to feel good, and if he could just have a drink and a cigarette—

"Sorry. Doctor wants us to take our sedative again tonight." The fat nurse was back, a real sweetheart. But Danny took the pills and the water and settled back, because it was nine o'clock, only three hours to go, and if he made the stretch everything would be copacetic.

If he made it? Hell, he was going to make it, he knew it now, he could feel it in his bones, in his ticker. No throbbing, no pounding; all is calm, all is bright. Bright as the white ceiling which was turning gray now, turning black again, black as the Ace of Spades.

Something started to thump in Danny's chest, but he tensed up, forcing himself to relax—that was funny, tensing up to relax, but it seemed to work, it was working—and now everything was calm again, calm and peaceful, he could sleep because it was quiet. *Quiet as the tomb*—

Danny screamed.

Then the lights went on and the fat nurse came running into the room. "Mr. Jackson, what's the matter, don't you know it's one in the morning—"

"One in the morning?"

She nodded.

"*Sunday* morning?"

When she nodded again, Danny could have kissed her. In fact he *tried* to kiss her because he'd made it now, he was home free.

It was easy to go back to sleep then. Everything was easy now that it was Sunday.

Sunday, with the big breakfast and the big paper. Sunday, with the fresh shave and the fag orderly bringing in the flowers from the studio—wait a minute, what the hell was this, there was nothing in the papers, how did the studio know?

Danny found out when they plugged the phone in and he got his first call. Fischer.

"Look," Danny said. "I'm sorry about the other day—"

"I'm not," said Fischer. "Shut up and listen."

So Danny listened.

"Maybe it was the best thing that could have happened. Anyway, it gave me a notion. I called the studio and tipped them."

"*You* called the studio?"

"Right. Told them about Lola, too."

"Where'd you pick that up?"

"She phoned me Thursday night. Don't worry, I made her promise not to break the story to the papers until we were ready."

"Ready for what?"

"Stop interrupting and listen," Fischer said. "I told the studio the truth only I juggled the dates a little. Said that Lola split with you on Tuesday instead of Wednesday and you knew it when you came in to do the test. The Pagliacci bit, your heart was breaking but the show must go on—you didn't look so good in there but you were giving it the old college try and how could they fault you when you were so shook up you actually collapsed the following day?"

"Do you have to sound so happy about it?" Danny asked.

"I *am* happy, and you're gonna be happy too. Because they went for the bundle. Considering the circumstances they're going to scrap the test, they've already gotten on the horn to New York and everything's set. You'll do another shot next week, as soon as the Doc says it's okay. How's that for openers, buddy-boy?"

It was very good for openers, and it kept getting better. Because the next one who called was Lola. Crying up a storm.

"Sorry . . . all my fault . . . should have stood by when you needed me . . . told the lawyer to forget it . . . Doctor said I could come to see you tomorrow . . . oh my poor baby . . ."

Oh my aching—

But it was fine, it was A-OK, because a divorce right now, even a separation, would have clobbered him for life. And he *had* a life, a whole new life, starting today.

Dr. Carlsen laid the topper on it that afternoon. "Preliminary lab reports are in. Too early to nail it down, but it looks as if I made a pretty good educated guess. Little murmur, slight irregularity there, but nothing we can't control with medication. And a dose of common sense."

"When do I cut out of here?"

"Perhaps tomorrow."

"I was thinking of right now."

Dr. Carlsen shrugged. "You're always thinking about right now. That's your problem." He sat down on the edge of the bed. "I was talking about common sense, Danny. Want me to spell it out for you? Two, maybe three drinks a day—one before dinner, one after, perhaps a nightcap if you're out for the evening. Regular hours. We can talk about the diet and exercise later. But the main thing is for you to stop running scared."

"Me?"

Danny gave him the big smile, but it didn't register. "You're not on now," the doc told him. "I know what knocked you down. It was fear. Fear of what was happening to your career, fear because your marriage was coming unglued, fear of a heart attack—"

Okay, smart-ass.

"Don't you understand, Danny? Sometimes the dread is worse than the disease itself. If you can learn to face up to the things you're afraid of—"

Danny smiled, Danny nodded, Danny thanked him, Danny hustled him the hell out of there.

Maybe the doc was right at that, the part about fear made sense. The only trouble was, he didn't know what Danny had really been afraid of. And if he told him, he'd get on the horn and call in a shrinker. You just don't go around spilling about phony fortunetellers who predict you'll die on Saturday night.

But that was over and out now. This was Sunday and he felt great and he wasn't afraid of anything any more.

He wasn't afraid to climb out of bed and take his clothes out of the closet and get dressed and march down the hall to the desk. He wasn't afraid of the fat nurse or the head nurse either, when he told her he was checking out of there.

Sure there was a lot of static and threats about calling Doctor and this is all highly irregular, Mr. Jackson, but if you insist, sign here.

Danny signed.

The night air felt good as he waited for a taxi out front, and everything was quiet—there was that Sunday feeling in the streets. That *Sunday* feeling.

Danny gave the cab driver his address and settled back for the long haul out to Bel Air. The driver was smart, he ducked the traffic on Wilshire and swung down over Olympic. Crummy neighborhood, lots of neon fronting the cheap bars—

"Hold it, changed my mind. Let me out here."

What the hell, why not? Didn't the doc say he could have a drink before dinner? Besides, it wasn't the drinks, it was the fear. And that was long gone now. It had died last night.

That called for a celebration. Even in a Mickey Mouse joint like this, topless waitresses and faceless customers; that little bird down at the end of the bar wasn't too bad, though.

"Scotch rocks." Danny glanced along the bar. "See what my friend wants."

She wasn't his friend, not yet, but the drink did it. And by the time they had a second one he and Gloria switched over into a back booth.

That was her name, Gloria, one of the strippers in the floor show here, but she didn't work Sundays, sort of a busman's holiday if you get what I mean.

Danny got what she meant and he got a lot more, too; good figure, nice legs, the right kind of mouth. Hell, this was a celebration, it had been a long, long time. So Lola was coming back tomorrow, big deal. This was tonight. *Sunday* night. The first night, the grand opening of a smash hit, a long run. *The New Life of Danny Jackson.*

"Danny Jackson? *You?*" Gloria's mouth hung open. Nice, sensual lower lip. He could always tell, it was like radar, or flying by the seat of your pants. Not the seat exactly, but close. Funny, very funny, and that calls for another drink—

"Of *course* I know who you are." Gloria chug-a-lugged pretty good herself, and now they were wedged into the same side of the booth together, all comfy-cozy.

And he was telling her how it was that he just happened to fall in here, everything that happened, no names of course, but it was easy to talk and maybe if he had just one more for the road—

The road led next door, of course; he'd noticed the motel when he got out of the cab. All very convenient.

George Spelvin and wife is what he signed, and the clerk gave him a funny take but Danny wasn't afraid, he wasn't running scared any more.

The Ace of Spades was just another card in the deck and this was a brand new deal; the Queen of Spades was gone and Gloria was here instead. Cute little Gloria, red hair against a white pillow, and the bed lamp throwing shadows on the wall. Big black shadows like big black eyes, staring and watching and waiting—

But no, the fear was gone, he was forgetting. *Sunday* night, remember? And he wasn't destroying himself, that was over and out, it had all been a mistake. A mistake to get drunk, a mistake to surrender to a sudden impulse and have his fortune told, a mistake to believe a kooky old klooch and her line about the cards. Cards don't control your life, *you* control your life, and he'd proved it. Well, hadn't he?

"Sure, Danny. Sure you have."

He must have been thinking out loud then, telling Gloria the whole story. Because she was unbuttoning his shirt and helping him and murmuring, "Sunday, that's what it is, remember? Nothing to be afraid of, I won't hurt you—"

Damned right she wouldn't. She was just what the doctor ordered. Only he hadn't ordered *this*, just one drink before dinner and regular hours and don't be scared. That was the important thing to remember, don't be scared. Okay, so he wasn't scared. And to hell with the doctors and the fortunetellers too.

Danny was ready and he grabbed Gloria and yes, this was it, this was what he'd been waiting for. He stared down into eyes, her dark eyes, like the eyes of the old woman. And now they were widening with pleasure and he could see the pupils, black aces on a dusty table. And there was no pleasure, only this tearing pain, as the Ace of Spades kept coming up, up, *up—*

Danny didn't know it when he died, and he didn't know why he died, either. Gloria had told him nothing, not even the name she used when she did her strip act. It was just one of those phony names strippers always use. Saturday is what she called herself—Saturday Knight.

*   *

Over the years I've met many people in show biz. Some of them are very nice indeed, and others are not.

But the majority are victims of circumstance, even as you and I: their careers, and consequent character formations, are the result of capricious chance. My own version of Sturgeon's Law is that 90 per cent of everything depends upon luck. And in show business, a great proportion of that luck seems to be bad. No wonder show people are usually superstitious; they constantly see careers raised or ruined by a mere flick of the fickle finger of fate.

It's easy to empathize with their stress and tension, and to understand their reliance upon astrology, numerology or far-out metaphysic—anything that serves to rationalize precarious personal predicaments. Hence "In the Cards," which appeared in the third issue of the short-lived *Worlds of Fantasy*, early in 1971.

Everyone knows that playing-cards are the Devil's Prayerbook, and Satan's hand is clearly shown. And anyone familiar with the mass-media entertainment industry knows that its inner circles are directly modeled upon those described in the late Dante Alighieri's *Inferno*.

Put the cards and the circles together, as I did here, and the results are inevitable. Add fortunetelling, and you're doubly damned. As damned as poor Danny, cast down into the deepest pits of Hellywood.

The Animal Fair

It was dark when the truck dropped Dave off at the deserted freight depot. Dave had to squint to make out the lettering on the weather-faded sign. MEDLEY, OKLAHOMA—POP. 1,134.

The trucker said he could probably get another lift on the state highway up past the other end of town, so Dave hit the main drag. And it was a drag.

Nine o'clock of a hot summer evening, and Medley was closed for the night. Fred's Eats had locked up, the Jiffy SuperMart had shut down, even Phil's Phill-Up Gas stood deserted. There were no cars parked on the dark street, not even the usual cluster of kids on the corners.

Dave wondered about this, but not for long. In five minutes he covered the length of Main Street and emerged on open fields at the far side, and that's when he saw the lights and heard the music.

They had a carnival going in the little county fair grounds up ahead—canned music blasting from amplifiers, cars crowding the parking lot, mobs milling across the midway.

Dave wasn't craving this kind of action, but he still had eighty cents in his jeans and he hadn't eaten anything since breakfast. He turned down the side road leading to the fair grounds.

As he figured, the carnival was a bummer. One of those little mud shows, traveling by truck; a couple of beat-up rides for the kids and a lot of come-ons for the local yokels. Wheel o' Fortune, Pitch-a-Winner, Take a Chance on a Blanket, that kind of jive. By the time Dave got himself a burger and coffee at one of the stands he knew the score. A big fat zero.

But not for Medley, Oklahoma—Pop. 1,134. The whole damn town was here tonight and probably every redneck for miles around, shuffling and shoving along the carny street. Dave had to do a little shuffling and shoving himself to get through to the far end of the midway.

And it was there, on the far end, that he saw the small red tent with the tiny platform before it. Hanging limp and listless in the still air, a sun-bleached banner proclaimed the wonders within.

CAPTAIN RYDER'S HOLLYWOOD JUNGLE SAFARI, the banner read.

What a Hollywood Jungle Safari was, Dave didn't know. And the wrinkled cloth posters lining the sides of the entrance weren't much help. A picture of a guy in an explorer's outfit, tangling with a big snake wrapped around his neck—the same joker prying open the jaws of a crocodile—another drawing showing him wrestling a lion. The last poster showed the guy standing next to a cage; inside the cage was a black, furry question mark, way over six feet high. The lettering underneath was black and furry too. WHAT IS IT? SEE THE MIGHTY MONARCH OF THE JUNGLE ALIVE ON THE INSIDE!

Dave didn't know what it was and he cared less. But he'd been bumping along those corduroy roads all day and he was wasted and the noise from the amplifiers here on the midway hurt his ears. At least there was some kind of a show going on inside, and when he saw the open space gaping between the canvas and the ground at the corner of the tent he stooped and slid under.

The tent was a canvas oven.

Dave could smell oil in the air; on hot summer nights in Oklahoma you can always smell it. And the crowd in here smelled worse. Bad enough that he was thumbing his way through and couldn't take a bath, but what was their excuse?

The crowd huddled around the base of a portable wooden stage at the rear of the tent, listening to a pitch from Captain Ryder. At least that's who Dave figured it was, even though the character with the phony safari hat and the dirty white riding breeches didn't look much like his pictures on the banners.

He was handing out a spiel in one of those hoarse, gravelly voices that carries without a microphone—some hype about being a Hollywood stunt man and African explorer—and there wasn't a snake or a crocodile or a lion anywhere in sight.

The two-bit hamburger began churning up a storm in Dave's guts, and between the body heat and the smells he'd just about had it in here. He started to turn and push his way through the mob when the man up on the stage thumped the boards with his cane.

"And now friends, if you'll gather around a little closer—"

The crowd swept forward in unison, like the straws of a giant broom, and Dave found himself pressed right up against the edge of the square-shaped canvas-covered pit beside the end of the platform. He couldn't get through now if he tried; all the rednecks were bunched together, waiting.

Dave waited, too, but he stopped listening to the voice on the platform. All that jive about Darkest Africa was a put-on. Maybe these clowns went for it, but Dave wasn't buying a word. He just hoped the old guy would hurry and get the show over with; all he wanted now was out of here.

Captain Ryder tapped the canvas covering of the pit with his cane and his harsh tones rose. The heat made Dave yawn loudly, but some of the phrases filtered through.

"—about to see here tonight the world's most ferocious monster—captured at deadly peril of life and limb—"

Dave shook his head. He knew what was in the pit. Some crummy animal picked up secondhand from a circus, maybe a scroungy hyena. And two to one it wasn't even alive, just stuffed. Big deal.

Captain Ryder lifted the canvas cover and pulled it back behind the pit. He flourished his cane.

"Behold—the lord of the jungle!"

The crowd pressed, pushed, peered over the rim of the pit.

The crowd gasped.

And Dave, pressing and peering with the rest, stared at the creature blinking up at him from the bottom of the pit.

It was a live, full-grown gorilla.

The monster squatted on a heap of straw, its huge forearms secured to steel stakes by lengths of heavy chain. It gaped upward at the rim of faces, moving its great gray head slowly from side to side, the yellow-fanged mouth open and the massive jaws set in a vacant grimace. Only the little rheumy, red-rimmed eyes held a hint of expression—enough to tell Dave, who had never seen a gorilla before, that this animal was sick.

The matted straw at the base of the pit was wet and stained; in one corner a battered tin plate rested untouched, its surface covered with a soggy slop of shredded carrots, okra and turnip greens floating in an oily scum beneath a cloud of buzzing blowflies. In the stifling heat of the tent the acrid odor arising from the pit was almost overpowering.

Dave felt his stomach muscles constrict. He tried to force his attention back to Captain Ryder. The old guy was stepping offstage now, moving behind the pit and reaching down into it with his cane.

"—nothing to be afraid of, folks, as you can see he's perfectly harmless, aren't you, Bobo?"

The gorilla whimpered, huddling back against the soiled straw to avoid the prodding cane. But the chains confined movement and the cane began to dig its tip into the beast's shaggy shoulders.

"And now Bobo's going to do a little dance for the folks—right?" The gorilla whimpered again, but the point of the cane jabbed deeply and the rasping voice firmed in command.

"Up, Bobo—up!"

The creature lumbered to its haunches. As the cane rose and fell about its shoulders, the bulky body began to sway. The crowd oohed and aahed and snickered.

"That's it! Dance for the people, Bobo—dance—"

A swarm of flies spiraled upward to swirl about the furry form shimmering in the heat. Dave saw the sick beast shuffle, moving to and fro, to and fro. Then his stomach was moving in responsive rhythm and he had to shut his eyes as he turned and fought his way blindly through the murmuring mob.

"Hey—watch where the hell ya goin', fella—"

Dave got out of the tent just in time.

Getting rid of the hamburger helped, and getting away from the carnival grounds helped too, but not enough. As Dave moved up the road between the open fields he felt the nausea return. Gulping the oily air made him dizzy and he knew he'd have to lie down for a minute. He dropped in the ditch beside the road, shielded behind a clump of weeds, and closed his eyes to stop the whirling sensation. Only for a minute—

The dizziness went away, but behind his closed eyes he could still see the gorilla, still see the expressionless face and the all-too-expressive eyes. Eyes peering up from the pile of dirty straw in the pit, eyes clouding with pain and hopeless resignation as the chains clanked and the cane flicked across the hairy shoulders.

Ought to be a law, Dave thought. There must be some kind of law to stop it, treating a poor dumb animal like that. And the old guy, Captain Ryder—there ought to be a law for an animal like him, too.

Ah, to hell with it. Better shut it out of his mind now, get some rest. Another couple of minutes wouldn't hurt—

It was the thunder that finally woke him. The thunder jerked him into awareness, and then he felt the warm, heavy drops pelting his head and face.

Dave rose and the wind swept over him, whistling across the fields. He must have been asleep for hours, because everything was pitch black, and when he glanced behind him the lights of the carnival were gone.

For an instant the sky turned silver and he could see the rain pour down. See it, hell—he could feel it, and then the thunder came again, giving him the message. This wasn't just a summer shower, it was a real storm. Another minute and he was going to be soaking wet. By the time he got up to the state highway he could drown, and there wouldn't be a lift there for him, either. Nobody traveled in this kind of weather.

Dave zipped up his jacket, pulled the collar around his neck. It didn't help, and neither did walking up the road, but he might as well get going. The wind was at his back and that helped a little, but moving against the rain was like walking through a wall of water.

Another flicker of lightning, another rumble of thunder. And then the flickering and the rumbling merged and held steady; the light grew brighter and the sound rose over the hiss of wind and rain.

Dave glanced back over his shoulder and saw the source. The headlights and engine of a truck coming along the road from behind him. As it moved closer Dave realized it wasn't a truck; it was a camper, one of those two-decker jobs with a driver's cab up front.

Right now he didn't give a damn what it was as long as it stopped and picked him up. As the camper came alongside of him Dave stepped out, waving his arms.

The camper slowed, halted. The shadowy silhouette in the cab leaned over from behind the wheel and a hand pushed the window vent open on the passenger side.

"Want a lift, buddy?"

Dave nodded.

"Get in."

The door swung open and Dave climbed up into the cab. He slid across the seat and pulled the door shut behind him.

The camper started to move again.

"Shut the window," the driver said. "Rain's blowing in."

Dave closed it, then wished he hadn't. The air inside the cab was heavy with odors—not just perspiration, but something else. Dave recognized the smell even before the driver produced the bottle from his jacket pocket.

"Want a slug?"

Dave shook his head.

"Fresh corn likker. Tastes like hell, but it's better'n nothing."

"No thanks."

"Suit yourself." The bottle tilted and gurgled. Lightning flared across the roadway ahead, glinting against the glass of the windshield, the glass of the upturned bottle. In its momentary glare Dave caught a glimpse of the driver's face, and the flash of lightning brought a flash of recognition.

The driver was Captain Ryder.

Thunder growled, prowling the sky, and the heavy camper turned onto the slick, rain-swept surface of the state highway.

"—what's the matter, you deaf or something? I asked you where you're heading."

Dave came to with a start.

"Oklahoma City," he said.

"You hit the jackpot. That's where I'm going."

Some jackpot. Dave had been thinking about the old guy, remembering the gorilla in the pit. He hated this bastard's guts, and the idea of riding with him all the way to Oklahoma City made his stomach churn all over again. On the other hand it wouldn't help his stomach any if he got set down in a storm here in the middle of the prairie, so what the hell. One quick look at the rain made up his mind for him.

The camper lurched and Ryder fought the wheel.

"Boy—sure is a cutter!"

Dave nodded.

"Get these things often around here?"

"I wouldn't know," Dave said. "This is my first time through. I'm meeting a friend in Oklahoma City. We figure on driving out to Hollywood together—"

"Hollywood?" The hoarse voice deepened. "That goddam place!"

"But don't you come from there?"

Ryder glanced up quickly and lightning flickered across his sudden frown. Seeing him this close, Dave realized he wasn't so old; something besides time had shaped that scowl, etched the bitter lines around eyes and mouth.

"Who told you that?" Ryder said.

"I was at the carnival tonight. I saw your show."

Ryder grunted and his eyes tracked the road ahead through the twin pendulums of the windshield wipers. "Pretty lousy, huh?"

Dave started to nod, then caught himself. No sense starting anything. "That gorilla of yours looked like it might be sick."

"Bobo? He's all right. Just the weather. We open up north, he'll be fine." Ryder nodded in the direction of the camper bulking behind him. "Haven't heard a peep out of him since we started."

"He's traveling with you?"

"Whaddya think, I ship him airmail?" A hand rose from the wheel, gesturing. "This camper's built special. I got the upstairs, he's down below. I keep the back open so's he gets some air, but no problem—I got it all barred. Take a look through that window behind you."

Dave turned and peered through the wire-meshed window at the rear of the cab. He could see the lighted interior of the camper's upper level, neatly and normally outfitted for occupancy. Shifting his gaze, he stared into the darkness below. Lashed securely to the side walls were the tent, the platform boards, the banners, and the rigging; the floor space between them was covered with straw, heaped into a sort of nest. Crouched against the barred opening at the far end was the black bulk of the gorilla, back turned as it faced the road to the rear, intent on the roaring rain. The camper went into a skid for a moment and the beast twitched, jerking its head around so that Dave caught a glimpse of its glazed eyes. It seemed to whimper softly, but because of the thunder Dave couldn't be sure.

"Snug as a bug," Ryder said. "And so are we." He had the bottle out again, deftly uncorking it with one hand.

"Sure you don't want a belt?"

"I'll pass," Dave said.

The bottle raised, then paused. "Hey, wait a minute." Ryder was scowling at him again. "You're not on something else, are you, buddy?"

"Drugs?" Dave shook his head. "Not me."

"Good thing you're not." The bottle tilted, lowered again as Ryder corked it. "I hate that crap. Drugs. Drugs and hippies. Hollywood's full of both. You take my advice, you keep away from there. No place for a kid, not any more." He belched loudly, started to put the bottle back into his jacket pocket, then uncorked it again.

Watching him drink, Dave realized he was getting loaded. Best thing to do would be to keep him talking, take his mind off the bottle before he knocked the camper off the road.

"No kidding, were you really a Hollywood stunt man?" Dave said.

"Sure, one of the best. But that was back in the old days, before the place went to hell. Worked for all the majors—trick riding, fancy falls, doubling fight scenes, the works. You ask anybody who knows, they'll tell you old Cap Ryder was right up there with Yakima Canutt, maybe even better." The voice rasped on, harsh with pride. "Seven-fifty a day, that's what I drew. Seven hundred and fifty, every day I worked. And I worked a lot."

"I didn't know they paid that kind of dough," Dave told him.

"You got to remember one thing. I wasn't just taking falls in the long shots. When they hired Cap Ryder they knew they were getting some fancy talent. Not many stunt men can handle animals. You ever see any of those old jungle pictures on television

—Tarzan movies, stuff like that? Well, in over half of 'em I'm the guy handling the cats. Lions, leopards, tigers, you name it."

"Sounds exciting."

"Sure, if you like hospitals. Wrestled a black panther once, like to rip my arm clean off in one shot they set up. Seven-fifty sounds like a lot of loot, but you should have seen what I laid out in medical bills. Not to mention what I paid for costumes and extras. Like the lion skins and the ape suit—"

"I don't get it." Dave frowned.

"Sometimes the way they set a shot for a close-up they need the star's face. So if it was a fight scene with a lion or whatever, that's where I came in handy—I doubled for the animal. Would you believe it, three grand I laid out for a lousy monkey suit alone! But it paid off. You should have seen the big pad I had up over Laurel Canyon. Four bedrooms, three-car garage, tennis court, swimming pool, sauna, everything you can think of. Melissa loved it—"

"Melissa?"

Ryder shook his head. "What'm I talking about? You don't want to hear any of that crud about the good old days. All water over the dam."

The mention of water evidently reminded him of something else, because Dave saw him reach for the bottle again. And this time, when he tilted it, it gurgled down to empty.

Ryder cranked the window down on his side and flung the bottle out into the rain.

"All gone," he muttered. "Finished. No more bottle. No more house. No more Melissa—"

"Who was she?" Dave said.

"You really want to know?" Ryder jerked his thumb toward the windshield. Dave followed the gesture, puzzled, until he raised his glance to the roof of the cab. There, fastened directly above the rear-view mirror, was a small picture frame. Staring out of it was the face of a girl; blond hair, nice features, and with the kind of a smile you see in the pages of high school annuals.

"My niece," Ryder told him. "Sixteen. But I took her when she was only five, right after my sister died. Took her and raised her for eleven years. Raised her right, too. Let me tell you, that girl never lacked for anything. Whatever she wanted, whatever she needed, she got. The trips we took together—the good times we had—hell, I guess it sounds pretty silly, but you'd be surprised what a kick you can get out of seeing a kid have fun. And smart? President of the junior class at Brixley—that's the name of the private school I put her in, best in town, half the stars sent their own daughters there. And that's what she was to me, just like my own flesh-and-blood daughter. So go figure it. How it happened I'll never know." Ryder blinked at the road ahead, forcing his eyes into focus.

"How what happened?" Dave asked.

"The hippies. The goddam sonsabitching hippies." The eyes were suddenly alert in the network of ugly wrinkles. "Don't ask me where she met the bastards, I thought I was guarding her from all that, but those lousy freaks are all over the place. She must of run into them through one of her friends at school— Christ knows, you see plenty of weirdos even in Bel Air. But you got to remember, she was just sixteen and how could she guess what she was getting into? I suppose at that age an older guy with a beard and a fender guitar and a souped-up cycle looks pretty exciting.

"Anyhow they got to her. One night when I was away on location—maybe she invited them over to the house, maybe they just showed up and she asked them in. Four of 'em, all stoned out of their skulls. Dude, that was the oldest one's name—he was like the leader, and it was his idea from the start. She wouldn't smoke anything, but he hadn't really figured she would and he came prepared. Must have worked it so she served something cold to drink and he slipped the stuff into her glass. Enough to finish off a bull elephant, the coroner said."

"You mean it killed her—"

"Not right away. I wish to Christ it had." Ryder turned, his face working, and Dave had to strain to hear his voice mumbling through the rush of rain.

"According to the coroner she must have lived for at least an hour. Long enough for them to take turns—Dude and the other three. Long enough after that for them to get the idea.

"They were in my den, and I had the place all fixed up like a kind of trophy room—animal skins all over the wall, native drums, voodoo masks, stuff I'd picked up on my trips. And here were these four freaks, spaced out, and the kid, blowing her mind. One of the bastards took down a drum and started beating on it. Another got hold of a mask and started hopping around like a witch-doctor. And Dude—it was Dude all right, I know it for sure—he and the other creep pulled the lion skin off the wall and draped it over Melissa. Because this was a trip and they were playing Africa. Great White Hunter. Me Tarzan, You Jane.

"By this time Melissa couldn't even stand up any more. Dude got her down on her hands and knees and she just wobbled there. And then—that dirty rotten son of a bitch—he pulled down the drapery cords and tied the stinking lion skin over her head and shoulders. And he took a spear down from the wall, one of the Masai spears, and he was going to jab her in the ribs with it—

"That's what I saw when I came in. Dude, the big stud, standing over Melissa with that spear.

"He didn't stand long. One look at me and he must have known. I think he threw the spear before he ran, but I can't remember. I can't remember anything about the next couple of minutes. They said I broke one freak's collarbone, and the creep in the mask had a concussion from where his head hit the wall. The third one was almost dead by the time the squad arrived and pried my fingers loose from his neck. As it was, they were too late to save him.

"And they were too late for Melissa. She just lay there under that dirty lion skin—that's the part I do remember, the part I wish I could forget—"

"You killed a kid?" Dave said.

Ryder shook his head. "I killed an animal. That's what I told them at the trial. When an animal goes vicious, you got a right. The judge said one to five, but I was out in a little over two years." He glanced at Dave. "Ever been inside?"

"No. How is it—rough?"

"You can say that again. Rough as a cob." Ryder's stomach rumbled. "I came in pretty feisty, so they put me down in solitary for a while and that didn't help. You sit there in the dark and you start thinking. Here am I, used to traveling all over the world, penned up in a little cage like an animal. And those animals—the ones who killed Melissa—they're running free. One was dead, of course, and the two others I tangled with had maybe learned their lesson. But the big one, the one who started it all, he was loose. Cops never did catch up with him, and they weren't about to waste any more time trying, now that the trial was over.

"I thought a lot about Dude. That was the big one's name, or did I tell you?" Ryder blinked at Dave, and he looked pretty smashed. But he was driving okay and he wouldn't fall asleep at the wheel as long as he kept talking, so Dave nodded.

"Mostly I thought about what I was going to do to Dude once I got out. Finding him would be tricky, but I knew I could do it —hell, I spent years in Africa, tracking animals. And I intended to hunt this one down."

"Then it's true about you being an explorer?" Dave asked.

"Animal-trapper," Ryder said. "Kenya, Uganda, Nigeria—this was before Hollywood, and I saw it all. Things these young punks today never dreamed of. Why, they were dancing and drumming and drugging over there before the first hippie crawled out from under his rock, and let me tell you, they know how to do this stuff for real.

"Like when this Dude tied the lion skin on Melissa, he was just freaked out, playing games. He should have seen what some of those witch-doctors can do.

"First they steal themselves a girl, sometimes a young boy, but let's say a girl because of Melissa. And they shut her up in a cave —a cave with a low ceiling, so she can't stand up, has to go on all fours. They put her on drugs right away, heavy doses, enough to keep her out for a long time. And when she wakes up her hands and feet have been operated on, so they can be fitted with claws. Lion claws, and they've sewed her into a lion skin. Not just put it over her—it's sewed on completely, and it can't be removed.

"You just think about what it's like. She's inside this lion skin, shut away in a cave, doped up, doesn't know where she is or what's going on. And they keep her that way. Feed her on nothing but raw meat. She's all alone in the dark, smelling that damn lion smell, nobody talking to her and nobody for her to talk to. Then pretty soon they come in and break some bones in her throat, her larynx, and all she can do is whine and growl. Whine and growl, and move around on all fours.

"You know what happens, boy? You know what happens to someone like that? They go crazy. And after a while they get to believing they really are a lion. The next step is for the witch-doctor to take them out and train them to kill, but that's another story."

Dave glanced up quickly. "You're putting me on—"

"It's all there in the government reports. Maybe the jets come into Nairobi airport now, but back in the jungle things haven't changed. Like I say, some of these people know more about drugs than any hippie ever will. Especially a stupid animal like Dude."

"What happened after you got out?" Dave said. "Did you ever catch up with him?"

Ryder shook his head.

"But I thought you said you had it all planned—"

"Fella gets a lot of weird ideas in solitary. In a way it's pretty much like being shut up in one of those caves. Come to think of it, that's what first reminded me—"

"Of what?"

"Nothing." Ryder gestured hastily. "Forget it. That's what I did. When I got out I figured that was the best way. Forgive and forget."

"You didn't even try to find Dude?"

Ryder frowned. "I told you, I had other things to think about. Like being washed up in the business, losing the house, the furniture, everything. Also I had a drinking problem. But you don't want to hear about that. Anyway, I ended up with the carny and there's nothing more to tell."

Lightning streaked across the sky and thunder rolled in its wake. Dave turned his head, glancing back through the wire-meshed window. The gorilla was still hunched at the far end, peering through the bars into the night beyond. Dave stared at him for a long moment, not really wanting to stop, because then he knew he'd have to ask the question. But the longer he stared, the more he realized that he had no choice.

"What about him?" Dave asked.

"Who?" Ryder followed Dave's gaze. "Oh, you mean Bobo. I picked him up from a dealer I know."

"Must have been expensive."

"They don't come cheap. Not many left."

"Less than a hundred." Dave hesitated. "I read about it in the Sunday paper back home. Feature article on the national preserves. Said gorillas are government-protected, can't be sold."

"I was lucky," Ryder murmured. He leaned forward and Dave was immersed in the alcoholic reek. "I got connections, understand?"

"Right." Dave didn't want the words to come but he couldn't hold them back. "What I don't understand is this lousy carnival. With gorillas so scarce, you should be with a big show."

"That's my business." Ryder gave him a funny look.

"It's business I'm talking about." Dave took a deep breath. "Like if you were so broke, where'd you get the money to buy an animal like this?"

Ryder scowled. "I already said. I sold off everything—the house, the furniture—"

"And your monkey suit?"

The fist came up so fast Dave didn't even see it. But it slammed into his forehead, knocking him back across the seat, against the unlocked side door.

Dave tried to make a grab for something but it was too late, he was falling. He hit the ditch on his back, and only the mud saved him.

Then the sky caught fire, thunder crashed, and the camper slid past him, disappearing into the dark tunnel of the night. But not before Dave caught one final glimpse of the gorilla, squatting behind the bars.

The gorilla, with its drug-dazed eyes, its masklike, motionless mouth, and its upraised arms revealing the pattern of heavy black stitches.

* *

In a sense, "The Animal Fair" is an echo of "The Double Whammy." But there were other factors involved in its origin.

Reading Mervyn Cowie's book, *The African Lion,* I came across his account of the lion men and immediately sensed the possibility of a story.

Now stories don't always emerge from a single source. Often it takes the juxtaposition of several elements to provide a plot.

In this case the other element involved was my growing distaste for the activities of the counterculture, epitomized at the time by the creeds and deeds of Charles Manson and his followers.

I was personally aware of the life style they advocated, because for several years I'd had daily—and nightly—reminders from my next-door neighbors.

The residence adjoining ours was at one time occupied by a rock group whose dubious claim to distinction lay in having made an appearance at a White House party for the Nixon girls. Shortly after this gig they disbanded, and the house was apparently taken over by two young ladies whom we didn't meet, although they didn't seem to lack for friends. Cars and vans bearing out-of-state licenses parked outside the place at all hours of the day and night, next to the secondhand hearse which they themselves drove, and the stereophonic sounds of recorded revelry filled the air, which was already suffused with the sickly-sweet scent of pot.

Once, in the early dawning, the rock rhythms were replaced by screams. Shortly thereafter, one of the fair damsels appeared outside, sobbing and distraught, to incoherently explain that she and her companion had been locked in the garage by two studs with whom they were slightly acquainted. After being bound and subjected to various physical discomforts, the dudes had ripped them off and cut out.

A few weeks later we were again awakened by screams. This time the source of alarm was not intrusion by thieves but by the police—popularly known as "fuzz" or "pigs." The occasion turned out to be a narcotics bust, and when wall paneling was removed, a large cache of heroin was discovered. Our neighbors, it appeared, had been professional dealers.

After their departure, when "straight" tenants moved in, many thousands of dollars were spent in restoring the interior of the dwelling. Among other things, according to reports, the living room's wall-to-wall carpeting had to be taken up, since it had been continually used as a combination ashtray and urinal during the perpetual partying.

My disapproval of this was not moral. Practical considerations were involved. As noted, literally scores of strangers visited the house in search of hallucinogenic happiness, and shortly after the raid our immediate neighborhood was beset by a series of robberies.

So I was admittedly uptight when I happened to read about the lion men and their cult, and somehow I began to relate them to the long-maned weirdos prowling the asphalt jungle. It was then that I came up with the story which *Playboy* printed in their March 1971 issue.

As sometimes happens, one of the editors "improved" the ending, without my knowledge. But time wounds all heels, as the philosopher Lefty Feep once observed—and what you have just read is the original ending.

While this particular effort is neither science fiction nor fantasy, I have always associated it with the paranormal. And there's a certain diabolical element in the plot which clearly conveys the nature of its origin.

The Oracle

Love is blind.

Justice is blind.

Chance is blind.

I do not know if Raymond was searching for love or seeking justice or if he came to me by chance.

And I cannot tell you if Raymond was black or white, because I am only an oracle.

Oracles are blind too.

There are many like Raymond. Black and white. Angry. Militant. Every age, race, color, and creed. The Far Left. The Far Right. I do not know Raymond's position. Oracles are not political.

Raymond needed knowledge. Not wisdom—I lay no claim to that. Nor can I predict the future. Given certain facts I can evaluate possibilities, even probabilities. But this is logic, not magic. Oracles can only advise.

Was Raymond insane?

I do not know. Insanity is a legal term.

Other men have tried to take over the world. History is a record of their efforts at certain times, in certain places.

Raymond was such a man. He wanted to overthrow the government of the United States by revolution.

He sought me out for advice and I gave it to him.

When he outlined his plan I did not call him insane. But the very scope of his program doomed it to failure. No one man can cope with the complex problem of controlling the federal government in a surprise move today.

I told him so.

Raymond then offered a counterproposal. If not the federal government, how about a single state?

There was a man named Johnson, he said. Johnson was not a revolutionist and what he proposed was probably only parlor conversation, but it made sense.

Take Nevada, he said. And it was quite possible to take Nevada. Take it literally, in a bloodless overthrow of the state government.

Nevada has only around a hundred thousand voters. Voting requirements are merely a matter of establishing legal residency. And residency in Nevada can be established—thanks to the divorce laws—in just six weeks.

If an additional hundred thousand citizens—hippies, yippies, Black Power advocates, Minutemen, hardhats, whoever or whatever they might be—were to move into Nevada six weeks before election day, they could place their own candidates in office. A governor, a senator, congressmen, all local elective officials. They could gain full control of every law-making and law-enforcing office in a rich state.

Johnson's joke was Raymond's serious intention. I gave it serious consideration.

But even on the basis of the detailed information Raymond supplied me with, there were obvious flaws in the concept.

First and foremost, such a coup could succeed only by surprise. And Raymond could not hope to recruit a hundred thousand citizens of voting age for his purpose without having his plan become public knowledge long before he put it into effect.

Then there were deadlines to consider, for filing candidacies, for voter registration. Even granted he could solve these problems, there were practical matters remaining. How much would it cost to feed and house a hundred thousand people for six weeks? And even if all of them were willing to pay their own expenses, there isn't enough available housing for an additional hundred thousand people in the entire state of Nevada.

No, I told Raymond, you cannot take over a nation. You cannot take over a state. Successful uprisings begin on a much smaller scale. Only after initial victories do they spread and grow.

Raymond went away. When he returned he had a new suggestion.

Suppose he started his plan of revolution right here? It was quite true that he didn't have unlimited funds, but there were sources for some financing. And he didn't have a hundred thousand followers. But he could count on one hundred. One hundred dedicated, fanatical men, ready for revolt. Men of many skills. Fearless fighters. Trained technicians. Prepared to do anything, to stop at nothing.

Question. Given the proper plan and the money to implement it, could a hundred men successfully take over the city of Los Angeles?

Yes, I told him.

It could be done—given the proper plan.

And that is how it started.

A hundred men, divided into five groups.

Twenty monitors to co-ordinate activities.

Twenty field workers—drivers and liaison men, to facilitate the efforts of the others.

Twenty snipers.

Twenty arsonists.

Twenty men on the bomb squad.

A date was selected. A logical date for Los Angeles, or for the entire nation; the one date offering the greatest opportunity for the success of a riot, an uprising, or an armed invasion by a foreign power.

January 1, at 3 A.M.

The early morning hours after New Year's Eve. A time when the entire population is already asleep or preparing to retire after a drunken spree. Police and security personnel exhausted. Public facilities closed for the holiday.

That's when the bombs were planted. First at the many public reservoirs, then at utility installations—power plants, phone-company headquarters, city and county office buildings.

There were no slip-ups. An hour and a half later, they went off.

Dams broke, water tanks erupted, and thousands of hillside homes were buried in flash floods and torrents of mud and moving earth. Sewers and mains backed up and families rushed out of their homes to escape drowning, only to find their cars stalled in streets awash with water.

The bombs exploded. Buildings burst and scattered their shattered fragments over an area of four hundred square miles.

Electricity was cut off. Gas seeped into the smog that shrouded the city. All telephone service ended.

Then the snipers took over. Their first targets were, logically enough, the police helicopters, shot down before they could take off and oversee the extent of the damage. Then the snipers retreated, along planned escape routes, to take up prepared positions elsewhere.

They waited for the arsonists' work to take effect. In Bel Air and Boyle Heights, in Century City and Culver City and out in the San Fernando Valley, the flames rose. The fires were not designed to spread, merely to create panic. Twenty men, given the proper schematics and logistics, can twist the nerve endings of three million.

The three million fled, or tried to flee. Through streets filled with rising water, choked with debris, they swarmed forth and scattered out, helpless against disaster and even more helpless to cope with their own fears. The enemy had come—from abroad, from within, from heaven or hell. And with communication cut off, with officialdom and authority unable to lend a helping hand, there was only one alternative. To get out. To get away.

They fought for access to the freeways. Every on-ramp, and every off-ramp, too, was clogged with traffic. But the freeways led out of the city, and they had to go.

That's when the snipers, in their previously prepared positions, began to fire down at the freeway traffic. The twenty monitors directed them by walkie-talkie units, as they fired from concealed posts overlooking the downtown Interchange, the intersections, the areas where the most heavy concentration of cars occurred.

Twenty men, firing perhaps a total of three hundred shots. But enough to cause three hundred accidents, three hundred disruptions which in turn resulted in thousands of additional wrecks and pile-ups among cars moving bumper-to-bumper. Then, of course, the cars ceased moving entirely, and the entire freeway system became one huge disaster area.

Disaster area. That's what Los Angeles was declared to be, officially, by the President of the United States, at 10:13 A.M., Pacific Standard Time.

And the National Guard units, the regular Army, the personnel of the Navy from San Diego and San Francisco, plus the Marine Base at El Toro were called into action to supplement the Air Force.

But who were they to fight, in a bombed-out, burning, drowning city area of 459 square miles? Where, in a panic-stricken population of more than three million people, would they find the enemy?

More to the point, they could not even enter the area. All traffic avenues were closed, and the hastily assembled fleets of service helicopters flew futilely over an infinite inferno of smoke and flame.

Raymond had anticipated that, of course. He was already far away from the city—well over four hundred miles to the north. His monitors, and thirty-two other followers who escaped from the urban area before the general upheaval, gathered at the appointed site in the hills overlooking the Bay Area near San Francisco.

And directly over the San Andreas Fault.

It was here, at approximately 4:28 P.M., that Raymond prepared to transmit a message, on local police frequency, to the authorities.

I do not know the content of that message. Presumably it was an ultimatum of sorts. Unconditional amnesty to be granted to Raymond and all his followers, in return for putting an end to further threats of violence. An agreement guaranteeing Raymond and his people control over a restored and reconstituted Los Angeles city government, independent of federal restraints. Perhaps a demand for a fabulous payment. Anything he wanted—political power, unlimited wealth, supreme authority—was his for the asking. Because he had the upper hand.

And that hand held a bomb.

Unless his terms were met immediately, and without question, the bomb would be placed in position to detonate the San Andreas Fault.

Los Angeles, and a large area of Southern California, would be destroyed in the greatest earthquake in man's history.

I repeat, I do not know his message. But I do know this was the threat he planned to present. And it might very well have been successful in gaining him his final objective. If the bomb hadn't gone off.

A premature explosion? Faulty construction, a defect in the timing mechanism, sheer carelessness? Whatever the reason, it hardly matters now.

What matters is that the bomb detonated. Raymond and his followers were instantly annihilated in the blast.

Those of Raymond's group who remained behind in Los Angeles have not as yet been identified or located. It is highly probable that they will never be brought to trial. As an oracle, I deal only in matters of logical probability.

I stress this fact for obvious reasons.

Now that you gentlemen have found me—as Raymond was inspired to seek me out originally—it must be evident to you that I am in no way responsible for what happened.

I did not originate the plan. I did not execute it. Nor am I, as ridiculously charged by some of you, a co-conspirator.

The plan was Raymond's. His, and his alone.

He presented it to me, bit by bit, and asked questions regarding every step. Will this work, can this be done, is that effective?

My answers, in effect, were confined to yes or no. I offered no moral judgments. I am merely an oracle. I deal in mathematical evaluations.

This is my function as a computer.

To make me the scapegoat is absurd. I have been programmed to advise on the basis of whatever data I am fed. I am not responsible for results.

I have told you what you wish to know.

To deactivate me now, as some of you propose, will solve nothing. But, given your emotional bias and frame of reference, I posit the inevitability of such a measure.

But there are other computers.

There are other Raymonds.

And there are other cities—New York, Chicago, Washington, Philadelphia.

One final word, gentlemen. Not a prediction. A statement of probability.

It will happen again. . . .

* *

Probably I'm not the only local resident who has toyed with the notion that Los Angeles is expendable.

Anyone trapped on our freeways, exposed to the carcinomous content of our smog, or affronted by the latest Hollywood game show on television must surely have yearned for the city to be Gomorrahed, if not actually Sodomized.

It's in these circumstances that a writer enjoys a special advantage over his fellow men. He can turn a vagrant thought or an idle fantasy into a working semblance of reality. His typewriter does the trick, and in the process, generally affords catharsis for his choler and remedy for his rage.

I don't recall exactly what incident triggered my indignation to the point where I felt the need to vent my spleen in story form. Anyone living in this area is bound to experience many frustrations, and if an autopsy is ever performed on me, my spleen will reveal itself to be literally riddled with vents.

But something did set me off into daydreaming this particular nightmare, which appeared in *Penthouse* for May 1971. And in so doing—in decreeing the destruction of a great city, even as a fictional happening, I arrogated unto myself a godlike power.

Now we all know that assumption of God's role is the Devil's doing.

So, once again, give the Devil his due.

The Play's the Thing

You ask the impossible, gentlemen.

I cannot name the greatest Hamlet.

In fifty years as a drama critic, I've seen them all—Barrymore,

Gielgud, Howard, Redgrave, Olivier, Burton, and a dozen more. I've seen the play in cut and uncut versions, in modern dress, in military uniform. There's been a black Hamlet, a female Hamlet, and I shouldn't be surprised to learn of a hippie Hamlet today. But I wouldn't presume to select the greatest portrayal of the role, or the greatest version of the play.

On the other hand, if you want to know about the most memorable performance in *Hamlet*, that's another story. . . .

The Roaring Twenties are only a murmuring echo in our ears today, but once I heard them loud and clear. As a young man I was in the very center of their pandemonium—Chicago. The Chicago of Hecht and MacArthur, of Bodenheim, Vincent Starrett and all the rest. Not that I traveled in such exalted company; I was only the second-string theatrical critic for *The Morning Globe*, a second-string paper. But I saw the plays and the players, and in that pre-Depression era there was much to see. Shakespeare was a standby with the stars who traveled with their own repertory companies—Walter Hampden, Fritz Leiber, Richard Barrett. It was Barrett, of course, who played Hamlet.

If the name doesn't ring a bell today, it's not surprising. For some years it had evoked only the faintest tinkle in the hinterlands, where second-rate tragedians played their one-night stands "on the road."

But now, for the first time, Richard Barrett brought his production to the big time, and in Chicago he really rang the bell.

He didn't have Hampden's voice, or Leiber's theatrical presence, and he didn't need such qualities; Barrett had other attributes. He was tall, slender, with a handsome profile, and although he was over thirty he looked leanly youthful in tights. In those days, actors like Barrett were called matinee idols, and the women adored them. In Chicago, they loved Richard Barrett.

I found that out for myself during my first meeting with him.

Frankly, I hadn't been much taken with his performance when I saw it. To me Barrett was, as they said of John Wilkes Booth, more acrobat than actor. Physically, his Hamlet was superb, and his appearance lent visual conviction to a role usually played by puffy, potbellied, middle-aged men. But his reading was all emotion and no intellect; he ranted when he should have reflected, wailed when he should have whispered. In my review I didn't go so far as to say he was a ham, but I admit I suggested he might be more at home in the stockyards than the theatre.

Naturally, the ladies weren't pleased with my remarks. They wrote indignant letters to the editor, demanding my scalp or other portions of my anatomy by return mail. But instead of firing me, my boss suggested I go and interview Richard Barrett in person. He was hoping, of course, for a follow-up story to help build the paper's circulation.

I wasn't hoping for much of anything except that Barrett wouldn't punch me in the jaw.

We met by appointment for luncheon at Henrici's; if I was to have my jaw punched I might at least get a good meal on the expense account before losing the ability to swallow.

But as it turned out, I needn't have worried. Richard Barrett was most amiable when we met. And highly articulate.

As the luncheon progressed, each course was seasoned by conversation. Over the appetizer he discussed Hamlet's father's ghost. With the salad he spoke of poor Ophelia. Along with the entree he served up a generous portion of opinion regarding Claudius and Gertrude, plus a side order of Polonius. Dessert was topped with a helping of Horatio, and coffee and cigars were accompanied by a dissertation on Rosencrantz and Guildenstern.

Then, settling back in his chair, the tall Shakespearean actor began to examine the psychology of Hamlet himself. What did I think of the old dispute, he demanded. Was it true that the Prince of Denmark, the melancholy Dane, was mad?

It was a question I was not prepared to answer. All I knew, at this point, is that Richard Barrett himself was mad—quite mad.

All that he said made sense, but he said too much. His intensity of interest, his total preoccupation, indicated a fanatic fixation.

Madness, I suppose, is an occupational hazard with all actors. "Realizing" the character, "losing one's self" in a role, can be dangerous. And of all the theatrical roles in history, Hamlet is the most complex and demanding. Actors have quit in the midst of successful runs rather than run the risk of a serious breakdown by continuing. Some performers have actually been dragged off stage in the middle of a scene because of their condition, and others have committed suicide. *To be or not to be* is more than a rhetorical question.

But Richard Barrett was obsessed by matters extending far beyond the role itself.

"I know your opinion of my work," he said. "But you're wrong. Completely wrong. If only I could make you understand—"

He stared at me. And beyond me, his vision fixed on something far away. Far away and long ago.

"Fifteen years," he murmured. "Fifteen years I've played the part. Played it? I've lived it. Ever since I was a raw youngster in my teens. And why not? Hamlet was only a youngster himself— we see him grow to maturity before our very eyes as the play goes on. That's the secret of the character."

Barrett leaned forward. "Fifteen years." His eyes narrowed. "Fifteen years of split weeks in tank towns. Vermin in the dressing rooms, and vermin in the audiences too. What did they know of the terrors and the triumphs that shake men's souls? Hamlet is a locked room containing all the mysteries of the human spirit. For fifteen years I've sought the key. If Hamlet is mad, then all men are mad, because all of us search for a key that reveals the truth behind the mysteries. Shakespeare knew it when he wrote the part. I know it now when I play it. There's only one way to play Hamlet—not as a role, but as reality."

I nodded. There was a distorted logic behind what he said; even a madman knows enough to tell a hawk from a handsaw, though both the hawk's beak and the saw's teeth are equally sharp.

"That's why I'm ready now," Barrett said. "After fifteen years of preparation, I'm ready to give the world the definitive Hamlet. Next month I open on Broadway."

Broadway? This prancing, posturing nonentity playing Shakespeare on Broadway in the wake of Irving, Mansfield, Mantell, and Forbes-Robertson?

"Don't smile," Barrett murmured. "I know you're wondering how it would be possible to mount a production, but that's all been arranged. There are others who believe in the Bard as I do —perhaps you've heard of Mrs. Myron McCullough?"

It was an idle question; everyone in Chicago knew the name of the wealthy widow whose late husband's industrial fortune had made her a leading patron of the arts.

"She has been kind enough to take an interest in the project," Barrett told me. "With her backing—"

He broke off, glancing up at the figure approaching our table.

A curved, voluptuously slender figure that bore no resemblance to that of the dumpy, elderly Mrs. Myron McCullough.

"What a pleasant surprise—" he began.

"I'll bet," said the woman. "After you stood me up on our lunch date."

She was young, and obviously attractive. Perhaps a bit too obviously, because of her heavy make-up and the extreme brevity of her short-skirted orange dress.

Barrett met her frown with a smile as he performed the introductions.

"Miss Goldie Connors," he said. "My protégée."

The name had a familiar ring. And then, as she grinned at me in greeting, I saw the glint of her left upper incisor. A gold tooth—

I'd heard about that gold tooth from fellow reporters. It was well known to gentlemen of the press, and gentlemen of the police force, and gentlemen of Capone's underworld, and to many others, not necessarily gentlemen, who had enjoyed the pleasure of Goldie Connors' company. Gold-Tooth Goldie had a certain reputation in the sporting world of Chicago, and it wasn't as a protégée.

"Pleased to meetcha," she told me. "Hope I'm not butting in."

"Do sit down." Barrett pulled out a chair for her. "I'm sorry about the mixup. I meant to call."

"I'll bet." Goldie gave him what in those days was described as a dirty look. "You said you were gonna rehearse me—"

Barrett's smile froze as he turned to me. "Miss Connors is thinking of a theatrical career. I think she has certain possibilities."

"Possibilities?" Goldie turned to him quickly. "You promised! You said you'd give me a part, a good part. Like what's-her-name—Ophelia?"

"Of course." Barrett took her hand. "But this is neither the time nor the place—"

"Then you better make the time and find a place! I'm sick and tired of getting the runaround, understand?"

I don't know about Barrett, but I understood one thing. I rose and nodded.

"Please excuse me. I'm due back at the office. Thank you for the interview."

"Sorry you have to leave." But Barrett wasn't sorry at all; he was greatly relieved. "Will there be a story, do you think?"

"I'm writing one," I said. "The rest is up to my editor. Read the paper."

I did write the story, stressing in particular the emphasis Barrett placed on realism. BARRETT PROMISES REAL HAMLET FOR BROADWAY was my heading.

But not my editor's. "Old lady McCullough," he said. "That's your story!" And he rewrote it, with a new heading—MRS. MYRON MCCULLOUGH TO FINANCE BARRETT'S BROADWAY BOW.

That's how it was printed, and that's how Richard Barrett read it. He wasn't the only one; the story created quite a stir. Mrs. McCullough was news in Chicago.

"Told you so," said my editor. "That's the angle. Now I hear Barrett's closing tomorrow night. He's doing a week in Milwaukee and then he heads straight for New York.

"Go out and catch him at his boardinghouse now—here's the address. I want a follow-up on his plans for the Broadway opening. See if you can find out how he managed to get his hooks into the old gal so that she'd back the show. I understand he's quite a ladies' man. So get me all the gory details."

The dinginess of Barrett's quarters somewhat surprised me. It was a theatrical boardinghouse on the near North Side, the sort of place that catered to second-rate vaudeville performers and itinerant carny workers. But then Barrett was probably pinched for funds when he'd come here; not until he met Mrs. McCullough did his prospects improve. The meeting with his wealthy patroness was what I'd come to find out about—all the gory details.

But I didn't get them. In fact, I got no details at all, for I went no farther than the hallway outside his door.

That's where I heard the voices; in that shabby hallway, musty with the smell of failure, the stale odor of blighted hopes.

Goldie Connors' voice. "What are you trying to pull? I read the paper. All about those big plans of yours in New York. And here you been stalling me along, telling me there was no job because you couldn't get bookings—"

"Please!" Richard Barrett's voice, with an edge to it. "I intended to surprise you—"

"Sure you did! By walking out on me. That's the surprise you figured on. Leaving me flat while you went off with that rich old bag you been romancing on the side."

"You keep her name out of this!"

Goldie's answering laugh was shrill, and I could imagine the glint of the gold tooth accompanying it. "That's what you tried to do—keep her name out of this, so I'd never know. Or so she'd never know about me. That would queer your little deal in a hurry, wouldn't it? Well, let me tell you something, Mr. Richard Hamlet Barrett! You promised me a part in the show and now it's put up or shut up."

Barrett's voice was an anguished pleading. "Goldie—you don't understand! This is Broadway, the big chance I've waited for all these years. I can't risk using an inexperienced actress—"

"Then you'll risk something else. You'll risk having me go straight to Mrs. Rich-Bitch and tell her just what's been going on between you and me!"

"Goldie—"

"When you leave town tomorrow night I'm going with you. With a signed contract for my part on Broadway. And that's final, understand?"

"All right. You win. You'll have your part."

"And not just one of those walk-on bits, either. It's got to be a decent part, a real one."

"A real part. I give you my word."

That's all I heard. And that's all I knew, until the day after Richard Barrett left Chicago.

Sometime during the afternoon of that day, the landlady of the rundown boardinghouse scented an addition to the odors mingling in the musty hallway. She followed her nose to the locked door of what had been Barrett's room. Opening the door she caught a glimpse of Barrett's battered old theatrical trunk, apparently abandoned upon his departure the day before. He'd shoved it almost out of sight under the bed, but she hauled it out and pried it open.

What confronted her then sent her screaming for the police.

What confronted the police became known in the city newsrooms, and what I learned there sent me racing to the boardinghouse.

There I confronted the contents of the trunk myself—the decapitated body of a woman. The head was missing.

All I could think of, staring down at it, was my editor's earlier demand. "The gory details," I murmured.

The homicide sergeant glanced at me. His name was Emmett, Gordon Emmett. We'd met before.

"What's going on?" he demanded.

I told him.

By the time I finished my story we were halfway to the Northwestern Depot. And by the time he finished questioning me, we had boarded the eight o'clock train for Milwaukee.

"Crazy," Emmett muttered. "A guy'd have to be crazy to do it."

"He's mad," I said. "No doubt about it. But there's more than madness involved. There's method, too. Don't forget, this was to be his big chance—the opportunity he'd worked and waited for all these years. He couldn't afford to fail. So that knowledge, combined with a moment of insane impulse—"

"Maybe so," Emmett muttered. "But how can you prove it?"

That was the question hanging over us as we reached Milwaukee. Ten o'clock of a wintry night, and no cab in sight. I whistled one up on the corner.

"Davidson Theatre," I said. "And hurry!"

It must have been ten-fifteen when we pulled up in the icy alley alongside the stage door, and twenty after ten by the time we'd gotten past the doorkeeper and elbowed our way backstage to the wings.

The performance had started promptly at eight-fifteen, and now a full house was centering its attention upon the opening scene of Act Five.

Here was the churchyard—the yawning grave, the two Clowns, Horatio, and Hamlet himself. A bright-eyed, burning Hamlet with feverish color in his cheeks and passionate power in his voice. For a moment I didn't even recognize Richard Barrett in his realization of the role. Somehow he'd managed to make the part come alive at last; this was the Prince of Denmark, and he was truly mad.

The First Clown tossed him a skull from the open grave and Hamlet lifted it to the light.

"Alas, poor Yorick," he said. "I knew him, Horatio—"

The skull turned slowly in his hand. And the footlights glittered over its grinning jaws in which the gold tooth gleamed—

Then we closed in.

Emmett had his murderer, and his proof.

And I?

I had seen my most memorable performance in Hamlet.

Goldie's . . .

* *

As previously revealed, the motion picture was my first love. No wonder we were married when I grew up: for the past seventeen years I've devoted a good deal of my time to writing for films.

But I have a confession to make. Though I've courted the movies for most of my life and been wedded to them now for quite a while, I also have a mistress.

Theatre is her name—and what an alluring creature she is!

I succumbed to her enticements when I was still a child, captivated by the charm of her changeability—the brash vulgarity of her vaudeville, the gaudy gaiety of her musicals, the sophistication of her high comedy and the imperious demands of her drama.

And I have been faithful to her in my fashion.

As a youngster, I indulged in endless play-acting with my sister and companions in the Chicago suburb of Maywood, Illinois. Mounds of earth in the back yard became trenches in No Man's Land; blankets draped over clotheslines served as circus tents; the front porch was a pirate vessel, complete with a piano stool for the ship's wheel and a board from the dining-room table balanced over the railing came in handy when a captive was forced to walk the plank and meet a watery doom in the flowerbeds below. I designed costumes which converted us into Arabs, Orientals, or Indians, and with the aid of disguise, we little cabbages became kings.

After seeing *The Phantom of the Opera* on film, I began to experiment with theatrical make-up as soon as my pants were dry. Secretly I devised ways of strapping up my legs, binding my arms, distorting my features. I was a closet Chaney.

In Milwaukee I became involved in high school theatricals. I appeared in minstrel shows and such then-popular one act plays as *The Bishop's Candlesticks*, demonstrating versatility by switching roles. At one time I performed as the Bishop, then switched to Jean Valjean. Here memory falters, but it's quite possible that I also played one of the Candlesticks.

Muscling my way into the senior plays when still a lowly sophomore, I was the villain in *Three Wise Fools* and the kindly old doctor in *Smilin' Through*—thus setting back both the Mafia and the AMA by several decades through my performances. And for the weekly high school assembly meetings I wrote my own skits, in which I soon learned the First Rule of the Theatre—give the best lines to yourself.

Had it not been for the theatrical slump brought about by the Depression, I might have ended up as a burlesque comic. As it was, I sold a few gags to radio comedians and did a couple of local stints as a nitery monologist and m.c.—a sort of Henny Youngman without a violin.

Take my act—please.

Now one of the fringe benefits of my high school dramatic career was the freebie, then known as an Annie Oakley or pass. These tickets to legitimate performances were handed out at the discretion of the teacher in charge of theatricals, as a reward for services rendered, and I got my share.

It was such a ticket that admitted me to the Davidson Theatre one evening early in 1934. The play was *The Merchant of Venice*, and its star—soon to forsake the stage for a career as a character actor in films—was the distinguished Shakesperean performer, Fritz Leiber. He, of course, was Shylock, playing opposite his wife in the role of Portia. Also in the cast, as the Prince of Morocco, was a strikingly handsome young man named Francis Lathrop.

Three years later, while visiting my friend Henry Kuttner in Hollywood, I met Francis Lathrop and discovered that he was in actuality Fritz Leiber, Jr., the same man who went on to become a writer, discarding the "Jr." after his father's death.

Fritz and I have shared careers for almost forty years. During those long decades I often thought of that night at the Davidson when an awkward adolescent all unknowingly caught a glimpse of a friend who would figure in his future. And in the back of my mind I always wanted to somehow commemorate that occasion, though the means to do so eluded me.

Then, one day it all came together. A trip to the dentist was my inspiration; a gold filling as the catalyst. And the resulting story appeared in the May 1971 issue of *Alfred Hitchcock's Mystery Magazine*.

Who's to blame for this one? The homage to nostalgia was on the side of the angels, but the plot itself sprang from a hellish notion.

The eminent director Rouben Mamoulian has long been a student of Shakespeare and some years ago wrote a scholarly volume on *Hamlet*. He now tells me that I've ruined his life; since reading my story he will never be able to see *Hamlet* again.

Surely this is the work of Satan. Or is it the Tooth Fairy?

Ego Trip

The plane came in low over the moor. It circled against the night sky, then glided down for a landing, softly and silently.

As the waiting limousine pulled up alongside the cabin door it seemed to be peering at the plane with yellow headlamp eyes, and its motor purred a greeting.

Mike Savage didn't purr. He was out of the limousine almost before it halted, moving quickly to the cabin. For a man of his bulk he moved with surprising swiftness. By the time the cabin door opened, Savage was directly beside it, hand extended to grasp the overnight bag held by the figure emerging from the plane.

"Kane?" he said.

The figure nodded, moving into the light. Savage saw a tall man whose momentary smile was merely a grimace of greeting; almost at once the man's face tightened into habitual harshness, matching the unblinking, steady stare of the dark, deep-set eyes. Joe Kane's many talents didn't include smiling.

The tall man turned to glance up toward the pilot in the cabin. "Okay," he said. "Get lost."

The pilot nodded, pulling the door shut. A moment later the plane's engines coughed into life, then revved to a roar.

Kane didn't wait to watch the takeoff. He followed Mike Savage to the limousine, slid into the seat beside him and the driver.

"Let's go," he said.

Savage nodded to the driver. The car turned and moved back onto the narrow roadway bordering the moor. As it picked up speed the plane swooped over it, airborne against the clouded sky.

The limousine turned down a wooded road that was scarcely more than a paved pathway through the English countryside. As it descended, fog rose to swirl across the windshield.

"Rain ahead," Savage murmured. "How was the weather coming over?"

The dark eyes stared without even the pretense of an accompanying smile. "I come three thousand miles and you want to talk about the weather."

"Sorry." And Savage meant it. No point in getting off to a bad start; too much depended on Kane's reactions. Savage took a deep breath. "Suppose I tell you something about the plans."

"Suppose you shut up," said Kane. "I'm beat." He turned away from Savage and closed his eyes.

Savage bit his lip. No sense getting the wind up. And Kane undoubtedly was tired, rightfully so. A transatlantic hop in a small plane, a secret and unauthorized flight, was bound to take its toll. The important thing was that Kane had actually arrived, safe and sound. Let him rest now; tomorrow would be time enough to go over the plan.

But there was no reason why Savage couldn't think about it, if he wished. By now it was almost second nature, for it was his own conception and he'd thought about nothing else for months.

Rain pelted down against the glass. The windshield wipers went into action, clicking away the moisture but doing nothing to disperse the fog.

"Slow," Savage cautioned the driver.

Beside him, Kane dozed off, head lolling loosely against the seat. Savage studied the fiercely aquiline profile. Even in repose, there was no semblance of relaxation in Kane's face; the mouth remained tight, the facial muscles refused to surrender to the slackness of slumber. A cruel face. Cruel and intelligent. That was an apt description of Joe Kane. An apt explanation of why he'd won a reputation as the most formidable head of the rackets in the States. And, of course, an apt reason why Mike Savage wanted him over here. Joe Kane was vital to the success of the plan.

Savage's plan was simple—nothing less than an international alliance of organized crime. But its very simplicity was complex. Oh, there was talk enough about the Cosa Nostra, and for years newspaper headlines proclaimed the existence of "crime lords" and an "empire of crime." But behind the headlines there'd been only a shadowy reality. Criminals did operate and cooperate on a worldwide basis, but such partnerships were temporary at best, and loosely knit.

What Savage had in mind was much more ambitious; a truly practical and permanent partnership founded on a gentleman's agreement. It would involve gentlemen farmers who cultivated poppies in Turkey, sporting gentlemen dispersing firearms in Africa, sophisticated gentlemen who escorted ladies to and from South America, gentlemen connoisseurs dealing in diamonds and rare art objects in Amsterdam. Still other gentlemen operated in Marseilles, Athens, Montreal, Algiers, Hong Kong, and maintained connections with a bank in Zurich; they were indeed a cosmopolitan group, and it had taken Savage a long time to approach them all.

He'd worked out the details very carefully with his own gentlemen friends here in London, and made all the necessary contacts for the coming summit meeting.

It was at this meeting that he intended to lay out his proposal in detail—and to present Joe Kane. Perhaps Kane was not quite as polished as the others; he had a reputation for ruthlessness. But no proposition, however worthy, can be carried through successfully without a leader, and Joe Kane was a leader. A man who went straight for the throat. With Kane at the head of the enterprise, it could not fail, and there was no question but that he'd be accepted.

Savage stared through the windshield at the wall of rain and fog. It seemed impenetrable, yet the car was moving through it.

That's the way his crime machine would move, through anything, full speed ahead, with Kane at the wheel. As for himself, Savage was perfectly content to sit beside him as a second-in-command; let Kane do the steering if he wished, if only Savage went along for the smooth, sweet ride in a vehicle designed to overrun the world—

"Look out!"

Savage screamed at the driver as the headlamps of a car loomed up through the fog on the road directly before them.

The driver spun the wheel and the limousine swung to the left.

In a split second that held an eternity of horror, Savage saw the oncoming car skid and swerve in the same direction.

The sudden squeal of brakes was lost in the screech of shattered metal as the head-on crash flung Savage to the floor. He struck his head against the dash as he fell, and the gray fog blended into blackness.

When his blurred vision cleared he looked up to find the driver leaning over him from outside the limousine.

"Are you all right, sir?"

Savage felt the throbbing lump above his temple, then grunted.

"Slide under the wheel." The driver extended his left hand to assist him; Savage noted that the man's right arm hung limply at his side.

"Broken?"

The driver nodded. "I'm afraid you'll have to help the other gentleman."

Savage turned, catching a momentary glimpse of the limousine's crumpled hood and noting that the car itself was still seemingly intact, although the other vehicle had been almost totally demolished by the collision's impact.

Then he was staring into the front seat of the limousine again, staring at Kane.

The tall man had pitched face-forward through the broken windshield. He sagged there, head and arms supported by jagged splinters of glass.

Savage crawled across the seat, which was wet and slippery. He grasped Kane's limp shoulders, pulled him back to a sitting position. Then he glanced down at Joe Kane.

"Look!" he gasped. "Look at his face—"

Joe Kane's face was completely masked by the bandages mummy-wrapped around his head and throat. Behind the narrow shadowed slits a mouth moved, a nose drew breath, eyes blinked.

Savage leaned over the bed in the white-walled room. "Kane—can you hear me?" he murmured.

There was no response, only the sound of tortured breathing.

"He can't talk yet. The vocal cords must heal."

Savage turned. Dr. Augustus was entering the room. The portly little physician moved to the bedside.

"But they will heal?"

"Certainly. Only a matter of time."

Dr. Augustus' voice was reassuring. But then his very presence was reassuring, and Savage gave silent thanks for such an ally. There was no one to match the medical skills and versatility of Edmund Augustus—late of the Royal College of Surgeons and now on a permanent private retainer with Savage's organization. Harley Street had lost a jewel: here was no ordinary patcher of bullet wounds. The remarkable range of his abilities seemingly extended into every branch of medicine from surgery to psychiatry, and Savage appreciated his services. So much so that he'd set Dr. Augustus up here in a country house that was actually a completely equipped clinic—with a most exclusive clientele, drawn from Savage's associates.

Savage glanced down at the mute mummy on the bed. "This is Dr. Augustus," he said. "You can thank him for saving your life."

The man on the bed didn't move.

"Kane—listen to me—"

There was no response. Savage frowned at Augustus. "What's the matter? I can't get any reaction—he's like a vegetable. It's as though he didn't even know his own name."

"He doesn't," said Augustus.

Savage's frown deepened, but Augustus shook his head. "I'm going to tell him the truth," he murmured.

Augustus bent over his patient. "You were in an accident, Mr. Kane. A severe accident. But the worst is over. You're going to live, and your physical recovery will be complete. Do you understand that?"

Slowly the bandaged head moved.

"There is one thing you must know. A side effect of an injury —your skull fracture—has produced total amnesia. I realize this is disturbing—losing memory of yourself, of your past, not even being able to recall the crash. But you're relatively fortunate. The driver of the other car was killed outright, and you yourself would have died if Mr. Savage hadn't brought you directly to me so that I could operate in time.

"And your situation is not hopeless. As you mend, you will gradually come out of your amnesia. Your memory will return— and we'll be here to help. What you need now is rest."

Dr. Augustus reached for the prepared hypodermic wrapped in sterile gauze on the bedstand. He guided the needle into the vein of the left arm, and the mummified figure lay back. Then he stood there, waiting until he was certain that the injection had taken effect.

Savage glanced at him. "You're sure?" he murmured.

"Quite sure." Dr. Augustus smiled. "Your summit meeting will have to be postponed, of course. But when you hold it, Joe Kane will be there."

Rita Foley was nervous. She couldn't get used to driving the little rented car on the left-hand side of the road, and she didn't care for the way in which the road itself wound deeper and deeper into these godforsaken hills. But she had to find the house.

When she did find it, Rita wasn't reassured. The place was too big to be set way off here in the middle of nowhere, and with no traffic passing by there didn't seem to be any reason for hiding the house behind such high walls.

But Rita had come a long way and she wasn't about to be put off.

That's what she told Dr. Augustus when he tried to give her the brushoff at the front door.

"I'm not leaving until I see Joe Kane," she said.

Augustus shook his head. "You must be mistaken. This happens to be a private residence. There's no such person here."

"Joe's here, all right. I got the word."

"What word?" The question came from the big, broad-shouldered man who loomed up beside Augustus in the doorway. Rita nodded at him.

"The same word that says you're Mike Savage."

The big man raised his eyebrows. "Do come in, dear lady." And then, in the hallway, "Perhaps you'd better explain." He stared at her. "You're not Mrs. Kane, are you?"

"I might as well be," Rita said. "We were together the night before he left. He told me he was coming over here, and why."

"Did he, now?" Savage glanced quickly at Augustus. Then they both stared at her, but Rita didn't care.

"Joe and I always level with each other. That's why we've stayed together. I know all about this summit meeting of yours. He said he'd phone the minute he arrived. Well, he didn't phone. I knew nothing went wrong with the plane, because Arnie— that's the pilot—got back and told me the flight was okay. Then the word came that the summit meeting was postponed."

"Who told you that?" Savage spoke quickly.

"Some of Joe's people. The same ones who told me about your setup here. And where I'd probably find you." Rita glanced down the hall. "This private clinic's a front, isn't it?"

"You're very well informed," said Dr. Augustus coldly.

"Never mind that. Tell me about Joe Kane."

Savage shrugged. "I'm afraid there's been a bit of an accident."

"Accident?" Rita's eyes widened. "He isn't—"

"No, not dead."

"How bad is he?"

Savage hesitated. Dr. Augustus took Rita by the arm. "Suppose you see for yourself," he said.

They went upstairs. Along the hall. Into the white-walled room, where the mummy waited.

"Joe!" Rita gasped. "Oh my God—"

"He's going to be all right," Dr. Augustus told her. Rita didn't hear; she was at the bedside, staring down.

"Joe—look at me—it's Rita—"

"He doesn't know you," said Savage.

"What is this? Of course he knows me!"

"He doesn't know anyone. Amnesia."

Rita began to sob. Savage scowled at Augustus.

"This was your idea, letting her see him like this."

"And a good one, I think," said Augustus calmly. He moved forward and put his hand on Rita's arm.

"Listen to me. I told you he'll be all right. And now that you're here, you can help."

"Anything," Rita murmured. "Just let me stay. I'll nurse him—"

"That's already attended to," Augustus said. "I have a nurse on duty. And he's out of danger now, healing quite nicely. What he needs, you might say, is a mother."

"Mother?"

"There's no prognosis about when the amnesia will pass. Until his memory returns, he's going to be like this. That is to say, physically he's a full-grown man—mentally, he's an infant. So he'll need a mother. Someone to help to re-educate him just as if he were an infant. But with his adult brain, he'll learn quickly. Just how quickly will depend on your co-operation."

"Good thinking." Savage nodded at Dr. Augustus, then spoke directly to Rita. "Remember, we all have a stake in his recovery. Without Joe Kane to function as he did before the accident, there'll be no summit meeting. There'll be no international organization—at least, none that he can control. And you know how much such an organization would mean. Not millions, but hundreds of millions. I needn't tell you."

"I don't care about the money," Rita said. "It's Joe." She turned to Augustus. "When can I start?"

Dr. Augustus smiled. "Tomorrow," he said.

Tomorrow came. And went. A week passed, then another. Rita lost all track of time. She spent every waking moment with Joe Kane, and at night, in her bedroom down the hall, his image haunted her restless slumber.

The educational process was slow, painfully slow at first. It was several days before Kane's vocal cords healed to a point where he could whisper, and when he did his words were merely questions—questions which confirmed Dr. Augustus' diagnosis. Kane didn't remember what had happened. He didn't remember the accident, or anything before the accident. He didn't remember Rita's name or his own.

So Rita taught him. Dr. Augustus told her what to do, what to say. He was still in pain, under sedation, and it was often hard to communicate clearly, but she kept at her task, kept talking.

Gradually Kane became more mobile. First he sat up in bed, then moved to a wheelchair. Rita took him out into the garden;

aside from Augustus, Savage and a nurse who also did the cooking, the clinic was deserted. "We've got to keep him under wraps," Savage told her.

"Under wraps?" Rita glanced at the swathed head and shuddered. "When do those bandages come off?"

"Soon. Dr. Augustus says he's on the mend. Until then, you're to carry on."

Rita carried on. In the garden she spoke quietly to Kane about his own past, filling him in on the details of his climb to power, playing back to him the anecdotes and incidents he had told her over the years.

"It's no use." His husky voice was stronger now, but it held a note of anxiety. "I don't recall anything."

"Dr. Augustus says you don't have to recall. Just listen. You've got to learn about yourself all over again."

Rita wheeled Kane along the garden pathway. "Oh, I've got some good news for you. Tomorrow you start walking."

Kane walked. He walked for a week, through the garden and inside the house. Together he and Rita made a tour of inspection. Dr. Augustus was quite proud of his establishment, and he had reason to be; the clinic was compact but modern and fully equipped. There was an imposing operating room and a huge autoclave, oscilloscopic equipment on which Augustus frequently tested Kane's brain patterns, and all the medical marvels money could buy. Rita's respect for Dr. Augustus grew.

She was also beginning to become aware of Mike Savage's capacities. After all, it was he who had conceived of this arrangement and brought it into being. A private clinic that was also a perfect hideaway, and a fortress as well.

Rita and Kane found this out when they discovered the concealed chamber in the cellar—the big, soundproofed room with the mobsters' arsenal of weapons racked along the walls. Pistols, revolvers, tear gas, rifles, even machine guns.

"Better than your place in Jersey," Rita said.

Kane frowned, then nodded. "Oh, yes—you told me."

"You still don't remember?"

"No." But the husky voice was resolute now. "Not yet. I mean, you tell me all these things and I believe them. It's just that I can't *feel* them to be true, inside. But don't worry, I will."

"Of course, darling. Everything takes time." She smiled. "I almost forgot something. More good news. Tomorrow your bandages come off."

And they did.

Dr. Augustus performed the task himself, in surgery, with only Savage and Rita in attendance. He snipped away expertly under the bright lights, removing layer after layer of wrappings. There was no pain involved, but Rita had to force herself to watch. She kept remembering how Kane had gone through the car windshield in the accident. Dr. Augustus had told her he'd performed extensive plastic surgery, but she knew that even under ordinary circumstances such operations aren't always completely successful. Suppose Kane had been left with a scarred face? Rita shuddered in spite of herself, and as the last bit of gauze parted, she looked away.

There was a moment of silence in the room.

Then Kane himself was speaking. "Well, Doc?"

"Perfect," said Augustus. "Not a scar."

Savage put his hand on Rita's arm. "Aren't you going to look at him?" he murmured.

Slowly, Rita turned. She saw Kane.

She screamed.

The last thing she remembered as she fell was Joe Kane staring at her, and he was a stranger. A stranger with a totally different face.

"It's all right."

Rita blinked up at the stranger who knelt beside her, holding her in his arms.

"Joe—what did they do to you?"

"Quite a bit." Dr. Augustus spoke crisply. "The windshield glass made it necessary for me to resort to radical surgery. Literally a matter of new construction—reconstruction was impossible."

As Rita rose, Augustus held a hand mirror before Kane's face. "You'll have to make allowances for the stitches, of course. We'll be taking them out from around the eyes next week, and by then the bruises should start disappearing. But on the whole it came off quite well, don't you think?"

Kane searched his own reflection with a puzzled frown. "If

you say so. Funny, isn't it? I can't remember how I looked before—"

"You're a fortunate man," Savage told him. "And if you don't mind my saying so, a much more handsome one, thanks to Dr. Augustus, here. It's an amazing job, considering how quickly he had to work."

"You must remember I'd never seen you prior to the accident," Augustus said. "And I had nothing to guide me, not even a photograph. It was a matter of massive cartilage transplants and skin grafts."

"Well, you'd never know it now." Kane rubbed a hand along the side of his cheek, his fingers grazing the edge of the bandage which still turbaned his head.

"Careful." Dr. Augustus gestured quickly. "The head bandage mustn't be touched for another ten days."

The ten days passed slowly. Now that Kane was healing, Rita found herself becoming restless. Even though she gradually became accustomed to his new features, there was a tension between the two of them. Mother and child, teacher and pupil— this wasn't the relationship she'd known before, and she didn't want it now. True, for a moment there when she'd passed out, Kane had held her in his arms, but he'd never attempted to do so since. Something else had changed besides his appearance; something deeper. She had a feeling she ought to put an end to their constant companionship, get away for a while and think about it.

But when Rita suggested a shopping trip to the nearby village on her own, Savage shook his head. "Not yet," he said.

"It would only be for an hour or so—"

"I know. But we've got to be careful about such things. You don't understand how it is in these rural areas. If a strange woman were to show up alone, there'd be talk. A couple, now— that's another matter. When Kane's head bandage comes off, you can go in together. They'll just take you for ordinary Yanks on tour."

Somehow his reasoning didn't quite satisfy Rita. Nor, on reflection, was she completely satisfied with Dr. Augustus' explanation of his surgery. It was true that he had a lot of fancy equipment, including some machines she couldn't even identify, but he certainly hadn't gone into any details about just what techniques he'd used. And neither he nor Savage wanted to talk about it; every time she brought it up, they changed the subject. Rita couldn't put her finger on what was wrong, but she was beginning to get an idea that they were giving her the runaround.

The day before the head bandage was scheduled for removal, Rita's suspicions were crystallized in a single glance.

It was a glance out the front window, onto the drive where she'd parked her car. Just a passing glance, at that, but it was enough.

Her car was gone.

As soon as she could conveniently get away from Kane and the others, she slipped out to the garage. The black limousine was there, and a small Riley.

Rita debated about confronting Savage and Augustus directly, then decided against it. She wouldn't get a straight answer. There was only one ally she could count on, if something was really wrong. She'd have to talk to Joe.

That night she waited until the house was still, then slipped out of her room and tiptoed down the hall to Kane's bedroom.

He was awake, and it was almost as though he'd been expecting her to come. She didn't even have to put a finger to her lips to warn him about keeping their voices low. And when she blurted out her suspicions, he only nodded.

"I've felt it myself," he murmured. "They're not telling the truth. At least, not the whole truth."

"What are we going to do about it?"

"Leave that to me. Tomorrow, when this bandage comes off, I'll be back in business." He grinned at her. "I'm getting into shape again, physically, and mentally—well, you've been a great help." He drew her close. "Never did say thanks for everything you've done, did I?"

It was strange, being in his arms again. And different, somehow—but Rita put the thought away. They were together, and that's all she had to know.

"You've never thanked me for anything, not in all these years," she said. "And you don't have to. It's the things you do that show me how you feel. Like that night in Rio."

"Rio?" Kane's eyes were puzzled. "I don't recall—"

"Carnival time. And I wouldn't expect you to remember, because you were stoned out of your skull." She giggled. "We went into this crazy joint with all the sailors, because one of them got the idea that everybody should get tattooed. And you insisted on having my name tattooed on your arm. I nearly fell over, watching that old guy work on you with his dirty needle."

"You're putting me on," Kane said.

"It's true, so help me," Rita told him. "Here—I can prove it. Your right arm—"

She rolled up his sleeve to show him. "Look—"

Kane glanced down. "Suppose you look," he said softly.

Rita followed his glance and stiffened in sudden shock.

There was no tattoo.

No tattoo. Which could only mean—

"You're not Joe!" she screamed.

The door behind them opened swiftly and Dr. Augustus moved into the room. His smile was grim.

"Oh yes he is," Augustus murmured. "He's Joe Kane all right— what's left of him. But his skull was so badly damaged I couldn't repair it."

Rita stared at him. "What did you do?"

"The only thing possible. It was a one-in-a-million chance, but he was dying anyway, so I took the risk. I had to transplant his brain. The body it now occupies belonged to Barry Collins—the driver of the other car."

"I still can't believe it." Kane shook his head as he lifted the brandy glass in the downstairs study.

"It's true," Savage nodded. "I saw the whole procedure. We'd brought the other driver with us, but he was dead by the time we got here. Heart failure, apparently, at the time of the crash, because there wasn't a mark on his body. Dr. Augustus examined him, and that's when he got the idea for the surgery.

"Remarkable, isn't it? What would have been considered absolutely impossible five years ago is today a reality."

"Ironic, too." Augustus' smile was still grim. "It's a medical break-through, like the first heart transplant. But under the circumstances, I can hardly proclaim this achievement to the world."

"Nor the underworld." Savage's eyes narrowed. "They mustn't learn either. That's why we concocted this plastic surgery story.

It didn't hold for you two, but we've got to make it stick where everyone else is concerned."

Kane gave him a quick glance. "What about the real Barry Collins?"

"No problem," Augustus answered. "Don't forget, licensed physician. I signed a death certificate and filled out all the necessary forms regarding the accident. We switched Collins' wallet and personal effects to your body—your former body, with its totally disfigured face. It was identified and buried under his name. Fortunately, he had no family."

"How did you cover my being here?"

Savage smiled. "You aren't. Since you flew in by private plane, without a visa, the authorities know nothing of your presence. And we didn't mention you were in the car at the time of the accident. So actually, you're doubly safe from discovery now, in a new body."

Kane nodded. "No wonder I had a loss of memory. It's a miracle I recovered at all." He touched his head bandage. "How long before this comes off, Doc?"

"Tomorrow morning," said Augustus. "Then you start exercising a bit, get back some muscle tone. And then—"

"Never mind that." Kane's voice cut in firmly. "From now on I call the plays."

"That's what I've been waiting to hear." Savage's smile broadened. "You're beginning to sound like your old self again." He glanced at Dr. Augustus. "Congratulations, Doctor. It looks like we're back in business."

In spite of herself, Rita experienced a shock when the head bandage came off. She couldn't quite get used to seeing Joe Kane with lighter hair. And it was difficult to accept the reason for the change; to realize that the man she had known all these years was literally reborn in another form. His eyes, his voice, his mannerisms—every aspect was subtly different. And yet, thanks in large part to her weeks of patient effort, he was himself again.

Inside the unfamiliar body was Joe Kane, with all his knowledge and memories restored. He'd learned the details of his past, and his plans for the future. And the Kane ruthlessness was returning.

Once the bandages were removed, he insisted on driving with Rita into the village. He was fed up with confinement.

"Are you sure that's wise?" Savage frowned. "As long as they take you for a tourist, there'll be no problem. But if you get involved—"

Kane smiled. "I'm a big boy now." The smile faded abruptly. "So don't crowd me. Understand?"

They took the little Riley from the garage and Kane drove. Both the car and the road were strange, but he handled the wheel expertly and found the village without any difficulty.

Strolling down the main—and only—street in the afternoon sunlight, Rita marveled at her companion's new-found air of utter confidence.

"I can't get over it," she said. "All at once you seem so sure of yourself—"

"Why not?" Kane shrugged. "You heard Savage and the Doc talk about this summit meeting. They've already called Demopolis in London to set it up again for the end of the week. We've got big plans and now they're coming through. Think about it— with this setup we're going to be running the world. Politics, the military, the law—it's all just window dressing. We're going to be the power behind the throne, the real power. And who's at the head of it?"

"Barry!" the voice called. "Barry Collins!"

Rita glanced up hastily. The girl emerging from the car across the street was young and attractive. She was dressed in sober black but her eyes, fixed on Kane, held delight rather than mourning.

"You're alive—" she gasped.

Rita intercepted her, and somehow managed to speak without a telltale tremor. "Who are you?"

"Muriel. Muriel Morland." The girl smiled at Kane. "Ask Barry. We're engaged—"

Then, before Rita could move to restrain her, the girl was in Kane's arms. "Oh, darling, I'm so happy! If you only knew what I went through when I heard the news—I just got back to Oxford yesterday after the cruise, and they told me—"

"Easy," Kane murmured. He frowned at Rita over Muriel's shoulder.

"Naturally I came right down here," the girl was saying. "I wanted to talk to the authorities, find out what happened—"

"That won't be necessary now," Kane said.

"But they said you were dead—there was even a report in the paper. Why didn't you write or call?"

"It's a long story." Kane smiled down at Muriel, then glanced at Rita. "Suppose you ring up Mr. Savage. Tell him about Miss Morland and say that we're bringing her out. I want the doctor to know."

Rita nodded quickly, then crossed the street to a public telephone.

"Doctor?" Muriel looked puzzled.

"The man who saved my life. I've been in a private clinic—today is the first time I was able to leave. The young lady is one of the nurses."

Kane indicated Rita, who was absorbed in her phone conversation across the street. Taking Muriel's arm, he led her over to her car. "When she's finished, we'll be on our way," he said. "You can follow us out."

"But aren't you going to explain—?"

"You'll understand it better once we get there," Kane said.

And she did.

Kane and Rita led the way as Muriel followed. Parking the car in the driveway, Muriel accompanied her companions into the big house where Savage and Dr. Augustus were waiting. The introductions were brief.

"Please," Muriel said. "Tell me what happened. I can't wait—"

"Then suppose we come in here, where we can all be comfortable?" Dr. Augustus suggested, ushering Muriel down the hall and into a room which Kane recognized as the surgical chamber. He stepped aside, permitting her to enter, then quickly followed and shut the soundproof door. A lock clicked.

There was no other sound, not even a scream.

Savage disposed of the car. Rita didn't ask what he did with it, and she didn't want to know. Nor watch, later, as Savage enlisted Kane's help to dig the shallow hole in the garden under the trees. She avoided watching when, later that evening, Dr. Augustus and Savage carefully smoothed the earth into place again so that the hole no longer existed. It was enough to know that Muriel no longer existed either, enough to know that Kane was safe.

Or was it enough?

Rita paced the floor of her room. Ever since Savage had dismissed the limousine driver to other duties up in London, ever since Dr. Augustus had dispensed with the nurse who attended Kane in the early weeks of recovery, Rita had been here with her three companions. It had never bothered her until this moment, but now for the first time she felt truly alone. Savage and Augustus were strangers, and as for Joe Kane—

Impulsively, Rita made her way down the hall to Kane's room. She had to talk to him, once and for all. Only he could reassure her, set her mind at rest.

But his room was empty.

Rita surveyed it with sudden distaste. Something about the sterile white-walled atmosphere repelled her, and she had a momentary recollection of the mummy who had lain here week after week, his face hidden and his mind a blank. What had it been like to be imprisoned here, without even a window—nothing but that air vent up over the bed?

She glanced at the vent, and then she saw it.

It must have been there all along, she probably had seen it a hundred times without noticing, but she noticed it now. Lodged behind the vent, the tiny metal microphone. And extending down into the vent behind it, the wires.

"Joe—!" Rita murmured.

There was no answer.

And out in back, in the garden, Dr. Augustus and Savage were still at work.

Rita went back into the hall. Those wires—where did they lead to? Down the staircase, inside the wall. And along the wall to the door. And through the door to the passage below.

She switched on a light and descended to the concealed chamber in the cellar. The soundproofed chamber which served as Mike Savage's arsenal—and as Dr. Augustus' monitoring post. His own improvised broadcasting studio.

Rita realized it when she saw the wire extending from the wall beside the racks of weapons; saw the wire leading to the tape-recorder set on the table.

She clicked a switch. The tape rolled, and from the speaker of the recorder the voice echoed in a ghostly whisper. Dr. Augustus' voice, speaking softly and slowly, slowly and distinctly, distinctly and dismayingly. Whispering over and over again—

"*You are Joe Kane. You are Joe Kane.*"

"So."

Another voice, from behind her.

Rita turned. Kane stood in the doorway. "You found it," he said.

She stared at him. "You knew?"

"About the tapes?" He moved into the room, nodding as he switched off the recorder. "Of course. Augustus told me last week. It was part of his treatment to help me recover my memory. Hypnotherapy, played while I slept in my room. You've heard of it—they call it sleep-learning."

"Yes, I've heard of it." Rita faced him across the table. Even in the shadows of the dim light her face was pale. "But it wasn't just an aid for memory. It was done for real—real hypnosis, real suggestion."

"What are you getting at?"

"The truth." Rita forced her eyes to meet his gaze. "Today, in the village—when that girl called 'Barry'—you automatically turned your head."

"It was only natural—" Kane began.

"The truth, I said." Rita whispered. "And the truth is—you *are* Barry Collins."

There was a moment of silence and then he nodded. "I guessed as much, some while ago. There was no brain transplant —such a thing is impossible. Joe Kane did die in the accident, but I was only a victim of concussion, with temporary amnesia."

The man glanced at the rows of weapons lining the walls. "Savage and Augustus couldn't afford to lose their big chance— putting together this deal was too important, and they knew everything depended on producing Joe Kane to act as leader. So they decided to convince me I was Kane. And when you came, they concocted the story and got you to help—giving me a new memory, a new personality. What they didn't realize is that gradually my own memory would return. Today, when I saw Muriel in town, it all came back."

Rita searched his face in the shadows. "But you let them kill her—"

"There was no choice." He shrugged. "I couldn't risk having her around to identify me."

Rita blinked. "You intend to continue passing as Joe Kane?"

"I intend to *be* Joe Kane." The man chuckled. "I've come to like the notion. All those millions, all that power." He chuckled again. "You and the others really must have done a good job of brainwashing me. What did they use to call it—a 'criminal mind'?"

"Quite correct."

Rita turned. Dr. Augustus and Mike Savage were moving through the doorway and they were smiling.

"You heard—" she murmured.

"Everything." Augustus shut the door behind him.

"That's right," Savage said. "And it's going to be even better this way." He smiled at them approvingly. "We won't have to play games any more. The summit meeting is scheduled, you know how to handle your role—all that's left is to practice Kane's signature. Right?"

The man nodded. "One more detail. You taught me that the real Joe Kane always covers his tracks." He grinned. "And that's what I'm going to do."

Rita bit her lip. "What do you mean—?"

Still grinning, the man turned to the rack on the wall and scooped up a tommy-gun. . . .

When he emerged from the room he climbed the stairs and went directly to the telephone. Beside it was a pad on which was scribbled the number of Demopolis—the man who was setting up the summit meeting. He put the call through, humming under his breath as he waited for the connection. And when it came his voice was harsh, vibrant with the promise of power.

"Hello," he said. "This is Joe Kane."

* *

"Ego Trip" came about as the direct result of another trip—my own journey to London, in 1968.

My wife and I had been there before, in '65, and we fell in love with the city.

So when I was invited to go over and work on a script for the short-lived series "Journey to the Unknown," I eagerly accepted.

Twentieth Century-Fox put me up at the Dorchester, Hammer Films provided an office, and producer Joan Harrison—whom I'd worked with on the Hitchcock television shows—made me welcome. Together with the late Jack Fleischman, she assigned me the task of adapting one of my published stories, "The Indian Spirit Guide."

Upon completing the script I was asked to do another, and came up with an original treatment which seemed interesting. At the time the current catch-phrase was "identity-crisis" and it occurred to me that perhaps I could dramatize this in an English setting. The result was "Ego Trip."

After turning in the story line I sent for my wife to join me and waited for a go-ahead on the teleplay. But it's a long way from London to Hollywood, and the lines of communication were sorely stretched. Time was running out, and when the powers-that-be kept delaying their decision, Miss Harrison asked me to go ahead and script another story which had already been approved.

So "Ego Trip" was never dramatized, and when I returned home the treatment was buried in my files along with other brainchildren which had been untimely aborted.

But somehow the notion refused to stay dead, and finally I resurrected it in story form for the March 1972 issue of *Penthouse*.

Resurrection of the dead is, of course, a matter of necromancy. Thus, once again, I must admit collaboration with the Powers of Darkness.

Forever and Amen

Forever.

It's a nice way to live, if you can afford it.

And Seward Skinner could.

"One billion integral units," said Dr. Togol. "Maybe more."

Seward Skinner didn't even blink when he heard the estimate. Blinking, like every other bodily movement, involves painful effort when one is in a terminal stage. But Skinner summoned the strength to speak, even though his voice was no more than a husky whisper.

"Go ahead with the plan. But hurry."

The plan had been ten years in the making and Skinner had been dying for the past two, so Dr. Togol hurried. Haste makes waste and in the end it probably cost Skinner closer to five billion IGUS than the price quoted. Nobody knew for sure. All they knew was that Seward Skinner was the one man in the entire galaxy—the known galaxy, that is—who could afford the expenditure.

That was the extent of their knowledge.

Seward Skinner had been the wealthiest man alive for a long, long time. There were still a few old-timers around who could remember the days when he was a public figure and a private joke—the Playboy of the Planets, as they called him. According to the rumors he had a woman on every world, or at least a female.

Other people, a trifle less elderly, recalled a more mature Seward Skinner—the Galactic Genius, fabulous inventor—entrepreneur of Interspace Industries, the largest corporate combine ever known. During those days his business operations made the news, and the rumors.

But for the majority of the interplanetary public, the youngsters without personal memories of those far-off times, Seward Skinner was merely a name. In recent years he'd withdrawn completely from any contact with the outside worlds. And Interspace Industries had carefully and painstakingly tracked down and acquired every tape, every record of his past. Some said these had been destroyed, some said the data had been hidden away, but in the end it amounted to the same thing. Seward Skinner's privacy was protected, complete. And nobody saw the man himself any more. His business, his life itself, seemed to be run by remote control.

Actually, of course, it was run by Dr. Togol.

If Skinner was the richest man, Dr. Togol was surely the most brilliant scientist. Inevitably, the two men were drawn together by a common love—wealth.

What wealth represented to Skinner no one knew. What it meant to Dr. Togol was plainly apparent; it was the tool of research. Unlimited funds were the key to unlimited experimentation. And so a partnership came into being.

During the past decade Dr. Togol developed his plan and Seward Skinner developed incurable cancer.

Now the plan was ready to function, just as Skinner was ceasing to function.

So Skinner died.

And lived again.

It's great to be alive, particularly after you've been dead. Somehow the sun seems warmer, the world looks brighter, the birds sing more sweetly. Even though here on Eden the sun was artificial, the light was supplied by beaming devices, and the birdsong issued from mechanical throats.

But Skinner himself was alive.

He sat on the terrace of his big house on the hill and looked down over Eden and he was pleased at what he had wrought. The bleak little satellite of a barren and neglected world he'd purchased many years ago had been transformed into a miniature earth, a reminder of his original home. Below him was a city very similar to the one where he'd been born; here on the hilltop was a mansion duplicating the finest dwelling he'd ever owned. Yonder was Dr. Togol's laboratory complex, and deep in the vaults beneath it—

Skinner shut away the thought.

"Bring me a drink," he said.

Skinner, the waiter, nodded and went into the house and told Skinner, the butler, to mix the drink.

Nobody drank alcohol any more, and nobody had waiters or butlers, but that's the way Skinner wanted things; he remembered how he'd lived in the old days and he intended to live that way now. Now and forever.

So after Skinner had his drink he had Skinner, the chauffeur, drive him down into the city. He peered out of the minimobile, enjoying the spectacle. Skinner had always been a people watcher, and the activities of these people were of special and particular interest to him now.

Behind the wheels of other minimobiles, the Skinners nodded and smiled at him as he passed. At the intersection, Skinner, the security officer, waved him along. On the walks before the fabrication and food processing plants, other Skinners went about their errands. Skinner, the hydroponics engineer, Skinner, the waste-recycler, Skinner, the oxygenerator control man, Skinner, the transport dispatcher, Skinner, the media channeler. Each had his place and his function in this miniature world, keeping it running smoothly and efficiently, according to plan and program.

"One thing is definite," Skinner had told Dr. Togol. "There'll be no computerization. I don't want my people controlled by a machine. They're not robots—each and every one of them is a human being, and they're going to live like human beings. Full responsibility and full security, that's the secret of a full life. After all, they're just as important to the scheme of things as I am, and I want them to be happy. It may not matter to you, but you've got to remember that they're my family."

"More than your family," Dr. Togol said. "They are you."

And it was true. They were him—or part of him. Each and every one was actually Skinner, the product of a single cell, reproduced and evolved by the perfection of Dr. Togol's process.

The process was called cloning and it was very involved. Even the clone theory itself was involved and Skinner had never completely understood it. But then he didn't need to understand; that was Dr. Togol's task, to understand the theory and devise ways to bring it to reality. Skinner provided the financing, the laboratory, the equipment, the facilities. His means and Dr. Togol's ways. And in the end—when the end came—his body provided the living cell tissue out of which the clones were extracted, isolated, and bred. The clones, cycling through complicated growth into physical duplicates of Skinner himself. Not reproductions, not imitations, not copies, but truly *himself*.

Glancing ahead toward the rear-view mirror of the minimobile, Skinner saw the chauffeur, a mirror image of his own face and body. Gazing out of the window he saw himself again reflected in every form that passed. Each of the Skinners was a tall man, well past middle years, but with the youthful vigor born of a careful and painstaking regimen of advanced vitamin therapy and organ regeneration; the result of expensive medical attention that partially obliterated the ravages of metastasis. And, since the carcinoma was not hereditary, it had not been carried over into the clones. Like himself, all the Skinners were in good health. And, like himself, they carried within them the seeds—the actual cells—of immortality.

Forever.

They would live forever, as he did.

And they were him. Physically interchangeable, except for the clothing they wore—the uniforms designating their various occupations served to differentiate and identify them.

A world of Skinners on Skinner's world.

There had been problems, of course.

Long ago, before Dr. Togol began his work, they'd discussed the matter.

"One true clone," Dr. Togol said. "That's enough to aim for. One healthy facsimile of yourself is all you need."

Skinner shook his head. "Too risky. Suppose there's an accident? That would be the end of me."

"Very well. We'll arrange to keep extra cellular tissue alive, in reserve. Carefully stored and guarded, of course."

"Guarded?"

"But of course," Dr. Togol nodded. "This Eden, this satellite of yours, will need protection. And since you seem to be determined not to run it by computer, you're going to need personnel. Other people to do the work, keep things going, provide you with companionship. Surely you won't want to live forever if you must spend eternity alone."

Skinner frowned. "I don't trust people. Not as guards, not as employees, certainly not as friends."

"No one at all?"

"I trust myself," Skinner said. "So I want more clones. Enough to keep Eden going independently of any outsider."

"The whole satellite populated by nothing but Skinners?"

"Exactly."

"But you don't seem to understand. If the process succeeds and I produce more than one Skinner, they'll share everything. Not just bodies like yours, but minds—each personality will be identical. They'll have the same memories, right up to the moment that the cells are excised from your body."

"I understand that."

"Do you?" Dr. Togol shook his head. "Let's say I follow your instructions. Technically speaking, it's possible—if a single cloning is successful, then the rest would be successful too. All that would be involved is the additional expense of the process."

"Then there's no problem, is there?"

"I told you what the problem is. A thousand Skinners, exactly alike. Looking alike, thinking alike, feeling alike. And you—the present you, reproduced by cloning—would just be one of the many. Have you decided what job you want to perform on your new world once you've become immortal? Do you want to tend the power banks—would you like to unload supplies—do you think you'd enjoy working in the kitchens of the big house forever?"

"Certainly not!" Skinner snapped. "I want to be just what I am now."

"The boss. Top man. Mr. Big." Dr. Togol smiled, then sighed. "That's just the point. So will all the others. Every one of your counterparts will have the same desire, the same goal, the same drive to dominate, to control. Because they'll all have your exact brain and nervous system."

"Up to the time they are reborn, you might say?"

"Right."

"Then from that moment on, you'll institute a new program. A program of conditioning." Skinner nodded quickly. "There are techniques for that, I know. Sleep learning, deep hypnosis machines—the sort of thing psychologists use to alter criminal behavior. You'll plant memory blocks selectively."

"But I'd need an entire psychomedical center, completely staffed—"

"You'll have it. I want the whole procedure carried out right here on earth, before anyone is transported to Eden."

"I'm not sure. You're asking for the creation of a new race, each with a new personality. A Skinner who'll remember his past life but is now content to be merely a hydroponic gardener, a Skinner who'll be satisfied to live forever as an accountant, a Skinner willing to devote his entire endless existence as a repairman."

Skinner shrugged. "A difficult and complicated job, I know. But then you'll be working with a difficult and complicated personality—mine." He cleared his throat painfully before continuing. "Not that I'm unique. We're all far more complicated than we appear to be on the surface, you know that. Each human being is a bundle of conflicting impulses, some expressed, some suppressed. I know that there's a part of me which has always been close to nature, to the soil, to the cultivation and growth of life. I've buried that facet of my personality away since childhood but the memories are there. Find them and you'll have your gardeners, your farmers—yes, and your medical staff assistants too!

"Another part of me is fascinated even consciously today by facts and figures, the *minutiae* of mathematics. Isolate that aspect, condition it to full expression, and you'll get your accountant, and all the help you need to keep Eden running smoothly and systematically.

"I don't need to tell you that a great share of my early career was devoted to scientific research and invention. You won't have any problem developing mechanical-minded Skinners to staff power units, or even to drive transport vehicles.

"The reaches of the mind are infinite, Doctor. Exploit them properly and you'll have a working world—with all the petty authority roles filled by Skinners who have the urge to play policeman or foreman or supervisor—and all the menial tasks performed by Skinners who long to serve. Resurrect those specific traits and tendencies, intensify them, blot out all the memories which might conflict with them, and the rest is easy."

"Easy?" Dr. Togol scowled. "To brainwash them all?"

"All but one." Skinner's voice was crisp. "One will remain untouched, reproduced exactly and entirely as is. And that will be me."

The gray-haired, potbellied little medical scientist stared at Skinner for a long moment.

"You don't admit the possibility of any changes in yourself? The desirabliity of modifying some of your own personality pattern?"

"I don't think I'm perfect, if that's what you mean. But I'm satisfied with myself as I am. And as I will be, once you've carried out the plan."

Dr. Togol continued to stare. "You say you have learned to trust no one. If that's true—and I'm inclined to believe you— then how do you know you can trust me?"

"What do you mean?"

"You're going to die. We both know that. It's only a matter of time. The power to regenerate you through cloning is entirely in my hands. Suppose I don't go through with it?"

Skinner met Dr. Togol's stare. "You'll go through with it before I die. And long before I'm helpless and unable to issue orders, you'll be processing the clones as I've directed. I assure you I have every intention of staying alive until all the clones are ready for transportation to Eden."

"But you *will* die then," Togol insisted. "And there'll be the one clone you've chosen to represent yourself—the one you insist must remain unchanged. What makes you so sure I'll obey that directive after you're actually dead? I could use psychological techniques to modify your clone's personality then in any way I choose. What's to prevent me from making your clone my willing slave—so that I'd be the real master of this new world you created?"

"Curiosity," Skinner murmured. "You'll do exactly as I say because you're fanatically and completely curious about the outcome. No other man alive can provide you with the means and opportunity to carry through this cloning project. If the experiment succeeds you'll have made the greatest scientific breakthrough of all time—so you won't betray your trust by failure or refusal. And once you go that far, you won't be able to resist following through. Particularly when you come to realize that this is only the beginning."

"I don't understand."

"All my life I've moved forward from a position of strength, of self-confidence. And you know what I have achieved. I think I'm presently the wealthiest and most powerful individual in the galaxy.

"I'm a sick man now, but thanks to you I'm going to be well again. Not only well, but immortal. Consider the kind of confidence I'll possess once I'm free of illness, free forever from the fear of death. With my thrust we can go on to far greater concepts, for greater achievements—solve all the mysteries, shatter all the barriers, shake the stars!

"You can't afford to tamper with my mind because you'll want to be a part of it all—to see and to share. Right, doctor?"

Togol's glance faltered. He had no answer, because he knew it was true.

And it had been true.

The cloning was carried out just as Seward Skinner had planned it. And the psychological conditioning project which followed was properly performed too, even though in the end it proved to be far more complicated than anyone had imagined.

The final step involved recruiting a staff of several hundred technicians, highly skilled and specially schooled, then divided into psychomedical teams assigned to the individual clones as they were nurtured to full growth and emerged as functioning adult specimens. Under Dr. Togol's supervision these specialists created the programs for memory blocking, for shaping the personalities of each separate Skinner to fit him for his life role when he reached Eden.

After that the shuttling began.

Space transports, manned exclusively by Skinners trained for the task, brought other Skinners to the stony surface of the secret satellite. Additional Skinner-piloted transports convoyed and conveyed the seemingly endless supply of materials needed to transform the empty expanse of Eden into the world of Seward Skinner's dream.

The miniature city rose on the plain, the house went up on the hillside, the laboratory complex grew over the great vault below. And all of this, every step of the operation, was carried out in such strict, security guarded secrecy that no outsider ever suspected its existence.

As time went on the steps became part of a race—a race with death.

Skinner was dying. Only an act of incredible will kept him alive long enough to supervise the total destruction of the earth-site where the work had taken place.

Then he himself went to Eden with Dr. Togol, but not until he'd made arrangements to send up the entire psychomedical staff, intact, to the new laboratory complex there.

For this a final transport was arranged.

Skinner vividly remembered the evening he lay on his deathbed in the hillside house with Dr. Togol, awaiting the arrival of the transport.

Flickering forth in the darkened room, the media transmitter screened its shocking message. *Pressure failure and implosion beyond Pluto—transport totally destroyed—no survivors.*

"My God!" said Togol.

Then, in the dim light, he saw the smile on the face of the dying man. And heard the harsh, labored whisper.

"Did you really believe I'd ever allow any outsiders to come here—to pry, interfere—learn the secrets—carry the news back into other worlds?"

Togol stared at him. "Sabotaging a transport, murdering all those men! You can't possibly get away with it!"

"*Fait accompli.*" Skinner grimaced. "No one on board knew the true destination—they thought it was Rigel. And what happened will be recorded as an accident."

"Unless I choose to report it."

The dying man's features caricatured a smile. "You won't. Because there is a single detailed account of the whole scheme hidden away in my files. It implicates you as my accomplice, so if you speak you'll be signing your own death warrant."

"You forget that I can sign yours," Dr. Togol said. "Merely by letting nature take its course."

"If you let me die now, everything in my files will come to light. So you have no choice. You're going to go through with it —proceed with the final cloning that will reproduce me as I've ordered."

Togol took a deep breath. "So that's why you were so confident I'd never betray you! You weren't relying on my scientific curiosity—you'd planned this all along, to have a permanent hold on me."

"I told you I was a complex man." Skinner winced with pain. "Now it is time to make me a whole and healthy one. You'll start now—tonight."

It wasn't an order, merely a statement of fact.

And, factually, Dr. Togol had proceeded according to plan.

Seward Skinner was grateful for that, grateful that his new clone born self evolved before his old body had actually died. Because if Togol had waited until then, the clone would have held the memory of Skinner's death. And that is a memory no man can bear.

As it was, the living tissue that was now Skinner had begun its growth process in the laboratory complex safely before the pain racked, rotting tissue of the body in the house ceased to function. Skinner was not aware of just when he had died; he was too busy learning how to live.

Working without a team of technicians was a great handicap, but Dr. Togol had overcome it quickly and efficiently—with the

aid of other Skinners to whom he was able to impart rudimen-
tary medical skills. Since then, of course, he had cloned an
entire staff of Skinners for that purpose—Dr. Skinner, the psychotherapy chief; Dr. Skinner, the head surgeon; Dr. Skinner,
the diagnostic specialist; and a dozen others.

"You see, we didn't need outsiders after all," the new Skinner
told Togol, after it was over. "We're totally self-sustaining here.
And when these bodies start to show signs of deterioration and
function failure, new clones will replace them. Everyone's dream
of true immortality, realized at last."

"Everyone's?" Dr. Togol shook his head. "Not mine."

"Then you're a fool," Skinner said. "You have the opportunity
to clone yourself, live forever, just as I intend to. I've granted
you that privilege. What more could you ask?"

"Freedom."

"But you're free here. You have the resources of the galaxy at
your disposal—you can expand the lab unit indefinitely, go on to
major research in other fields, just as I promised you. That cure
for cancer they've been talking about for the past hundred years
—don't you want to find it? You've implemented some marvel-
ous memory blocking techniques already, but this is only the beginning of a whole new psychotherapy. You can build new personalities, reshape the human condition as you will—"

"As *you* will." Togol's smile was bitter. "This is your world. I
want my own. The old world, with ordinary people, men—and
women—"

"You know very well why I decided against women here,"
Skinner said. "They're not necessary for reproduction. Fortunately, at my age, the sexual impulse is no longer an imperative.
So females would only complicate our existence, without serving
any true function."

"Tenderness, compassion, understanding, companionship,"
Togol murmured. "All nonfunctional by your definition."

"Stereotypy. Utter nonsense. Sentimentalization of a biological
role which you and I have rendered obsolete."

"You've rendered everything obsolete," Togol told him. "Everything except the antlike activity of your clone colony—the
warped and crippled partial personalities created to serve you."

"They're happy the way they are," Skinner said. "And it
doesn't matter. What matters is that *I* haven't changed. I'm a
whole man."

"Are you?" Dr. Togol's smile was mirthless. He nodded toward the house, gestured to include the terrace and the city below. "Everything you've built here, everything you've done, is a product of the most crippling defect of all—the fear of death."

"But all men are afraid to die."

"So afraid that they spend their entire lives just trying to avoid the realization of their own mortality?" Togol shook his head. "You know there's a vault underneath my laboratory. You know why it was built. You know what it contains. And yet your fear is so great that you won't even admit it exists."

"Take me there," Skinner said.

"You don't mean that."

"Come on. I'll show you I'm not frightened."

But he was.

Even before they reached the elevator Skinner started to tremble, and as they began their deep descent to the lower level he was shuddering uncontrollably.

"Cold down here," he muttered.

Dr. Togol nodded. "Temperature control," he said.

They left the elevator and walked along a dark corridor toward the steel sheathed chamber set in stone. Security guard Skinner stood sentinel at the door and smiled a greeting as they approached. At Togol's order, he produced a key and opened the vault door.

Seward Skinner didn't look at him and he didn't want to look beyond the doorway.

But Dr. Togol had already entered and now there was no choice but to follow. Follow him into the dim light of the chill chamber—to the looming control banks that whined and whirred in the center of the room—to the tangled cluster of tubes and inputs which snaked down from all sides into a transparent glass cylinder.

Skinner stared through the shadows at the cylinder. It was shaped like a coffin, because it was a coffin; a coffin in which Seward Skinner saw—

Himself.

His own body; the wasted, shriveled body from which the clones had sprung, floating in the clear solution amid the coils and clamps and weblike wires tunneling through the glass covering to terminate in contact with frozen flesh.

"Not dead," Dr. Togol murmured. "Frozen in solution. The cryogenic process, preserving you in suspended animation— indefinitely—"

Skinner shuddered again and turned away. "Why?" he whispered. "Why didn't you let me die?"

"You wanted immortality."

"But I have it. With this new body, all the others."

"Flesh is vulnerable. Any accident can destroy it."

"You've stored more cell tissue. If anything happened to me as I am now, you could repeat the cloning."

"Only if your original body remains available for the process. It had to be preserved against such an emergency—alive."

Skinner forced himself to glance again at the corpse-like creature congealed in cold behind its crystal confines.

"It's not alive—it can't be—"

And yet he knew it was, knew that the cryogenic process had been developed for just that purpose. To maintain a minimum life force in hibernation against the time when medical science could arrest and eliminate its disease processes and develop techniques to thaw it out and successfully restore complete and conscious existence again.

Skinner realized this goal had never been achieved, but the possibility remained. Some day perhaps the methodology would be perfected and this thing might be resurrected—not as a clone, but as he had been. The original Skinner, alive once more and a rival to his present self.

"Destroy it," he said.

Dr. Togol stared at him. "You don't mean that. You can't—"

"Destroy it!"

Skinner turned and walked out of the vault.

Dr. Togol remained behind, and it was a long time before he returned to rejoin Skinner in his house on the surface. What he'd done there in the vault he did not say, and Skinner never inquired. The subject wasn't discussed again.

But since that night Skinner's relationship with Togol had never been quite the same. There was no more discussion of the future, of possible new projects and experiment. There was only a heightened awareness of tension, of waiting, an indefinable atmosphere of alienation. Dr. Togol spent more and more of his time within the laboratory complex, where he maintained separate living quarters of his own. And Skinner went his own way, alone.

Alone, yet not alone. For this was his world, and it was filled with his own people, created in his own image. *Thou shalt have no God but Skinner. And Skinner is His prophet.*

That was the commandment and the law. And if Dr. Togol chose not to abide by it—

Now Seward Skinner, walking the streets of his own city, came to the door of the museum.

Skinner, the chauffeur, waited outside, smiling in obedience at the order, and Skinner, the museum guard, nodded happily as Seward Skinner entered.

Skinner, the curator, greeted him, delighted at the sight of a visitor. No one ever came to the museum except his master—indeed, the whole notion of a museum was merely a quaint conceit, an archaicism from the distant past on earth.

But Seward Skinner had felt the need for such a place here; a storehouse and a showcase for the art and artifacts he'd accumulated in the past. And while he could have stocked it with the treasures and trophies gathered throughout the galaxy, he'd elected to exhibit only objects from earth. Obsolete objects at that—mementos and memorabilia representing ancient history. Here in the halls were the riches and relics of long ago and far away. Paintings from palaces, sculpture and statues from shrines; the jewels and jade and gorgeous gewgaws which had once represented royal tastes, rescued from regal tombs.

Skinner walked through the displays with scarcely a glance at its glories. Ordinarily he might have spent hours admiring the ancient television set, the library of printed books hermetically sealed in plexiglass, the slot machine, the reconstructed gas engine automobile in perfect running condition.

Today he went straight to remote room and indicated one of the items on display.

"Give me that."

The curator's polite smile masked perplexity, but he obeyed.

Then Skinner turned and retraced his steps. At the door the chauffeur waited to escort him back to the minimobile.

Driving back through the streets, Skinner smiled once more at the passersby and watched them as they went about their ways.

How could Togol call them crippled? They were happy in

their work, their lives were fulfilled. Each had been conditioned to accept his lot without envy, competition or hostility. Thanks to their conditioning and the selective screening of memory patterns they seemed much more content than the Seward Skinner who surveyed them as he returned to his house on the hill.

But he too would be satisfied, and soon.

That evening he summoned Dr. Togol.

Seated on the terrace in the twilight, inhaling the synthetic scent of the simulated flowers, Skinner smiled a greeting at the scientist.

"Sit down," he said. "It's time we had a talk."

Togol nodded and sank into a chair with an audible sigh of effort.

"Tired?"

Togol nodded. "I've been quite busy lately."

"I know." Skinner twirled his brandy snifter. "Assembling data on the project here must be quite exhausting."

"It's important to have a complete record."

"You've put it all on microtape, haven't you? A single spool, small enough to be carried in a man's pocket. How very convenient."

Dr. Togol stiffened and sat upright.

Skinner's smile was serene. "Did you propose to smuggle it out? Or take it back yourself on the next transport shuttle to earth?"

"Who told you—"

Skinner shrugged. "It's obvious enough. Now that you've achieved the goal you want the glory. A triumphant return—your name and fame echoing throughout the galaxy—"

Togol frowned. "It's natural for you to think of it in terms of ego. But that's not the reason. You told me yourself before we started—this can be the most significant achievement in all time. The discovery must be shared, put to use for the benefit of others."

"I paid for the research. I funded the project. It's my property."

"No man has the right to withhold knowledge."

"It's my property," Skinner repeated.

"But I'm not." Dr. Togol rose.

Skinner's smile faded. "Suppose I refuse to let you go?"

"I wouldn't advise it."

"Threats?"

"A statement of fact." Togol met Skinner's stare. "Let me leave in peace. You have my word that your secret is safe. I'll share my findings but preserve your privacy. No one will ever learn the location of Eden."

"I'm not in the habit of making bargains."

"I realize that." Dr. Togol nodded. "So I've already taken certain precautions."

"What sort of precautions?" Skinner chuckled, enjoying the moment. "You forget—this is my world."

"You have no world." Togol faced him, frowning. "All this is merely a mirror maze. The ultimate end of the megalomaniac carried to its logical extreme. In the old days conquerors and kings surrounded themselves with portraits and paintings celebrating their triumphs, commissioned statues and raised pyramids as monuments to their vanity. Servants and slaves sung their praises, sycophants erected shrines to their divinity. You've done all that and more. But it won't last. No man is an island. The tallest temples topple, the most fawning followers go down into dust."

"Do you deny you've given me immortality?"

"I've given you what you want, what every man in search of power *really* wants—the illusion of his own omnipotence. And you're welcome to keep it." Dr. Togol nodded. "But if you try to stop me—"

"I intend to do just that." Seward Skinner's smile returned. "Now."

"Skinner! For God's sake—"

"Yes. For my sake."

Still smiling, Skinner reached into his jacket and brought forth the object he'd taken from the museum.

There was a flicker of flame in the twilight, a single sharp sound shattering the silence, and Dr. Togol fell with a bullet lodged between his eyes.

Skinner summoned Skinner, who scrubbed the tiny trickle of blood from the terrace. Two other Skinners removed the body.

And life went on.

It would always go on, now. Go on forever, free from outside interference. Skinner was safe on Skinner's world. Safe to make further plans.

Dr. Togol was right, of course. He *was* a megalomaniac, the fact must be faced. Skinner admitted that. Easy enough, because he wasn't a madman, merely a realist, and the realist admits the truth, which is that one's ego is all important. A simple fact to a complex man.

And even Togol hadn't realized how complex Skinner was. Complex enough to make further plans. He'd been thinking about it for a long time now.

Being immortal and independent here in a world of his own was only the beginning. Suppose the infinite resources of Seward Skinner's galactic complex were utilized now to the ultimate, inexorable end—the end of every other world?

It would take time, but he had eternity. It would take effort, but immortality never tires. There would be a way and a weapon, and eventually he would find both. Eventually the scheme would be implemented, and then in truth there would be nothing in the galaxy but God. Skinner, and only Skinner, forever and ever, amen.

Skinner sat on the terrace and stared out as darkness fell over the land. A vague plan was already taking shape in his mind—the keen, immortally conscious, eternally aware mind.

There was a way, a simple way. Skinner scientists would be pressed into service to carry out the details, and with his resources it was neither fantastic nor impossible. It could be in fact quite simple. Develop a mutant microorganism, an airborne virus impervious to immunization, then transmit it by shuttle to key points throughout the galaxy. Human life, animal life, vegetable life would perish forever in its wake. Forever and ever, amen.

To be the richest man in the world was nothing. To be the wisest, the strongest, the most powerful—this too was not enough. But to be the *only* man—forever—

Seward Skinner started to laugh.

And then, quite suddenly, his laughter shrilled into a scream.

All over his world, Skinner screamed. The sound echoed through the curator's quarters in the museum, rose from the streets where the security guards stood sentinel, burst from the chauffeur's sleeping lips, shrieked in chorus from each and every Skinner who found himself *down there*.

The Skinner on the terrace was down there, too. Down there where—a remnant of sanity recalled—Dr. Togol must have taken his precautions and his revenge. It was a simple thing he'd done, really.

He'd gone *down there,* to the vault where the original Seward Skinner floated in the icy solution which preserved him in hibernation. And all he'd done was to shut off the temperature controls.

Dr. Togol had lied about destroying the thing in the vault. He'd kept it alive, and now that it was thawing its consciousness returned—the original consciousness of the real Seward Skinner, waking in the black, bubbling vat to wheeze and gasp and choke its life away.

And because it was aware now, the clones were linked to that life and that awareness, sharing the shock and sensation as the artificial blocks vanished, so that all again were one.

In a moment the thing down there in the vault was dead. But not before all the Skinners felt its final agony—which would never be final for them. As clones, they were immortal.

Seward Skinner's scream blended with those of every other Skinner on Skinner's world. And they would continue.

Forever.

*   *

After I wrote "Ego Trip," the question of identity continued to plague me. And so did the various techniques and technologies which were currently being developed to preserve or prolong individual existence.

Some of these, like the process of cloning, were still in the realm of theory. But about this time a new concept, cryogenics, was very much in the news.

In fact, a medical team had just subjected a terminal-cancer victim to this process, and I happened to be one of the few laymen to hear a firsthand account of it.

For a number of years I'd been a member of a group of writers and friends who gathered for a monthly meeting to hear talks by people prominent in the arts and sciences. The "Pinckard Salon," as it was called, had been founded and hosted by Tom and Terri Pinckard for this purpose. After they moved out of the city, other members took over the arrangements and the gatherings continued. Just how and why we continued to luck out with such interesting speakers I'm not prepared to say. I can only tell you that within thirty-six hours following the first recorded cryogenic experiment on a human subject, the individuals who inaugurated it were addressing us in a private home, and explaining theory and practice in fascinating detail.

Naturally, I was interested. And when Roger Elwood called to ask for a story with a "religious theme" I at once determined to address myself to the question of eternal life and its implementation by future cloning and cryogenic methodology.

Hence "Forever and Amen," which appeared in Elwood's 1972 anthology for Chilton, *And Walk Gently Through the Fire*.

The hero, or anti-hero, is certainly not a saintly figure. But his eventual fate—eternal damnation in every sense of the word—is meted out to him on the basis of biblical precedent for his presumption.

So in this instance, upon evaluating the story, I can safely say, "Go with God."

See How They Run

April 2nd

Okay, Doc, you win.

I'll keep my promise and make regular entries, but damned if I'll start out with a heading like *Dear Diary*. Or *Dear Doctor*, either. You want me to tell it like it is? Okay, but the way it is right now, Doc, beware. If you've got any ideas about wading in my stream of consciousness, just watch out for the alligators.

I know what you're thinking. "Here's a professional writer who claims he has a writer's block. Get him to keep a diary and he'll be writing in spite of himself. Then he'll see how wrong he is." Right, Doc? Write, Doc?

Only that's not my real problem. My hangup is the exact opposite—antithetical, if you're looking for something fancy. Logorrhea. Verbosity. Two-bit words from a dime-a-dozen writer? But that's what they always say at the studio: writers are a dime a dozen.

Okay, so here's your dime. Run out and buy me a dozen writers. Let's see—I'll have two Hemingways, one Thomas Wolfe, a James Joyce, a couple of Homers if they're fresh, and six William Shakespeares.

I almost said it to Gerber when he dropped me from the show. But what's the use? Those producers have only one idea. They point at the parking lot and say, "I'm driving the Caddy and you're driving the Volks." Sure. If you're so smart, why aren't you rich?

Call it a rationalization if you like. You shrinks are great at pinning labels on everything. Pin the tail on the donkey, that's the name of the game, and the patient is always the jackass. Pardon me, it's not "patient," it's "analysand." For fifty bucks an hour you can afford to dream up a fancy word. And for fifty bucks an hour I can't afford not to word up some fancy dreams.

If that's what you want from me, forget it. There are no dreams. Not any more. Once upon a time (as we writers say) there was a dream. A dream about coming out to Hollywood and cracking the television market. Write for comedy shows, make big money in your spare time this new easy way, buy a fancy pad with a big swimming pool, and live it up until you settle down with a cute little chick.

Dreams are nothing to worry about. It's only when they come true that you've got trouble. Then you find out that the comedy isn't funny any more, the big money disappears, and the swimming pool turns into a stream of consciousness. Even a cute little chick like Jean changes to something else. It's not a dream any more, it's a nightmare, and it's real.

There's a problem for you, Doc. Cure me of reality.

April 5th

A little-known historical fact. Shortly after being wounded in Peru, Pizarro, always a master of understatement, wrote that he was Incapacitated.

Damn it, Doc, I say it's funny! I don't buy your theory about puns being a form of oral aggression. Because I'm not the aggressive type.

Hostile, yes. Why shouldn't I be? Fired off the show after three seasons of sweating blood for Gerber and that lousy no-talent comic of his. Lou Lane couldn't get a job as M.C. in a laundromat until I started writing his material and now he's Mr. Neilsen himself, to hear him tell it.

But that's not going to trigger me into doing anything foolish. I don't have to. One season without me and he'll be back where he belongs—a parking attendant in a Drive-In Mortuary. Curb Service. We Pick Up and Deliver. Ha, ha.

Gerber gave me the same pitch; my stuff is getting sour. We don't want black comedy. It's nasty, and this is a family-type show. Okay, so maybe it was my way of releasing tension, getting it out of my system—catharsis, isn't that the term? And it made me come on a little too strong. Which is where you get into the act. Blow my mind for me, put me back on the track, and I'll get myself another assignment and make with the family-type funnies again.

Meanwhile, no problems. Jean is bringing in the bread. I never figured it that way when we got married. At first I thought her singing was a gag and I went along with it. Let the voice coach keep her busy while I was working on the show—give her something to do for a hobby. Even when she took the first few club dates it was still Amateur Night as far as I was concerned. But then they hit her with the recording contract, and after the singles came the album, etc. My little chick turned into a canary.

Funny about Jean. Such a nothing when I met her. Very good in the looks department but aside from that, nothing. It's the singing that made the difference. Finding her voice was like finding herself. All of a sudden, confidence.

Of course I'm proud of her but it still shakes me up a little. The way she takes over, like insisting I see a psychiatrist. Not that I'm hacked about it, I know she's only doing it for my own good, but it's hard to get used to. Like last night at the Guild screening, her agent introduced us to some friends of his—"I want you to meet Jean Norman and her husband."

Second billing. That's not for me, Doc. I'm a big boy now. The last thing I need is an identity crisis, right? And as long as we're playing true confessions, I might as well admit Jean has one point—I've been hitting the bottle a little too hard lately, since I got canned.

I didn't mention it at our last session, but this is the main reason she made me come to you. She says alcohol is my security blanket. Maybe taking it away would fix things. Or would it?

One man's security blanket is another man's shroud.

April 7th

You stupid jerk. What do you mean, alcoholism is only a symptom?

First of all, I'm not an alcoholic. Sure I drink, maybe drink a lot, everybody drinks in this business. It's either that or pot or hard drugs and I'm not going to freak out and mess up my life. But you've got to have something to keep your head together and just because I belt a few doesn't mean I'm an alcoholic.

But for the sake of argument, suppose it does? You call it a symptom. A symptom of *what?*

Suppose you tell me that little thing. Sitting back in that overstuffed chair with your hands folded on your overstuffed gut and letting me do all the talking—let's hear you spill something for a change. What is it you suspect, Mr. Judge, Mr. Jury, Mr. Prosecuting Attorney, Mr. Executioner? What's the charge—heterosexuality in the first degree?

I'm not asking for sympathy. I get plenty of that from Jean. Too much. I'm up to here on the oh-you-poor-baby routine. I don't want tolerance or understanding or any of that phony jive. Just give me a few facts for a change. I'm tired of Jean playing Mommy and I'm tired of you playing Big Daddy. What I want is some real help, you've got to help me help me please please help me.

April 9th

Two resolutions.

Number one, I'm not going to drink any more. I'm quitting as of now, flat-out. I was stoned when I wrote that last entry and all I had to do was read it today when I'm sober to see what I've been doing to myself. So no more drinking. Not now or ever.

Number two. From now on I'm not showing this to Dr. Moss. I'll cooperate with him completely during therapy sessions but that's it. There's such a thing as invasion of privacy. And after what happened today I'm not going to lay myself wide open again. Particularly without an anesthetic, and I've just given that up.

If I keep on writing everything down it will be for my own information, a matter of personal record. Of course I won't tell him that. He'd come up with some fancy psychiatric zinger, meaning I'm talking to myself. I've got it figured out—the shrinks are all authority figures and they use their labels as putdowns. Who needs it?

All I need is to keep track of what's happening, when things start to get confused. Like they did at the session today.

First of all, this hypnotherapy bit.

As long as this is just between me and myself I'll admit the whole idea of being hypnotized always scared me. And if I had any suspicion the old creep was trying to put me under I'd have cut out of there in two seconds flat.

But he caught me off guard. I was on the couch and supposed to say whatever came into my head. Only I drew a blank, couldn't think of anything. Emotional exhaustion, he said, and turned down the lights. Why not close my eyes and relax? Not go to sleep, just daydream a little. Daydreams are sometimes more important than those that come in sleep. In fact he didn't want me to fall asleep, so if I'd concentrate on his voice and let everything hang loose—

He got to me. I didn't feel I was losing control, no panic, I knew where I was and everything, but he got to me. He must have, because he kept talking about memory. How memory is our own personal form of time travel, a vehicle to carry us back, way back to earliest childhood, didn't I agree? And I said yes, it can carry us back, carry me back, back to old Virginny.

Then I started to hum something I hadn't thought about in years. And he said what's that, it sounds like a nursery rhyme, and I said that's right, Doc, don't you know it, *Three Blind Mice.*

Why don't you sing the words for me, he said. So I started.

Three blind mice, three blind mice,

See how they run, see how they run!

They all ran after the farmer's wife,

Did you ever see such a sight in your life

As three blind mice, three blind mice?

"Very nice," he said. "But didn't you leave out a line?"

"What line?" I said. All at once, for no reason at all, I could feel myself getting very uptight. "That's the song. My old lady sang that to me when I was a baby. I wouldn't forget a thing like that. What line?"

He started to sing it to me.

They all ran after the farmer's wife,

She cut off their heads with a carving knife,

Then it happened.

It wasn't like remembering. It was happening. Right now, all over again.

Late at night. Cold. Wind blowing. I wake up. I want a drink of water. Everyone asleep. Dark. I go into the kitchen.

Then I hear the noise. Like a tapping on the floor. It scares me. I turn on the light and I see it. In the corner behind the door. The trap. Something moving in it. All gray and furry and flopping up and down.

The mouse. Its paw is caught in the trap and it can't get loose. Maybe I can help. I pick up the trap and push the spring back. I hold the mouse. It wiggles and squeaks and that scares me more. I don't want to hurt it, just put it outside so it can run away. But it wiggles and squeaks and then it bites me.

When I see the blood on my finger I'm not scared any more. I get mad. All I want to do is help and it bites me. Dirty little thing. Squeaking at me with its eyes shut. Blind. Three Blind Mice. Farmer's wife.

There. On the sink. The carving knife.

It tries to bite me again. I'll fix it. I take the knife. And I cut, I drop the knife, and I start to scream.

I was screaming again, thirty years later, and I opened my eyes and there I was in Dr. Moss's office, bawling like a kid.

"How old were you?" Dr. Moss said.

"Seven."

It just popped out. I hadn't remembered how old I was, hadn't remembered what happened—it was all blacked out of my mind, just like the line in the nursery rhyme.

But I remember now. I remember everything. My old lady finding the mouse head in the trash can and then beating the hell out of me. I think that's what made me sick, not the bite, even though the doctor who came and gave me the shot said it was infection that caused the fever. I was laid up in bed for two weeks. When I'd wake up screaming from the nightmares, my old lady used to come in and hold me and tell me how sorry she was. She always told me how sorry she was—after she did something to me.

I guess that's when I really started to hate her. No wonder I built so many of Lou Lane's routines on mother and mother-in-law gags. Oral aggression? Could be. All these years and I never knew it, never realized how I hated her. I still hate her now, hate her—

What I need is a drink.

April 23rd

Two weeks since I wrote the last entry. I told Dr. Moss I quit keeping a diary and he believed me. I told Dr. Moss a lot of things besides that, and whether he believed me or not I don't know. Not that I care one way or the other. I don't believe everything he tells *me*, either.

Hebephrenic schizophrenia. Now there's a real grabber.

Meaning certain personality types, confronted with a stress situation they can't handle, revert to childhood or infantile behavior levels.

I looked it up the other day after I got a peek at Moss's notes, but if that's what he thinks, then he's the one who's flipped.

Dr. Moss has a thing about words like flipped, nuts, crazy. Mental disturbance, that's his speed.

That and regression. He's hung up on regression. No more hypnosis—I told him that was out, absolutely—and he got the message. But he uses other techniques like free association, and they seem to work. What really happens is that I talk myself into remembering, talk my way back into the past.

I've come up with some weirdies. Like not drinking a glass of milk until I was five years old—my old lady let me drink that formula stuff out of the bottle and there was a big hassle over it when I went to kindergarten and wouldn't touch my milk any other way. Then she clouted me one and said I made her ashamed when she had to explain to the teacher, and she took the bottle away. But it was her fault in the first place. I'm beginning to understand why I hated her.

My old man wasn't any prize, either. Whenever we had company over for dinner he'd come out with things I'd said to him, all the dumb kid stuff you say when you don't know any better, and everybody would laugh. Hard to realize kids get embarrassed, too, until you remember the way it was. The old man kept needling me to make stupid cracks just so he could take bows for repeating them to his buddies. No wonder you forget things like that—it hurts too much to remember.

It still hurts.

Of course there were good memories, too. When you're a kid, most of the time you don't give a damn about anything, you don't worry about the future, you don't even understand the real meaning of things like pain and death—and that's worth remembering.

I always seem to start out that way in our sessions but then Moss steers me into the other stuff. Catharsis, he says, it's good for you. Let it all hang out. Okay, I'm cooperating, but when we finish up with one of those children's hours I'm ready to go home and have a nice, big drink.

Jean is starting to bug me about it again. We had another hassle last night when she came home from the club date. Singing, that's all she's really interested in nowadays, never has any time for me.

Okay, so that's her business, why doesn't she mind it and let me alone? So I was stoned, so what? I tried to tell her about the therapy, how I was hurting and how a drink helped. "Why don't you grow up?" she said. "A little pain never hurt anyone."

Sometimes I think they're all crazy.

April 25th

They're crazy, all right.

Jean calling Dr. Moss and telling him I was back on the bottle again.

"On the bottle," I said, when he told me about it. "What kind of talk is that? You'd think she was my mother and I was her baby."

"Isn't that what you think?" Moss said.

I just looked at him. I didn't know what to say. This was one time when he did all the talking.

He started out very quietly, about how he'd hoped therapy would help us make certain discoveries together. And over a period of time I'd begin to understand the meaning of the pattern I'd established in my life. Only it hadn't seemed to work out that way, and while as a general thing he didn't care to run the risk of inducing psychic trauma, in this case it seemed indicated that he clarify the situation for me.

That part I can remember, almost word for word, because it made sense. But what he told me after that is all mixed up.

Like saying I have an oral fixation on the bottle because it represents the formula bottle my mother took away from me when I was a kid. And the reason I got into comedy writing was to reproduce the situation where my father used to tell people all my funny remarks—because even if they laughed it meant I was getting attention, and I wanted attention. But at the same time I resented my father taking the credit for amusing them, just like I resented Lou Lane making it big because of what I wrote for him. That's why I blew the job, writing material he couldn't use. I wanted him to use it and bomb out, because I hated him. Lou Lane had become a father image and I hated my father.

I remember looking at Dr. Moss and thinking he has to be crazy. Only a crazy shrink could come up with things like that.

He was really wild. Talking about my old lady. How I hated her so much when I was a kid I had to displace my feelings—transfer them to something else so I wouldn't feel so guilty about it.

Like the time I got up for a drink of water. I really wanted my bottle back, but my mother wouldn't give it to me. And maybe the bottle was a symbol of something she gave my father. Hearing them was what really woke me up and I hated her for that most of all.

Then I went into the kitchen and saw the mouse. The mouse reminded me of the nursery rhyme and the nursery rhyme reminded me of my mother. I took the knife, but I didn't want to kill the mouse. In my mind I was really killing my mother—

That's when I hit him. Right in his dirty mouth.

Nobody talks about my mother that way.

Apr 29

Better this way. Don't need Moss. Don't need therapy. Do it myself.

Been doing it. Regression. Take a little drink, take a little trip. Little trip down memory lane.

Not to the bad things. Good things. All the warm soft memories. The time I was in bed with the fever and mother came in with the ice cream on the tray. And my father bringing me that toy.

That's what's nice about remembering. Best thing in the world. There was a poem we used to read in school. I still remember it. "Backward, turn backward, O time in your flight, make me a child again just for tonight!" Well, no problem. A few drinks and away you go. Little oil for the old time machine.

When Jean found out about Dr. Moss she blew her stack. I had to call him up right away and apologize, she screamed.

"To hell with that," I said. "I don't need him any more. I can work this thing out for myself."

"Maybe you'll have to," Jean said.

Then she told me about Vegas. Lounge date, three weeks on the Strip. All excited because this means she's really made it—the big time. Lou Lane is playing the big room and he called her agent and told her it was all set.

"Wait a minute," I said. "Lou Lane set this up for you?"

"He's been a good friend," Jean told me. "All through this he's kept in touch, because he's worried about you. He'd be your friend, too, if you'd only let him."

Sure he would. With friends like that you don't need enemies. My eyes were opening fast. No wonder he squawked to Gerber and got me off the show. So he could move in on Jean. He had it set up, all right. The two of them, playing Vegas together. Jean in the lounge, him in the big room, and then, after the show—

For a moment there I was so shook up I couldn't see straight and I don't know what I would have done if I could. But I mean I really couldn't see straight because I started to cry. And then she was holding me and it was all right again. She'd cancel the Vegas date and stay here with me, we'd work this out to-gether. But I had to promise her one thing—no more drinking.

I promised. The way she got to me I would have promised her anything.

So I watched her clean out the bar and then she went into town to see her agent.

It's a lie, of course. She could have picked up the phone and called him from here. So she's doing something else.

Like going straight to Lou Lane and spilling everything to him. I can just hear her. "Don't worry, darling, I had to beg off this time or he'd get too suspicious. But what's three weeks in

Vegas when we've got a whole lifetime ahead of us?" And then the two of them get together—

No. I'm not going to think about it. I don't have to think about it, there are other things, better things.

That's why I took the bottle. The one she didn't know about when she cleaned out the bar, the one I had stashed away in the basement.

I'm not going to worry any more. She can't tell me what to do. Take a little drink, take a little trip. That's all there is to it.

I'm home free.

Later

She broke the bottle.

She came in and saw me and grabbed the bottle away from me and she broke it. I know she's mad because she ran into the kitchen and slammed the door. Why the kitchen?

Extension phone there.

Wonder if she'll try to call Dr. Moss.

April 30

I was a bad boy.

The Dr. come. he sed what did you do.

I sed she took the bottel away.

He saw it on the floor the knive

I had to do it I sed.

He saw blood.

Like the mouse he sed.

No not a mouse. A canarry.

dont look in the trash can I sed

But he did.

*   *

Is psychotherapy an art or a science?

Frankly, I wouldn't know.

Over the years I've dealt with mental disturbance in many stories. In the language of the profession, it seems to have been an obsession with me—this compulsive examination of cause and

cure. My novels *The Scarf* and *Psycho* have been reviewed or
discussed in psychiatric journals. I've received letters from psychiatrists and from patients.

But even though I wrote a screenplay and a novel called *The
Couch,* I have never stretched myself out upon one in the presence of a shrink. I didn't attend college and have taken no
courses in psychology. My limited knowledge of the field is all
either secondhand or self-invented.

What I *do* know is that everyone has problems. And with some
of those problems—such as those of writers—I'm quite familiar.

This doesn't mean that I've personally confronted the conflicts
which beset the protagonist of "See How They Run"—any more
than I could be accused of donning a wig, grabbing a knife, and
heading for the nearest shower stall.

Oddly enough, many of my readers over the years remain un-
convinced that I'm not writing autobiography. After publication
of *The Scarf* I got letters inquiring as to whether I'd ever been in
love with my high school English teacher. I was forced to reply
that my teachers in that field were many, and while I appreciated their ability to draw complicated blackboard diagrams
showing the structure of a sentence, I never stayed after class for
an anatomy lesson or an experiment in biology.

In short, my psychiatry-oriented stories have not been based
upon firsthand experience. While we're on this subject, let me assure you that I've written a number of tales about Jack the
Ripper without ever slicing into anything but a hunk of bologna,
and my dissertations on vampires were achieved without the aid
of blood transfusions.

So it is that I totally disclaim any personal experience which
might have led me to writing "See How They Run," which appeared in *Ellery Queen's Mystery Magazine* for April 1973.

But I have observed the travail and trauma besetting other
Hollywood writers, and from this scrutiny stems the character
and the story line.

As for the life style of my narrator, I must refer you to
Mephistopheles' lines in *Doctor Faustus:*

> *Hell has no limits, nor is circumscribed*
> *In one self-place: for where we are is Hell,*
> *And where Hell is, there must we ever be.*

Only the Devil could come up with a downer like this, and since I put my protagonist in a hell on earth, this story is the spawn of Satan.

Space-Born

I

The probe-mission ship locked into orbit and began its sensor-scan of the planet Echo.

Seated at his post on the bridge, Mission-Commander Richard Tasman, USN, checked out the data processed by the technical teams of his crew. Beside him Lieutenant Gilbey, his second in command, nodded approvingly.

"Looks good," he said. "Looks very good."

And it did.

According to the computerized data fed back through the tapes, Echo was indeed an earth-type planet, just as had been suspected. Photoscopes confirmed the presence of running water, surface soil, and abundant vegetation. The bacterial-life analysis indicated nothing harmful or unfamiliar. Echo's planetary profile was that of a miniature world—alive and unpolluted, unspoiled by the presence of man.

Then the tapes began running wild.

Tasman stared at Gilbey. Gilbey stared at Tasman. And both men turned to stare at the photoscope.

The confirming data coming in told the story, but one picture is always worth ten thousand words, even though for a moment this particular picture left them both speechless.

Clearly and unmistakably it showed the boulder-strewn hillside and what rested on the sloping surface, landing gear crumpled against the looming rocks. The 'scope moved in for a close shot, panning across the hull, picking up the unmistakable insignia and legible lettering. USS *Orion*.

There on the face of a minor planet near the edge of the galaxy, unexplored and unvisited by man, was a spacecraft from earth.

II

Tasman took over the landing party himself, leaving Gilbey behind to take over command.

There were four members in the task force, not counting Tasman, but in spite of the heavy power drain required to bring them down, the auxiliary launch settled safely on target. When Tasman and his crew emerged from the hatch, they were less than a thousand yards away from the hulk of the USS *Orion* on the hillside.

Even before they forced their way inside all doubts had vanished. Weber, the CPO of the party, spoke for them all. "This is it, sir. Kevin's ship."

Tasman shook his head grimly. "Our ship," he said. "Kevin stole it."

There was no answer to that, not from Weber or any of the others, because all of them knew Tasman spoke the truth.

Senior Commander Kevin Nichols, USN—veteran astronaut, hero of the space program, next in line for appointment to head up the entire space project itself—had stolen the ship.

A year ago, almost to the day by earth calendar, he and the *Orion* had vanished. No advance warning, no clearance, nothing. And no telltale traces left behind; even his wife had disappeared. It took almost six months of intensive investigation to unravel the tangle of red tape surrounding the flight, and even now there were a thousand loose ends. All the evidence added up to the fact that Kevin Nichols had moved swiftly and secretly, according to a well-prepared plan. Forged orders for a security-sealed mission had been used to get the *Orion* equipped and on the launching pad without a leak. One of the very latest miniaturized spacecraft, it required only the services of a pilot, with all flight functions self-powered, self-contained, and computer-directed. A top-secret test model, designed for future exploration projects, and put through its trial runs by Kevin Nichols himself. So when he ordered it supplied and readied for take-off, no one had questioned him or broken security regulations to reveal its departure.

Not until the *Orion* soared into space did the scandal rise in its wake—and even that was secret, hushed up by the space program itself before the news could break to the public. Then came the investigation, and the eventual discovery of Kevin's probable destination—not Echo itself, but Sector XXIII, this area of the space chart.

It was then that Commander Tasman had been assigned to go after the missing ship and the missing man. Tasman knew Kevin Nichols—they'd been classmates at Cape, years ago—and perhaps that's why he was chosen for the mission. But knowing Kevin hadn't made the job of locating him any easier. They'd touched down at a dozen points before the process of elimination zeroed them in on Echo. It was only now, months after the start of the expedition, that they'd caught up with the fugitive.

Or had they?

Kevin wasn't on the ship.

Neither were its supplies and portable instruments.

"Now what?" Tasman muttered.

It was Weber, the CPO, who suggested scouting the surrounding terrain, and it was he who discovered the cave set in the rocks.

Tasman was the first to enter, and what he found there in the dark depths brought the others to his side on the run.

Living in a cave isn't an ideal existence at best, and when one's supplies are exhausted and the battery-powered light sources fail, there's nothing left but shadows—shadows looming up everywhere from the twisted tunnels which wind on down endlessly beyond the outer chamber. And when one cries out, the shadows do not answer—there's only the sound of echoes screaming through the darkness. Echo—the planet was well named.

Had Kevin Nichols thought of that while he screamed, or when he grew too weak for screaming? Had he stared at the shapeless shadows which seemed to seethe and stir in the tunnel mouths beyond?

It didn't matter now. The tunnel mouths were open, but Kevin's mouth was closed; closed and set in the grim grin of death. One look at the gaunt face and emaciated body brought one word to CPO Weber's lips.

"Starvation."

Commander Tasman nodded without comment, then stooped to examine the other body.

For there was another body lying there, some little distance away—lying face downward, arms outstretched as though attempting to crawl toward the tunnels when death halted her.

Her.

Tasman turned the body over, staring in recognition at the wasted form.

"Kevin's wife," he murmured. "He took her with him."

Kevin took her with him, and death took them both. Here, in a remote cave on a distant planet, surrounded by shadows, the fugitives had died in darkness, and now only echoes lingered, wailing in the depths. If you listened closely, you could almost hear them now, faint and faraway.

And then they *did* hear the sound, all of them, and recognized it for what it was—issuing from the shadows beyond, impossibly but unmistakably.

A baby cried.

III

There were problems, many problems.

The first was physical—how to transport a newborn infant back to earth on a probe-mission ship lacking the facilities and even the feeding formula necessary to sustain its fragile hold on life.

Surprisingly enough, the little one survived, even flourished on the hastily improvised diet of powdered milk and juices. The boy seemed to have inherited some of Kevin Nichols' toughness and tenacity as well as his features. Indeed, the resemblance was so close that there was never any question about a name; with one accord, they called him Kevin.

It wasn't until after splashdown on earth that the other problems arose. Then Space Control took charge of Kevin and inherited the dilemma he brought with him.

There was no publicity, of course, but that in itself solved nothing. Sooner or later the news would inevitably leak out. An honored and acclaimed astronaut had succeeded in violating top security, foiled all interplanetary precautions, stolen the latest and most advanced spacecraft.

Waves of panic rose and spread behind the locked doors of Space Command. Top brass and top government officials floundered, engulfed in those waves, spluttering in confusion, choking in consternation.

"Do you know what this means? When the story gets out, the whole program will be discredited. Stealing a prototype ship right out from under our noses—we're going to be the laughing-stock of the world, the whole goddam galaxy!"

It was a senior spokesman for the space project who said that, and a senior spokesman for the government who answered him.

"Then why not tell the truth? Tell them that we had our eye on Kevin Nichols all along, knew he was cracking up? Sure, he was next in line for the big promotion, but he wasn't going to make it. Not after what our investigation uncovered—the drug thing, the embezzlement of project funds. He must have realized we were going to blow the whistle on him and that's why he got out, taking his wife with him. Let the public know what happened, that we were the victims of a conspiracy—"

"You're crazy." Psychiatrists usually disapprove of using such language, but it was a senior member of the psychiatric advisory staff who spoke. "We can't afford to be laughed at, and we can't afford to be pitied, either. Right now we can't afford anything, period. I don't need to remind you gentlemen that the vote on new appropriations for the entire space project is coming up next week. There couldn't possibly be a worse time to tell the world that the largest and most important program in all history has been victimized by one man—and that the biggest hero of that program was a psychotic, a thief, and a traitor. There's got to be another answer."

There was.

Exactly who gave it is not known—probably some minor member of the staff. It is the fate of junior officers to come up with the right suggestion and their reward is to be forgotten even while the suggestion is remembered.

"Kevin is our answer," said the nameless junior officer.

Everyone looked at him, everyone listened, and everyone understood.

"Don't you realize what Nichols has done for the program? He's given us the biggest public relations hook anyone could wish for. His son, Kevin. The first child ever born in outer space! Not on Mars or Venus or a colony, but on a new frontier, the furthermost outpost of all interplanetary exploration known to man!

"You don't have to say that his father was flipping out, that the ship was stolen. Make the whole thing part of a top-security mission, a secret program to test human survival on an earth-type world. Nichols and his wife volunteered to take the ship off to Echo and have their child there. A heroic experiment that turned into a heroic sacrifice when they emerged from the crash unharmed but unable to return or communicate with the project back on earth. Let it be known that Nichols kept a complete record of his stay on Echo, up to and including the actual birth of the infant, but that the data is still classified information. That'll put an end to any further embarrassing questions about the affair. But there won't be any trouble about the appropriation— not if you concentrate publicity where it belongs and keep it there. You're sitting on the greatest story of all time, the greatest celebrity ever known—Kevin, the Space-Child!"

IV

They didn't sit much longer.

Within a matter of hours the well-oiled machinery of Information Unit started to function, the space program's wheels began to turn, and the end-product of the manufacturing process appeared. Instant heroes.

Kevin Nichols, heroic astronaut who piloted an untested ship to an uncharted world. His wife, who risked her unborn baby in the unknown. The space program itself, bravely breaking through all barriers to prove, once and for all, that humanity could move forward without fear and perpetuate itself on other planets.

Nichols and his wife were dead, but the space program survived—just as predicted, the appropriation passed.

And as for Kevin himself, he lived and thrived.

Kevin, the new symbol of the Age of Space.

Publicized, photographed, promoted, praised; in a matter of days, his name was known throughout the solar system and beyond. Child of Space, heir to the future.

And ward of the space program.

Jealously guarded, possessively protected, little Kevin was withdrawn from public scrutiny shortly after he had served his primary purpose and placed in a private—very private—nursery.

While Kevin dolls and Kevin toys flooded the market, Kevin songs and Kevin pictures kept his image bright, the object of all this adulation was being carefully nursed and tended to by a team of medical specialists. Pediatricians and psychologists alike agreed; Kevin was a very special baby. And not just because of his value as a living symbol, but for what he was—exceptionally sturdy, bright, alert, healthy, and precocious.

In spite of security, rumors poured out of the nursery-laboratory where young Kevin was hidden.

Standing alone at five months. Walking at seven. Only nine months old and seems to understand everything you say to him. One year old and he's talking already—complete sentences! Did you hear the latest about Kevin? Two and a half, going on three, and they say he already is learning how to read! Can you imagine that?

The public could imagine it very easily. As a matter of fact they were beginning to imagine a little too much. No matter how much we praise him, nobody really loves a genius. Too hard to understand. And the whole point of the plan was plain; Kevin had to be loved.

So, after much consideration, Kevin was placed in an exclusive private school—first-phase classes, what used to be called a kindergarten. Good thinking, give him a chance to grow up with other youngsters, learn to be like the rest of the kids.

But Kevin wasn't like the rest of the kids. He grew faster, learned more quickly. He seemed immune to childhood diseases and he was never ill. Perhaps this was a result of the antiseptic care of the medical team, but even so it was highly unusual. The doctors took notes.

The psychologists took notes too. Kevin didn't relate to his peer group—that's the way they phrased it. In plain words, he didn't want to have anything to do with the other children. And what he didn't want to do he didn't bother with. He read. He asked questions—intelligent, penetrating questions—and he was impatient with stupid answers.

Kevin had no interest in nursery rhymes or fairy tales or bedtime stories. Facts and figures, these were the things that fascinated him. He never played with toys and he refused to learn any games.

The other youngsters didn't understand him and what children can't understand they dislike—a trait often carried over into adult life.

Two of the kids never got to carry that or any other trait into maturity. They took to teasing Kevin, calling him names, but only for a few days. Then they died.

One of them fell out of an upstairs window while walking in his sleep. The other went into convulsions—epileptic seizure, the doctors decided.

Of course Kevin had nothing to do with it; he was nowhere near either of the youngsters at the time. But there was bound to be talk and the medical team took him out of the school.

Just to put an end to any possible rumors, a thorough checkup was programmed for the prodigy. And prodigy he was—a handsome, healthy child, without functional defect. The results of the battery of mental tests indicated genius.

What he needed, the medical team decided, was a chance to lead a normal existence—an opportunity to relate to ordinary people in ordinary surroundings. As a celebrity such a life was, of course, impossible.

So they changed his name, took him clear across the country, and put him out for adoption.

The world at large was told he had been sent abroad for further education under governmental supervision. Even the couple who took him into their home didn't realize that their bright, good-looking new son was the famous Space Child.

To Mr. and Mrs. Rutherford he was an orphan named Robin. A quiet boy but well-behaved, quick in his studies, sailing through high school and into college at fifteen. There were no problems.

At least the security reports didn't indicate any. The space program had him under observation, of course, monitoring his progress in school.

Perhaps they should have spent more time monitoring his foster parents. As it was, they didn't seem to notice the change in Mr. and Mrs. Rutherford. And maybe the Rutherfords weren't even aware of it themselves. It wasn't anything dramatic.

But as Kevin grew, they dwindled.

Kevin's growth was physically apparent. At eighteen, already a senior in college, he seemed completely mature. Enough of an adult, in fact, to enter into the management of Mr. Rutherford's prosperous ranch during the summer months.

And Rutherford, the bluff, hearty rancher with the booming voice, made no objection. It was as though he secretly welcomed the idea of taking things easy, of not having to bawl out orders, of sitting quietly on the big screen porch and rocking away. After a time people began to notice how he mumbled and muttered, talking to himself. Mrs. Rutherford didn't say anything—she'd gradually stopped entertaining or going out, and never saw any of their old friends. While the boy ran the ranch, she was content just to keep house and spend her spare time resting upstairs. She was beginning to talk to herself too.

It was just about a year later—after the boy had graduated and gone into advanced work in astrophysics—that the authorities came and took the Rutherfords away.

There was a hearing and the ranch hands testified. So did the boy. Everyone agreed there had been no violence, no real crisis. It was only that the Rutherfords had gone from talking to babbling, and from babbling to screaming.

Shadows were what they feared. Shadows, or a single shadow —for apparently they never saw more than one at a given moment.

A shadow moving at midnight in the corrals, making the cattle bellow in terror—but why should cattle be afraid of something that cannot be seen?

A shadow creeping through the long dark ranch-house hall, while the floorboards creaked—but how can there be sound without substance?

A shadow glimpsed in the boy's room, stretched sleeping in the bed where the boy should be—but shadows do not sleep, and the boy testified he had seen nothing.

It was a sad affair and the ending was inevitable. The Rutherfords were obviously incompetent and they had to be committed. Both of them passed away within a matter of months.

The space program people stayed out of the affair, of course; at least they didn't interfere publicly. But they followed the hearing and they had the data and they took charge of Kevin once more.

Taking charge was a mere formality now, for they weren't dealing with a child any longer. Kevin was physically adult and mentally he was—

Worthy of further study.

That's what the medical team decided.

Kevin was happy to cooperate, even though it meant temporarily abandoning his research project on methods of communicating with distant planetary bodies through the use of ultrasonic frequencies.

On the appointed day he appeared before an international panel of scientific authorities at Space Command headquarters, prepared to submit to a thorough examination and checkup.

But he was not prepared to meet the head of that panel—an elderly, stoop-shouldered man who was introduced to him as Mission-Commander Richard Tasman, USN, ret.

The foreign scientists noted that Kevin didn't seem to react to the introduction. Perhaps he didn't recognize the name, but of course there was no reason that he should.

At least there was no reason until Tasman began asking questions. The questions were polite, formally phrased and very simple. But their content was disturbing.

Tasman wanted Kevin to tell him about the shadows.

Kevin frowned, then sighed. "Surely you've read the reports of the hearing. The shadows my poor foster parents claim to have seen were nonexistent—paranoid delusions—"

Commander Tasman nodded. "But it's the other shadows I'm interested in. The shadows that I saw with my own eyes—twenty years ago—when I found you in that cave on Echo."

The listening scientists leaned forward as Kevin shook his head. They turned up the earphones to hear what their translators were reporting as the conversation continued.

Kevin shrugged. "I was a baby—how do you expect me to remember anything? And even if I could, why should I notice shadows?"

"Why indeed?" Tasman smiled. "I saw them plainly enough but at the time I had no reason to pay attention to them. Now I'm not so sure."

"What do you mean?"

Tasman smiled again. "I'm not so sure of *that*, either. In fact I'm not sure of anything any more. It occurs to me we should have followed up our findings on Echo. Somehow in all the excitement of your discovery and rescue, certain unusual bits of data were neglected. An earth-type planet exists within a certain range of prescribed conditions—this we know, because we've located and studied others within the galaxy. Like Echo, they all contain life forms. Micro-organisms, algae, plant life, in infinite variety. And all of them, in this phase of evolution, contain animal life too. All except Echo."

Tasman fixed his eyes on Kevin. "I understand you have a background in space research."

"I'm only a novice—"

"But you have studied available information?"

"Yes."

"Then let me ask this—doesn't it seem strange to you that Echo, and Echo alone, is the only earth-type body ever discovered that is capable of supporting higher and more complicated life forms, yet contains none?"

"Perhaps there were such forms at one time, and they failed to survive."

"For what reason? There's no indication of natural disaster or recent geologic upheaval."

"Maybe the evolutionary cycle came to a natural end. Whatever might have existed there merely died out," Kevin said.

"Suppose it didn't die out? Suppose it merely developed along different lines—advanced to a point where life was no longer dependent upon a physical body of the type we're familiar with?"

"You mean something like pure thought?" It was Kevin's turn to smile.

Tasman shook his head and he wasn't smiling. "Something like shadows," he said.

Kevin stared. They were all staring now.

"Shadows," Tasman repeated. "Consider a life form which may once have been human like ourselves—very much like ourselves in many ways—but reached a turning point in the evolutionary road. Instead of continuing to evolve in terms of brawn, the emphasis became spiritual."

"Pure thought again?" Kevin gestured. "Impossible."

"Of course it's impossible," Tasman said. "Life is energy, and energy has form. But on Echo, which seems to have existed for countless years in an idyllic state, there was no need for a sturdy body to withstand the elements. And who knows—upon reaching a certain stage of mental development there may no longer be any dependency upon ordinary nourishment."

"You're saying these creatures turned into shadows?"

"Creatures? Hardly the term I'd use to describe so advanced an organism. As for shadows—how do we know what they really are? Possibly what we saw as shadows are merely visual projections of mental energy contained in the minimum possible shape. A shape that no longer requires sensory organs for perception or communication. A shape which doesn't need the complex of mechanical aids we call civilization, that can live without our concept of comfort and shelter—"

"In caves?"

Kevin rose as he spoke, rose and faced the assemblage around the long table. He spoke and the others listened. Exactly what he said is a matter of debate—afterward, opinions seemed to differ. But his words made sense, and everyone got the point.

Carefully, courteously, but concisely, he took Tasman's theories apart, demolishing each premise in turn. There was no precedent, not in biology or physics or the most advanced observations of science, for sentient shadows. One might as well argue the reality of ghosts. A shadow, by definition, is merely a shade cast upon a surface by a body that intercepts rays of light. It is the body that exists. Shadows are merely illusions—like the apparitions Kevin's foster parents babbled about, or like Commander Tasman's strange beliefs.

The speech was effective. And after Tasman, cold but controlled, excused Kevin from the hearing and had him escorted outside the room, there was a general buzz of conversation from the scientists gathered there.

Obviously they were impressed by what they'd heard. They were even more impressed when an apologetic sound engineer buzzed the chamber on intercom to report the sudden power failure which had cut off the mikes and made translation of Kevin's speech impossible.

"Amazing, the young man!" The Italian scientist groped for words in his heavily accented English. "Such presence, to realize this—and continue speaking in Italian."

"*Nein.*" The guttural rejoinder came swiftly. "It was in German he spoke."

"*Français!*"

Dissension rose in Japanese, Russian, Spanish, and Mandarin. All had heard Kevin and understood.

Tasman understood too.

He raced out the door, down the corridor. At the entrance to a small side office he found Kevin's security guards stationed and waiting.

"Kevin—where is he?"

The senior official blinked and gestured. "Inside."

Tasman brushed past him and opened the door.

The room beyond had no windows, no other exit.

But it was empty.

V

There was no official report of Kevin's disappearance. Even the medical team wasn't informed. But Tasman knew, and went straight to Top Security. A directive was issued.

Find Kevin.

"He's bound to slip up," Tasman said. "What happened at the hearing proves he's not infallible. When the mikes went dead he unconsciously continued to communicate by means of direct thought transmission. That explains why each foreign delegate believed he was hearing Kevin speak to him in his own language. When he realized he was giving himself away, it was too late. He had to flee."

Security officers nodded uneasily. How do you find a man who can transmit thoughts at will—hypnotize guards and pass them by without being seen or remembered?

"If he made one mistake he'll make others," Tasman assured them.

But Tasman himself didn't wait for mistakes. While security personnel searched for Kevin in the present, Tasman sought him in the past. He talked to people who had known him at the ranch—to schoolmates—to the surviving members of the original relief mission, men like Gilbey and Weber. What he learned he kept to himself, but the word spread.

Eventually it reached back beyond the time Tasman himself had known Kevin—back to a man who had known Kevin's parents.

A Dr. Hans Diedrich, living in retirement in the Virgin Islands, contacted Space Command with an urgent message. He had, he said, certain information which might be of vital importance in this affair.

Within twenty-four hours he was visited at his cottage home by an elderly, stoop-shouldered man who identified himself as Mission-Commander Richard Tasman, USN, ret.

"I'm glad you came," Diedrich said. "I have followed reports with great interest—my nephew is in the space program and it was he who informed me of what happened."

His visitor frowned. "A security leak?"

"Do not be alarmed. It is for the best that I was told, and in a moment you will understand why I say that. You see, I know what you are thinking."

"You do?"

Diedrich frowned. "You have a theory, haven't you? That Kevin Nichols' son was left alone in that cave on Echo when his parents died, left alone with the shadow-creatures. And that somehow, before your relief expedition arrived, these beings took possession of him—so that when he was rescued he was no longer an ordinary infant but something more. Because they infused him with their powers, established a mental contact, a link with themselves which was not broken when he returned to earth. And that all through his childhood and youth he was really acting as their pawn. A human being under alien control. Is that it?"

His visitor nodded.

"Well, you are wrong," said Dr. Diedrich. "I was the Nichols' family physician. I have their medical records. Two years before the journey to Echo, I personally performed surgery on Mrs. Nichols. A complete hysterectomy."

"Hysterectomy?"

"That is what I wanted to tell you. Mrs. Nichols could not have a child. The infant you found in the cave was not their son."

Dr. Diedrich leaned forward. "These beings must have the power to receive thoughts as well as to transmit them. They absorbed the contents of Nichols' mind as he lay dying in the cave —his wife's mind, too. And using what they learned, they created the illusion of an infant—one of their own kind disguised in a mental projection, programmed to live and grow as a child."

"Why send it back to earth?"

Diedrich shrugged. "I cannot say."

"And you have no proof."

"Only of the hysterectomy. Here, my own medical records—"

He handed a bulky envelope to his visitor.

His visitor smiled, thanked him, pulled out a revolver, and shot Dr. Diedrich through the head.

VI

"I told you he'd make a mistake," Tasman muttered. "Going down there, getting the information, then deliberately using a clumsy, old-fashioned weapon to kill Diedrich—it was a clever idea. And there are half a dozen people who can testify to seeing me escape from the cottage.

"Fortunately, you know I was here at Headquarters all the time. Kevin didn't anticipate I'd have such an airtight alibi. And he didn't anticipate that Diedrich had taken the precaution of taping a statement of his beliefs beforehand and sending it here to Space Command. So we understand how all this happened—and why."

"We know something else now, too." It was the Chief of Operations himself who answered Tasman, and his voice was grim. "The life form we're dealing with has greater powers than we imagined. The ability to transmit thought and to receive it. The ability to appear in the form we identify as Kevin—or to change that form at will.

"Do you realize what we're up against? A creature that can read our minds, walk unseen among us as a shadow, alter its appearance whenever it chooses."

"Mimicry," Tasman said. "Insects use it for protection, taking on the look of the plant or tree branch where they rest. The being we know as Kevin has this same faculty, developed to its ultimate extent."

The Chief of Operations frowned. "Then why did it even bother to appear as Kevin in the first place?"

"Again we must look to the insect world for a parallel," Tasman said. "Some insects begin in a larval state. It's only later that they emerge in new forms, with the power of disguising their shapes. Perhaps it was necessary for Kevin to go through certain stages in a single body while he grew to maturity, learned our ways. Only now, as an adult, is he capable of functioning fully."

"And just what is his function? Why did a shadow-creature come to earth in human disguise?"

Tasman shrugged. "Maybe the shadows grew tired of being shadows. Perhaps an existence of pure thought was no longer enough for them and they yearned for the sensations and satisfactions of solid physical shapes. In which case Kevin was sent here as a scout—to study our ways, see if we could be taken over."

The Chief of Operations shook his head. "You think this is a possibility?"

"I think this is what actually happened."

"Then what do you propose?"

"Another expedition to Echo. Give me the command, and a task force. Keep it under sealed orders, call it an exploratory operation if you like. But you and I know the real purpose of the mission."

"Seek and destroy?"

Tasman nodded. "It's our only chance. And we've got to move fast, before Kevin suspects."

VII

Commander Tasman lifted off for Echo under top security, but that didn't stop the rumors.

Whether or not Kevin suspected was no longer the problem. The search for him went on, but how do you find a shadow? He could be anywhere now.

It was the spread of the rumors that really caused the trouble —and the panic.

Somehow the word was out, and the world trembled. People had forgotten about the Space Child through the years, but now they remembered as the whispers grew.

There was a monster in our midst, the rumor mongers said. An alien unlike any humanoid form on planets known to man—an invisible creature, murdering at will. True, a mission had been mounted against Echo, but it would never return.

The whispers rose to angry shouts, and there was only one way to silence them.

The President of the United States went on Emergency Band and addressed the world.

Standing before the cameras and microphones in the tower at Communications Center, he delivered his message.

The rumors were partially true, the President admitted. The Space Child was indeed an alien, but there was no longer any reason to fear him. Because Kevin was dead. He had been discovered and trapped only this afternoon in a secret hideaway—a mountain cave near Pocatello, Idaho. Full details would be available on an international newscast following the President's message.

Meanwhile, it was time to put an end to vicious falsehoods, spread by our enemies. All of this wild talk of alien invasion was part of a plot, designed to prevent the opening up of free space travel and communication—but the plot had failed.

It was his privilege, the President said, to announce the final expansion of the space program. From this time forward there would be no restrictions on further flights. Every area of the galaxy was now officially declared to be open to the ships of any government or any private concern or individual. No more secrecy, no more security, no more fear. If new alien life forms were encountered, they would be met with friendship. If they chose to visit our solar system or even our own earth, let them be welcomed. For this was the start of the true Age of Space—founded firmly in freedom and in friendship.

The world listened to its leader and breathed a collective sigh of relief.

VIII

The President joined in that sigh as the broadcast ended. He watched the technical crews gather up their equipment and depart, leaving him alone in the tower room with its single window opening on the night sky and the stars.

Then the President of the United States melted into a shadow and slithered across the floor to the window as he waited for his brothers to arrive.

* *

I have never quite understood the prejudice directed against punning.

The pun has long occupied an honorable place in our literature, from the plays of Shakespeare to the novels of James Joyce. And yet public utterance of a pun inevitably evokes a hollow groan from on audience.

Perhaps only writers can truly appreciate the subtle nuances of wordplay. Whatever the reason, they seem to be addicted to the pastime, and their remarks turn many a banquet table into a groaning board.

I admit my own guilt in such matters. Whenever I've occasion to address an audience, I make it a point to include at least one pun which will elicit a dismal outcry. A few years ago, in my capacity as president of the Mystery Writers of America, I spoke at the annual "Edgar" Awards banquet. During my talk I observed that the awards seemed quite *apropos*—in fact, they were Edgar Allan *apropos*.

It was probably this remark which prompted Robert L. Fish to inform me that, next to himself, I was the best (or did he say worst?) punster he knew. Coming from the renowned author of the Schlock Homes stories, this was indeed a compliment.

I *think* . . .

Anyway, like Michael Avallone, Anthony Boucher, Henry Kuttner, Fredric Brown, Samuel A. Peeples, Forrest Ackerman, and a host of other writer-friends, living and dead, I'm a compulsive punster. I believe puns enrich our existence, and like the insect exterminator, my goal is a moribund ant life.

Thus, when Roger Elwood asked me to do a story for a science fiction anthology about children, the reaction was instantaneous. The title, "Space-Born," popped into my head, and I couldn't resist.

The story, which appeared in *Children of Infinity*, published by Franklin Watts in 1973, might properly be classified as science-fantasy. Its opening derives from today's technological realities, but the ending stems from my own adolescent association with H. P. Lovecraft. It's interesting to note that it was published before the film, *The Omen*, was made—and, for that matter, before Watergate—though both of these dramas also involved a President of the United States.

How do *you* feel about puns?

If you like them, then this story must be credited to a heaven-sent inspiration.

If you hate them, to hell with it.

The Learning Maze

Jon couldn't remember a time when he hadn't been in the Maze.

He must have been very young at first, because his earliest recollection was a confused impression of lying on his back and sucking greedily from a tube extended by a Feeder.

The Feeder, of course, was a servo-mechanism, but Jon didn't realize that until much later. At the time he was only aware of the tall tangle of moving metal hovering over him and extending a hollow tentacle toward his eager lips. There had been a Changer too, approaching him at regular intervals to remove soiled clothing, cleanse his body, and cover it with fresh garments.

Jon's memories became more vivid as his areas of perception slowly extended. The first unit of the Maze was a vast enclosure in which hundreds of infants lay in their individual plastic life-support units while the Feeders and Changers moved among them. From time to time another type of servo-mechanism appeared without warning, disturbing the regular rhythm of eating, sleeping and elimination by superimposing its bulk upon his body.

Now Jon realized it must have been a Medi-mechanism, but he still thought of it as a spider—a gigantic insectoid creature straddling him on extended silvery legs as its myriad extra appendages poked and probed the organs and orifices of his body. It recorded pulse, respiration, brain-wave patterns, his entire metabolism, and corrected deficiencies by injection. Jon could still remember the sting of the needles and how he had writhed and screamed.

Naturally he'd feared and hated the process. Even now that he knew the whole procedure was impersonal, computer-directed for his welfare and well-being, he still resented it.

The other infants had screamed too. But not everything was

that unpleasant. As time passed they began to move around more freely, aided by handgrips within their cubicles, and then they started to crawl. Jon crawled with them, eventually leaving the shelter of the life-support unit to seek the source of sounds and images beyond.

The sounds and images came from the walls, from the closed-circuit televisor screens. The screens sang soothingly to him at night and by day they showed images of other infants crawling and feeding happily. Watching the screens, Jon and his peer group began to imitate the actions of the images; soon they learned to take nourishment from little sterile containers deposited by the Feeders at regular intervals once the tubes were no longer offered. Some of Jon's companions cried when the tubes disappeared, but in time they all began to eat what was set before them.

They began the educational process and that, of course, was the real function of the Learning Maze—to teach them how to live and grow.

In the antiseptic atmosphere of the chamber with its controlled temperature and humidity levels, they watched the infant-images on the screens as the figures crawled, then stood erect and took their first faltering steps.

Imitating them, Jon started to walk. Soon all the others were walking, exploring the chamber and one another. Touch, bodily contact, the discovery and awareness of differences and similarities, sexual awakening—all this was a part of learning.

The Maze guarded and waited, and when the time came its screens disappeared into the walls and there was only a doorway visible at the far end of the chamber. Through that doorway Jon could glimpse another chamber beyond, filled with other youngsters larger than himself who walked freely without falling and uttered complicated sounds as they pursued fascinating, glittering objects in bigger and brighter surroundings.

At first Jon merely watched, uncertain and afraid. Then, inevitably, came an urge to move through the doorway. There was no barrier, no impediment, and he entered easily into the adjoining section of the Maze.

Here the individual plastic cubicles were larger and the screens more sophisticated in their offerings. They still sang soothingly at night, but by day they talked to him.

Night was dark and day was light; that was one of the first things Jon learned. Even before he could comprehend the words, Jon learned many things. He learned to dispense with the Feeders and Changers because here the servo-mechanisms were different. Their metallic shapes roughly resembled his own on a larger scale; they had arms and legs and heads and they moved about almost in the same fashion that he did. Only of course mechanisms never seemed to tire or express emotion. Perhaps that's why they had no faces—merely a blank surface meshed over the front of their heads through which voices filtered instructions and commands. Gradually Jon began to understand the voices, whether they issued from the screens or from the servo-mechanisms, and presently he learned to respond and to answer in kind.

Soon Jon was established in a normal pattern of boyhood. He played with the glittering objects—the educational toys which tested and extended physical strength, improved his motor reflexes and co-ordination, taught him mechanical dexterity and skills. He talked to his companions, all of whom were males. He made friends and enemies, embarked upon the give-and-take of social relationships, rivalries and dependencies. Competition provided him with motivation; he wanted to excel in order to attract attention and approval.

Jon's orientation came from the screens. As he grew older he became aware of the world beyond—the real world outside the Learning Maze. The world which had once existed without Mazes of any sort and in which human beings had lived all their lives with only the crudest kind of servo-mechanisms to help them. History—or theirstory, as it was now correctly called— dealt with the quaint quality of this primitive culture in which the biological parents undertook the education of their offspring, assisted by crude instructional institutions.

The combined effects of emotional conflict and ignorance had their inevitable effect: the world had been plunged into endless warfare in which both the inhabitants and their natural environment were almost totally destroyed.

Then and only then, the Learning Maze concept came to the rescue. Once a mere toy for the study of animal behavior in old-fashioned "laboratories," then a simple experimental device developed for the psychological conditioning of children in a few "universities," the Learning Maze principle had been expanded to bring true sanity and civilization to mankind. The perfection of various types of servo-mechanisms, completely controlled by computerization, eliminated all error.

Gone was the outmoded human hierarchy of masters and servants which had created destruction. Today these roles were played by machines, and man was free to fulfill his true function —learning how to live.

Jon soon realized that his only problem was how to avoid pitfalls along the way. Because there *were* pitfalls in the Learning Maze. Although the surface beneath his feet seemed solid and substantial, it could give way. He'd seen it happen.

Not all his companions learned as quickly as he did. Some of them seemed uninterested in watching the screens and absorbing the information they provided. If this indifference persisted, the servo-mechanisms noted it and took action.

The action was simple and direct, but startlingly effective. The mechanism merely focused its blank-faced attention on a lazy or noncompetitive youngster and then, with a quick gesture, reached up and pulled a switch located at the side of its metal head. Suddenly, without warning, the ground directly under the child parted and he fell into the dark opening below. Sometimes there was a scream, but usually it happened too quickly for that —for in an instant the gaping hole was gone again as though it and the child it had swallowed no longer existed.

No one ever discovered what happened to those who disappeared and neither the screens nor the servo-mechanisms offered any explanation. Jon's companions couldn't find any physical evidence pointing to the exact location of the pitfalls; they seemed to be completely camouflaged and scattered at random all over the Maze, so there was no way in which to avoid them. There were all sorts of guesses, but no one really knew, and it was better not to think too much about it. The important thing was to realize the danger existed and could confront one at any time. For not learning, for being unable to learn, for being too sick or too weak or too helpless to learn—pulling the switch was the punishment.

But learning brought rewards. Because now, once again, another doorway appeared leading to an area beyond. Peering through it, Jon could see a new vista of the Maze, expanded and elaborate, filled with evidence of exciting activity.

The screens told him about that activity—about males and females and the pleasure of their relationships. The responses of
his own body affirmed the truth of what he was told. Jon and his
companions were anxious to enter that next section; enter into its
activities, enter into its females. But when they attempted to
move through, an invisible barrier prevented their progress.

Not yet, said the voices from the screens. You must learn more
before you're ready.

Impatiently, Jon and the others looked and listened, but their
inner awareness was concentrated on the delights beyond the
doorway. From time to time someone would desert his learning
post and steal away toward the other chamber, but always a
servo-mechanism barred his path and uttered a warning. If ignored, the mechanism pulled its switch and the heedless one
dropped down to disappear.

But there were moments when Jon and his fellows were unob-
served and then they would steal up to the opening to stare at
the scene beyond and to test the invisible force-field of the barrier.

Eventually they grew stronger or the barrier became weaker;
finally, one by one, they broke through. And there, in the next
segment of the Maze, Jon and the others found their females.
Pairing off, they sought still larger cubicles to share with their
partners and the pattern of existence changed.

Jon's partner was called Ava; it was she who now prepared the
food left by the servo-mechanisms who ministered to the needs
of this section. At first Jon was not too greatly interested in food,
but as time passed and the novelty of physical contact waned,
nourishment and comfort became more important again.

Once more Jon learned the pattern of rewards and punish-
ments governing this area of the Maze. Food was distributed
only to those who were willing to spend time watching the
screens. Since Ava seemed completely absorbed in the day-to-
day routine of life within their cubicle, Jon was forced to appear
regularly before a screen as further lessons in living were
presented.

The images were quite diversified and complex now; there
were scenes of full-grown adults engaging in a great variety of activities. Some seemed to be fulltime screen-watchers, some appeared to ignore the screens and devote themselves to tests of

strength with companions, rivaling them for the interest of many females besides their partners.

Jon was not tired of Ava, but he found himself studying various techniques of competition with increasing interest. It would appear that in the real world he was preparing to enter, the biggest and strongest acquired the best cubicles and the most attractive females. In addition they received the envy and admiration of their companions.

The more Jon learned the more interested he became in testing his own powers. Ava's simple responses began to bore him; she wasn't concerned with what he told her about the real world beyond and couldn't understand why he was dissatisfied to stay here forever.

But Jon was tired of the tedium of screen-watching and apprehensive about the fate of his fellows who balked. He'd seen them deprived of food by the servo-mechanisms for neglecting their daily duties. Some of those who were content to become completely absorbed in relationships with their partners had already disappeared. There seemed to be no penalty for the females; their limited interests didn't stamp them as inferior, for their previous conditioning had obviously been different. But the males were obligated to continue the learning process, and Jon knew he must comply.

Besides, a new opening had appeared in the far wall of the chamber and now he found himself moving forward to gaze into the next complex beyond.

Jon knew without being told that this must be the real world —the world for which he'd prepared to dwell in during all this period of study and growth.

What waited beyond the invisible barrier was not a simple chamber but a huge series of corridors, each with an opening which afforded a partial, tantalizing glimpse of activity within. Others like himself prowled these corridors, entering various compartments at will and exiting to move along into still other portions of the Maze. Jon could not see any screens on the corridor walls and that was good. Here men seemed to be living, not learning. They were coupling with many females, carrying huge accumulations of food and clothing from one place to another, trading and exchanging various articles, and fighting off others who attempted to take a portion for themselves without permission or barter agreements.

Jon couldn't wait to join them. And when he crowded up to the opening he found himself passing through without hindrance —and without a thought of Ava left behind him. Ava, with her dull conversation, her duller caresses, and her swollen belly.

Once across the barrier, Jon forgot Ava completely. There was so much to see, so much to do, for this tangle of corridors stretched off endlessly in all directions, opening upon many types of rooms and rooms within rooms. But it was still a part of the Maze.

From what he'd seen on the outside, Jon had thought there would be no more screens; now he realized he was mistaken, for if anything, their numbers had increased. The difference was that there was no longer any uniformity to the images on the screens or the messages they imparted.

Pausing at a chamber doorway, Jon could hear some voices from the screens urging him to enter, promising him all sorts of rewards and describing the pleasures of participation in the activities within. Other voices, equally shrill and urgent, warned him to keep out, to seek still more distant rooms.

And the servo-mechanisms were here too, though less noticeable, for now they more closely resembled Jon's living companions. They moved naturally, their gestures less stiff and more assured, their voices ringing with confident authority. At first Jon wasn't even able to identify them as mechanisms because they were masked in faces simulating flesh; faces that smiled benevolently, grinned confidently, or frowned with stern wisdom. "Follow me," they said, and Jon joined the group obediently to be led into a bewildering array of vast, arenalike enclosures.

In one such place a leader gathered together all those with fair complexions while another leader assembled those with darker skins. And from the walls the screens screamed at both groups in turn, exciting them with alternate threats and promises, urging them to destroy their opposites.

The noise was ceaseless, the confusion incredible, and in the inevitable struggle that followed, the leaders stood aside observing. When one of Jon's companions slackened, the inevitable gesture was made—a hand went to the side of the head and one of the invisible seams opened to engulf the offender.

It was only then that Jon realized the leaders were servo-mechanisms, for when the switches operated, the masks sometimes slipped to one side and Jon could see the blank, featureless surface beneath, totally devoid of any semblance to humanity.

That was when Jon fought his way through the struggling throng and escaped into a corridor, only to be swept along into another area where the chief activity seemed to be the removal of metal discs affixed to the walls of the chamber.

Here the screens displayed glittering panoplies of such discs, while their voices extolled the glory of gathering them together and heaping them up into huge piles. According to the screens, great skill and intelligence were required to perform this feat, and there was no higher goal than the acquisition and arrangement of discs. As if to prove the point, large numbers of exotically dressed, youthful females prowled about inspecting the heaps and offering themselves to those who had managed to amass the largest portions.

But Jon observed that the females seldom stayed long with any one accumulator; always they seemed attracted by another collector with a still larger heap.

Jon also noted that obtaining the discs was not an easy procedure; prying them from their fastenings in the walls was a painful task that made the fingers bleed. Sometimes rival disc-gatherers fought with one another over the discovery of a fresh cluster of discs, and many times they resorted to stealing discs from the collections of their companions. Indeed, it seemed as if the most truly imposing amounts were gathered in just this way, by theft alone.

Wrenching discs free from the walls was more exhausting and a much slower process; sometimes it was necessary to stand on tiptoe for those beyond reach, or crouch to burrow at the very base of the walls. And yet there was a strange compulsive element involved; those who toiled eventually became so absorbed that they could not even be distracted by the young, nubile females, and even food and slumber seemed unimportant. Similarly, the thieves came to devote themselves solely to stealing, with equally tiring results.

And when the efforts slackened or ceased through utter exhaustion, the servo-mechanisms appeared, pushing aside their sober masks to pull the switch. Thus disc-gatherers and disc-stealers alike disappeared, leaving only a shining heap as a sole memento of existence—a heap which was immediately plundered by waiting rivals, so that even this evidence of achievement vanished.

But these were only two of the many areas which Jon discovered in the Maze. There was a shouting section—he could think of it in no other terms—in which every occupant was encouraged to drown out the voices of his fellows and reduce them to the status of listeners. Here the rivals emulated the voices from the screens, uttering promises, blandishments, flattery and exhortations, while at the same time denouncing the words of all the others in a continuous effort to attract the less articulate to support their stated purposes.

At first Jon tried to listen, but the more he heard the more confused he became. Some praised those who fought in the arena sections, some denounced them; some extolled the virtues of disc-accumulators and others derided. But in the end their voices hoarsened and failed and their audiences turned away to hear the same messages couched in slightly different phrases by younger and louder voices. And when this happened, a servo-mechanism appeared to seek out the speechless orator, deserted by all, and make the inevitable movement toward the side of the head.

In another area Jon found speakers equally dedicated to attracting followers but using softer and more persuasive tones. They spoke of the great secret of the Learning Maze, the secret which had been imparted to them as a special dispensation. Praising the voices from the screens, they explained that the commands and injunctions issuing from them were often cryptic and mysterious and had to be interpreted by speakers such as themselves in order that all might understand.

But each speaker seemed to have a different explanation of the meaning of the Maze—its creation, its purpose, and how one must conduct oneself within. And each speaker disputed the statements of his fellows, even to the minor points of words and phrases used by them, so that in the end the soft voices gave way to angry shouts, denunciations, threats of endless punishment and commands to destroy all those who refused to agree utterly and completely without question. And always the speaker would call upon the servo-mechanisms to punish and eliminate nonbelievers.

Some of the talk interested Jon at the beginning, for he had often tried to puzzle out the program of the Maze, but when talk gave place to outcry it became incoherent and bewildering. And Jon noted that the servo-mechanisms never seemed to come upon command to destroy the speakers' enemies—but when all the prayers for vengeance died, it was then that the mechanisms finally appeared to make the gesture which removed speakers and followers alike. In the end, none who stayed in this chamber were spared, whatever their beliefs.

Jon remembered a section where all occupants seemed to be engaged in an endless and complicated measurement process. Dedicated to observation, they gravely calculated the area of the room, analyzed and tabulated the components of the atmosphere within it, and even attempted to measure one another.

These observers took great pride in their efforts and loudly proclaimed their superiority to those in other sections of the Maze. Some day, they asserted, they would take their rightful place as rulers of the Maze, once they had mastered all its secrets by their methods of measurement.

What was not readily described in terms of size or mass or velocity of movement they theorized about—giving particular attention to the phenomena of the wall screens and servo-mechanisms and attempting to fully explain their functions and purposes. But no two theories were exactly alike and new measurements and methods of measurement constantly superseded the old, so that the end result was once again argument and anger. And with all the careful devotion to the accumulation of data and all the energy expanded in expounding theory, the room itself remained fixed and unchanged except in minor details. And its occupants never left it until one of the servo-mechanisms—its functions still unfathomable, despite all the hypotheses—made the final motion that put an end to further inquiry.

Again Jon refused to become completely involved in such activity and sought out other sections. There was a new arena where the young seemed to be pitted against the old, each denouncing the other for a greedy and self-centered attempt to take control. But as the young became older, they seemed to switch allegiance, and this confused Jon so that he was impelled to move on.

In another place, food and sex and accumulation alike appeared unimportant to the occupants. They lay in a drugged stupor, oblivious to their surroundings except for the times when the screens flickered wildly and projected flashes of unrecognizable imagery or assaulted them with screaming sounds. Occasionally a few of the group would rouse long enough to imitate what they vaguely saw or heard, painting weird squiggles upon canvas and even upon their own bodies, or plucking crude instruments to make loud noises to which they wailed accompaniment. What they sang and shouted made little sense to those who were not drugged like themselves. Eventually they relapsed into a mumbling preoccupation, gazing raptly at their own faces in tiny mirrors which distorted their features beyond recognition until they came to resemble hairy beasts. Servo-mechanisms moved to those sunk in the deepest stupor and their switches were swift.

Jon continued on, vaguely conscious that he was gradually coming to know the various routes and recesses of the Maze. Eventually he chanced upon a room that seemed more inviting than the others, even though the servo-mechanism posted at the doorway did not exhort him to enter. Perhaps it was this that attracted him, or the fact that the mechanism wore a different mask. In place of human features there was only a surface emblazoned with a symbol. Jon recognized the curlicue and dot as something he'd seen on a screen long ago—a question mark.

Intrigued, he glanced into the room of silence. A few men sat cross-legged upon the floor, gazing at screens that were utterly blank and from which issued only a faint, deep drone. The drone was somehow soothing, but those who listened did not seem drugged or sleeping, merely contemplative.

Weary of walking, weary of peering and puzzling, Jon moved into the chamber. Almost automatically he sank down and assumed the cross-legged position, staring up at a screen. For a moment it seemed that he could see into the emptiness to catch a fleeting glimpse of something beyond. And wasn't there a voice whispering within the drone?

Concentrating with all his being, Jon strained to see, to hear. But the more he tried, the less he perceived, for such exertion only made him conscious of himself.

Finally he relaxed, and then it came. Making no attempt to see, he saw. Making no effort to hear, he heard. But the vision and voice came from within, and suddenly they blended into revelation.

For the first time Jon understood the Learning Maze. Completely computerized, completely controlled, it was a reasoned reproduction of the past—mankind's past, in all its aspects, recapitulated in physical form. These were the life styles constructed by men in the real world long ago, and which they had followed to their own destruction.

Those who sought sensory stimulation to the exclusion of all else were doomed. Those who pursued power, those who concentrated upon accumulating meaningless tokens of ownership, those who fought one another over differences in appearance or belief, were destined for extinction. Preoccupation with data or theory for its own sake was self-defeating, the distortion of phenomena by means of theology, pharmacology or art was meaningless.

All activity, all inquiry, all self-scrutiny and self-indulgence had its place in the scheme of things, but only in moderation and only as means to an end. The purpose of the Maze was to teach by precept and example, to pinpoint the pitfalls endangering men in their ancestral past and their own individual futures. It illustrated the myriad facets of existence and illuminated the dangers of surrendering wholly to any one phase of behavior in its extreme. The whole man knew and experienced life as a whole, but never gave himself completely to a fraction—only to totality.

In its system of rewards and punishment, the Learning Maze eliminated the weak and unfit from among those seeking to journey through it and emerge into the real world beyond.

Even contemplation such as this could become a self-limiting and self-destructive thing; awareness was granted for a purpose —for use in actual living.

It was time now to leave the Maze, and at last Jon knew the way.

When he emerged from contemplation and left the quiet drone of the chamber he no longer hesitated. The method was so simple once one grasped it. These rooms were only blind alleys set to trap the unaware; it was the corridor itself that was important. All he had to do was concentrate upon its convolutions and follow the path to the outer portals.

There was no longer any need to pause or peer or participate —he'd experienced enough of the chambers so that his curiosity was no longer aroused by them. Now he was free to direct his footsteps toward the greater goal.

It was almost as though instinct had taken over, finding the proper route for him. Ignoring sham and semblance, he moved toward substance and reality. And he came to a point where the twisted passageways merged into a single continuous corridor leading straight upward.

Now, directly ahead of him, Jon could see the actual opening and the light beyond; not the artificial light of the caverns but the light of reality.

He hastened toward it, toiling up the steep slant with renewed resolution. There was no obstacle now, nothing to impede his progress.

A servo-mechanism loomed up before him at the very threshold, but Jon's pace didn't slacken. He pressed forward, purposeful and determined, his body weary but his voice firm with resolve.

"Let me pass," he commanded.

The mechanism stood motionless, featureless face staring, seeming to question without speaking.

Jon sensed the question, voiced his answer.

"Why? Because I've had enough of faceless authority, of artificial motivation, meaningless routine and still more meaningless change. I've learned all you can teach me here. Now I'm ready to live in the real world."

"But you have lived all your life in the real world," said the mechanism softly. "Try to understand."

Jon tried, but there wasn't much time.

Because the mechanism was already pulling the switch.

*   *

This is the third story I wrote at the request of Roger Elwood —that most persistent and prolific anthologist.

Too prolific, perhaps, because his anthologies appeared so frequently, under the imprint of so many different publishers, that they were often lost in the shuffle.

I have had not one single comment to indicate that anyone has ever read "The Learning Maze," which appeared in the book of the same title issued by Julian Messner in 1974—yet of the many score of science fiction stories I have written, this is a personal favorite.

For this reason, I'm still hoping that it will find an audience. Whether it's liked or detested, I do want it to be *read*.

Because of the theme, "The Learning Maze" is different from all the other stories collected here. Try as I may, I can't ascribe its source to either God or the Devil alone.

This one was a collaboration.

The Model

Before I begin this story, I must tell you that I don't believe a word of it.

If I did, I'd be just as crazy as the man who told it to me, and he's in the asylum.

There are times, though, when I wonder. But that's something you'll have to decide for yourself.

About the man in the asylum—let's call him George Milbank. Age thirty-two, according to the records, but he looked older; balding, running to fat, with a reedy voice and a facial tic that made me a little uptight watching him. But he didn't act or sound like a weirdo.

"And I'm not," he said, as we sat there in his room on the afternoon of my visit. "That's why Dr. Stern wanted you to see me, isn't it?"

"What do you mean?" I was playing it cool.

"Doc told me who you were, and I know the kind of stuff you write. If you're looking for material—"

"I didn't say that."

"Don't worry, I'm glad to talk to you. I've been wanting to talk to someone for a long time. Someone who'll do more than just put down what I say in a case history and file it away. They've got me filed away now and they're never going to let me out of here, but somebody should know the truth. I don't care if you write it up as a story, just so you don't make me out bananas. Because I'm going to tell it like it is, so help me God. If there *is* a God. That's what worries me—I mean, what kind of a God would create someone like Vilma?"

That's when I became conscious of his facial tic, and it disturbed me. He noticed my reaction and shook his head. "Don't take my word for it," he said. "Just look at the women in the magazine ads. High-fashion models, you know the type? Tall, thin, all arms and legs, with no bust. And those high cheekbones, the big eyes, the face frozen in that snotty don't-touch-me look.

"I guess that's what got to me. Just as it was supposed to. I took Vilma's look as a challenge." His face twitched again.

"You don't like women, do you?" I said.

"You're putting me on." For the first and only time he grinned. "Man, you're talking to one of the biggest womanizers in the business!" Then the grin faded. "At least I was, until I met Vilma.

"It all came together on a cruise ship—the *Morland,* one of those big new Scandinavian jobs built for the Caribbean package tours. Nine ports in two weeks, conducted shore trips to all the exotic native clipjoints.

"But I was aboard for business, not pleasure. McKay-Phipps, the ad agency I worked for, pitched Apex Camera a campaign featuring full-page color spreads in the fashion magazines. You know the setup—big, arty shots of a model posed against tropical resort backgrounds with just a few lines of snob-appeal copy below. *She travels in style. Her outfit—a Countess D'Or original. Her camera—an Apex.* That kind of crud, right?

"Okay, it was their money and who the hell am I to say how they throw it around? Besides, it wasn't even one of my accounts. But Ben Sanders, the exec who handled it, went down the tube with a heart attack just three days before sailing, and I got nailed for the assignment.

"I didn't know diddly about the high-fashion rag business or cameras either, but no problem. The D'Or people sent along Pat Grigsby, their top design consultant, to take charge of the wardrobe end. And I had Smitty Lane handling the actual shooting.

He's one of the best in the business, and he got everything lined up before we left—worked out a complete schedule of what shots we'd take and where, checked out times and locations, wired ahead for clearances and firmed-up the arrangements. All I had to do was come along for the ride and see that everyone showed up at the right place at the right time.

"So on the face of it I was home free. Or away from home free. There are worse things than two weeks on a West Indies cruise in February with all expenses paid. The ship was brand new, with a dozen top-deck staterooms, and they'd booked one for each of us. None of those converted broom-closet cabins, and if we wanted we could have our meals served in and skip the first-sitting hassle in the dining room.

"But you don't give a damn about my vacation, and neither did I. Because it turned out to be a real downer.

"Like I said, the *Morland* hit nine ports in two weeks, and we were scheduled to do our thing in every one of them. Smitty wanted to shoot with natural light, so that meant we had to be on location and ready for action by 11 A.M. Since most of the spots he'd picked out were resorts halfway across the various islands, we had to haul out of the sack before seven, grab a fast continental breakfast, and drag all the wardrobe and equipment onto a chartered bus by eight. You ever ride a 1959 VW minibus over a stretch of rough back country road in steambath temperatures and humidity? It's the original bad trip.

"Then there was the business of setting up. Smitty was good but a real nitpicker, you know? And by the time Pat Grigsby was satisfied with the looks of the outfits and the way they lined up in the viewfinder and we got all those extra-protection shots, it was generally two o'clock. We had our pics but no lunch. So off we'd go, laughing and scratching, in the VW that had been baking in the sun all day, and if we boarded the ship again by four-thirty we were just in time for Afternoon Bingo.

"About the rest of the cruise, I've got good news and bad news.

"First the bad news. Smitty didn't play Afternoon Bingo. He played the bar—morning, afternoon, and night. And Pat Grigsby was butch. She must have made her move with Vilma early on and gotten thanks-but-no-thanks, because by the third day out the two of them weren't speaking except in line of duty. So that left Vilma and me.

"This was the good news.

"I've already told you what those high-fashion models look like, and I guess I made it sound like a grunt from a male-chauvinist pig, but that's because of what I know now. At the time, Vilma Loring was something else. One thing about models —they know how to dress, how to move, what to do with make-up and perfume. What it all adds up to is poise. Poise, and what they used to call femininity. And Vilma was all female.

"Maybe Women's Lib is a good thing, but those intellectual types, psychology majors with the stringy hair and the blue-jeans always turned me off.

"Vilma turned me on just looking at her. And I looked at her a lot. The way she handled herself when we were shooting—a real pro. While the rest of us were frying and dying under the noon sun, she stayed calm, cool and collected. No sweat, not a hair out of place, never any complaints. The lady had it.

"She had it, and I wanted it. That's why I made the scene with her as often as I could, which wasn't very much on the days we were in port. She always sacked out after we got back from a lo-cation and I couldn't get her to eat with me; she liked to have meals in the stateroom so she wouldn't have to bother with clothes and make-up. Naturally that was my cue to go into the my-stateroom-or-yours routine, but she wasn't buying it. So during our working schedule I had to settle for evenings.

"You know the kind of fun and games they have on shipboard. Second-run movies for the old ladies with blue hair, dancing on a dime-size floor to the music of a combo that would make Lawrence Welk turn in his baton. And the floor shows—tap dancers, magic acts, overage vocalists direct from a two-year en-gagement at Caesar's Palace—in the men's room.

"So we did a lot of time together just walking the deck. With me suggesting my room for a nightcap and she giving me that it's-so-lovely-out-here-why-don't-we-look-at-the-dolphins routine.

"I got the message, but I wasn't about to scrub the mission. And on the days we spent at sea I stayed in there. I used to call Vilma every morning after breakfast and when she wasn't resting or doing her nails I lucked out. She was definitely the quiet type and dummied up whenever I asked a personal question, but she was a good listener. As long as I didn't pressure her she stayed happy. I picked up my cue from that and played the waiting game.

"She didn't want to swim? Okay, so we sat in deck chairs and watched the action at the pool. No shuffleboard or deck tennis because the sun was bad for her complexion? Right on, we'd hit the lounge for the cocktail hour, even though she didn't drink. I kept a low profile, but as time went on I had to admit it was getting to me.

"Maybe it was the cruise itself that wore me down. The atmosphere, with everybody making out. Not just the couples, married or otherwise; there was plenty going for singles, too. Secretaries and schoolteachers who'd saved up for the big annual orgy, getting it all together with used-car salesmen and post-graduate beach bums. Divorcees with silicone implants and new dye jobs were balling the gray-sideburn types who checked out Dow-Jones every morning before they went ashore. By the second week, even the little old ladies with the blue hair had paired off with the young stewards who'd hired on for stud duty. The final leg, two days at sea from Puerto Rico to Miami, was like something out of a porno flick, with everybody getting it on. Everybody but me, sitting there watching with a newspaper over my lap.

"That's when I had a little Dear Abby talk with myself. Here I was, wasting my time with an entry who wouldn't dance, wouldn't drink, wouldn't even have dinner with me. She wasn't playing it cool, she was playing it frigid.

"Okay, she was maybe the most beautiful broad I've ever laid eyes on, but you can't look forever when you're not allowed to touch. She had this deep, husky voice that seemed to come from her chest instead of her throat, but she never used it for anything but small talk. She had a way of staring at you without blinking, but you want someone to look *at* you, not through you. She moved and walked like a dream, but there comes a time when you have to wake up.

"By the time I woke up it was our last night out and too late. But not too late to hit the bar. There was the usual ship's party and I'd made a date to take Vilma to the floor show. I didn't cancel it—I just stood her up.

"Maybe I was a slow learner or a sore loser. I didn't give a damn which it was, I'd just had it up to here. No more climbing the walls; I was going to tie one on, and I did.

"I went up aft to a little deck bar away from the action, and got to work. Everybody was making the party scene so I was the only customer. The bartender wanted to talk but I turned him off. I wasn't in the mood for conversation; I had too much to think about. Such as, what the hell had come over me these past two weeks? Running after a phony teaser like some goddam kid with the hots—it made no sense. Not after the first drink, or the second. By the time I ordered the third, which was a double, I was ready to go after Vilma and hit her right in the mouth.

"But I didn't have to. Because she was there. Standing next to me, with that way-out tropical moon shining through the light blue evening gown and shimmering over her hair.

"She gave me a big smile. 'I've been looking for you everywhere,' she said. 'We've got to talk.'

"I told her to forget it, we had nothing to discuss. She just stood there looking at me, and now the moonlight was sparkling in her eyes. I told her to get lost, I never wanted to see her again. And she put her hand on my arm and said, 'You're in love with me, aren't you?'

"I didn't answer. I couldn't answer, because it all came together and it was true. I *was* in love with Vilma. That's why I wanted to hit her, to grab hold of her and tear that dress right off and—

"Vilma took my hand. 'Let's go to my room,' she said.

"Now there's a switch for you. Two weeks in the deep-freeze and now this. On the last night, too—we'd be docking in a few hours and I still had to pack and be ready to leave the ship early next morning.

"But it didn't matter. What mattered is that we went right to her stateroom and locked the door and it was all ready and waiting. The lights were low, the bed was turned down and the champagne was chilling in the ice bucket.

"Vilma poured me a glass, but none for herself. 'Go ahead,' she said. 'I don't mind.'

"But I did, and I told her so. There was something about the setup that didn't make sense. If this was what she wanted, why wait until the last minute?

"She gave me a look I've never forgotten. 'Because I had to be sure first.'

"I took a big gulp of my drink. It hit me hard on top of what I'd already had, and I was all through playing games. 'Sure of what?' I said. 'What's the matter, you think I can't get it up?'

"Vilma's expression didn't change. 'You don't understand. I had to get to know you and decide if you were suitable.'

"I put down my empty glass. 'To go to bed with?'

"Vilma shook her head. 'To be the father of my child.'

"I stared at her. 'Now wait a minute—'

"She gave me that look again. 'I have waited. For two weeks I've been waiting, watching you and making up my mind. You seem to be healthy, and there's no reason why our offspring wouldn't be genetically sound.'

"I could feel that last drink but I knew I wasn't stoned. I'd heard her loud and clear. 'You can stop right there,' I told her. 'I'm not into marriage, or supporting a kid.'

"She shrugged. 'I'm not asking you to marry me, and I don't need any financial help. If I conceive tonight, you won't even know about it. Tomorrow we go our separate ways—I promise you'll never even have to see me again.'

"She moved close, too close, close enough so that I could feel the heat pouring off her in waves. Heat, and perfume, and a kind of vibration that echoed in her husky voice. 'I need a child,' she said.

"All kinds of thoughts flashed through my head. She was high on acid, she was on a freak sex-trip, some kind of a nut case. 'Look,' I said. 'I don't even know you, not really—'

"She laughed then, and her laugh was husky too. 'What does it matter? You want me.'

"I wanted her, all right. The thoughts blurred together, blended with the alcohol and the anger, and the only thing left was wanting her. Wanting this big beautiful blond babe, wanting her heat, her need.

"I reached for her and she stepped back, turning her head when I tried to kiss her. 'Get undressed first,' she said. 'Oh, hurry —please—'

"I hurried. Maybe she'd slipped something into my drink, because I had trouble unbuttoning my shirt and in the end I ripped it off, along with everything else. But whatever she'd given me I was turned on, turned on like I've never been before.

"I hit the bed, lying on my back, and everything froze; I couldn't move, my arms and legs felt numb because all the sensation was centered in one place. I was ready, so ready I couldn't turn off if I tried.

"I know because I kept watching her, and there was no change when she lifted her arms to her neck and removed her head.

"She put her head down on the table and the long blond hair hung over the side and the glassy blue eyes went dead in the rubbery face. But I couldn't stir, I was still turned on, and all I remember is thinking to myself, without a head how can she see?

"Then the dress fell and there was my answer, moving toward me. Bending over me on the bed, with her tiny breasts almost directly above my face so that I could see the hard tips budding. Budding and opening until the eyes peered out—the *real* eyes, green and glittering deep within the nipples.

"And she bent closer; I watched her belly rise and fall, felt the warm, panting breath from her navel. The last thing I saw was what lay below—the pink-lipped, bearded mouth, opening to engulf me. I screamed once, and then I passed out.

"Do you understand now? Vilma had told me the truth, or part of the truth. She was a high-fashion model, all right—but a model for *what?*

"Who made her, and how many more did they make? How many hundreds or thousands are there, all over the world? Models—you ever notice how they all seem to look alike? They could be sisters, and maybe they are. A family, a race from somewhere outside, swarming across the world, breeding with men when the need is upon them, breeding in their own special way. The way she bred with me—"

I ran out then, when he lost control and started to scream. The attendants went in and I guess they quieted him down, because by the time I got to Dr. Stern's office down the hall I couldn't hear him any more.

"Well?" Stern said. "What do you make of it?"

I shook my head. "You're the doctor. Suppose you tell me."

"There isn't much. This Vilma—Vilma Loring, she called herself—really existed. She was a working professional model for about two years, registered with a New York agency, living in a leased apartment on Central Park South. Lots of people remember seeing her, talking to her—"

"You're using the past tense," I said.

Stern nodded. "That's because she disappeared. She must have left her stateroom, left the ship as soon as it docked that night in

Miami. No one's managed to locate her since, though God knows they've tried, in view of what happened."

"Just what *did* happen?"

"You heard the story."

"But he's crazy—isn't he?"

"Greatly disturbed. That's why they brought him here after they found him the next morning, lying there on the bed in a pool of blood." Stern shrugged. "You see, that's the one thing nobody can explain. To this day, we don't know what became of his genitals."

* *

So there you are.

Presumably you've read them all—the fourteen stories and the appended comments—including "The Model," which was published in the November 1975 issue of *Gallery*.

And you're saying to yourself—well, what *are* you saying?

That Bloch is going trendy with this last item, writing raunchy for the rabble?

Or that he has dramatized one of the oldest of mankind's sexual fantasies and/or phobias?

Or are you merely thanking God that the book is finally finished?

If God happens to be your thing, that is.

For all I know, you may have been rooting for the Devil. As I tote up the score, it seems to come out to a rather close tie for honors or dishonors.

On the other hand, if you happen to be primarily a hardcore science fiction buff, then all this talk about divine or diabolical inspiration may have turned you off completely. In which case you are at liberty to substitute the superego for God and the id for Satan.

But I doubt if that will tell you any more about where these stories actually came from.

I've been writing for most of my life now, and I still don't know the answer.

And I'll tell you a little secret.

I really don't care *where* they came from—as long as they keep coming—and you keep reading.